Contents

PROLOGUE	1
CHAPTER 1	4
CHAPTER 2	11
CHAPTER 3	22
CHAPTER 4	29
CHAPTER 5	38
CHAPTER 6	45
CHAPTER 7	56
CHAPTER 8	80
CHAPTER 9	90
CHAPTER 10	99
CHAPTER 11	111
CHAPTER 12	120
CHAPTER 13	136
CHAPTER 14	148
CHAPTER 15	171
CHAPTER 16	183
CHAPTER 17	196
CHAPTER 18	211
CHAPTER 19	217

CHAPTER 20	222
CHAPTER 21	233
Epilogue	248

PROLOGUE

The sun was high in the sky, barely a cloud to be seen. A slight breeze kissed his face in the hot noon. Eyes closed, he pictured his home; the fields of golden wheat to the south, the sound of his wife humming in the garden as she tended her flowers, the hustle and bustle of the village nearby.

"Sir!" A heavy voice called, cutting through his thoughts. "The armies are in position."

Glancing down across the blackened plains below, he could see the armies of Therago; dwarf, men, felian, gnome and elf.

Strange, he thought as he looked up to the hordes of greyish brown demonic creatures, *how it takes this to unite us.*

"Are we prepared?" He asked, his voice weary. "I want this to be the end of it Falcio."

Falcio looked over at him, his green feline eyes heavy with exhaustion and lose.

"I hope that too," he replied. "I want to see my wife and children again."

"One way or another you will see them again, my old friend. I worry more for the land and if it can be saved."

"It will be, Avanthar," came a woman's voice, soft and enchanting. "Never underestimate nature's will to endure."

"I do not doubt that Seleena," he replied to the wood elf. "But what of the toll on its people?"

Seleena looked over at him, her long auburn hair framing her delicate face, emerald green eyes staring back into his silver. The black and gold robes she wore flowed over her small elegant frame.

"When this is over," Falcio began. "What are you going to do?"

"Go back home to my wife," Avanthar replied, without hesitation. "Help rebuild my village, bring life back to my farm."

"Ha, Avanthar the farmer," Falcio said wistfully. "That is something I would like to see."

Glancing from left to right, Avanthar could see the other few hundred Knights of Medusal; warriors, wizards, rangers, assassins, barbarians, and paladins from every race, each with powers, granted from the gods and immortals, to protect the realm from the mordian. Creatures filled with blood lust, wanting nothing but to kill, devour and destroy. Nothing more than mindless beasts, or so it had seemed. Over time it had become obvious that there was an intelligence behind them, leading them. Within the first few years most of the larger nations were destroyed, millions dead and a blight took hold of the land, corrupting anything and everything it touched.

"It's time," Avanthar called out as he donned his helm. "You all have your orders. I will see you at the end of this."

With that the Knights dispersed and joined the other armies. Off in the distance a horn bellowed and catapults fired. The final battle had begun.

***

The sun had begun to set. The battle, long and bloody, was over, Avanthar walked amidst the field, helm lost, blade covered in the black oil like blood of the mordian, the black and gold lion crested cloak he wore was in tatters. He knelt down beside a body, his silver eyes filled with sorrow.

"Go my friend," Avanthar said as he closed Falcio's eyes. "Be with your family."

He looked up, as he felt a hand on his shoulder, to see Seleena's emerald eyes, her face pale with exhaustion.

"Come Avanthar," she said to him. "Let us be gone from this place. We will give him a proper burial."

Nodding, Avanthar stood and turned. Seleena smiled as

she saw a small bloom push its way through the blighted soil. Turning, she placed a hand over her belly, knowing that there was hope, not only for Therago but also for the child growing within her.

CHAPTER 1

The dwarven city of Ysegarde, located in the mountains of Gramore, built right into the mountains themselves. It was probably the biggest trade city in all of Eastern Therago; built next to a massive lake, a huge fissure in the rocks lead right to the ocean giving Ysegarde one of the only trade routes to the island nation of Sandara, along with the huge fishing industry, making Ysegarde extremely wealthy.

The young gnome skipped through the street, the houses towering over her, but she loved it. She could not wait to get home to giver her mother the silks she was sent to retrieve, for her new dress.

A flash of red light from the nearby alley caught her attention. Overtaken by curiosity, the young gnome ventured into the now dark alley. It was quiet, too quiet. She was suddenly scared, everything felt wrong. She turned to leave, when suddenly a hand grabbed her. She screamed.

***

Avalon, capital city of the high elf nation of Avantharia, founded by the great King Avanthar nearly three thousand years ago. When the country was founded, Therago was in a time of turmoil as war had ravaged the realm. Much of the history of the time was lost but what is remembered were the sacrifices of great heroes that stood to protect the land. Avanthar being one of these heroes that started from humble origins, only to return a King.

The young elf ran through the city streets, cutting between buildings and darting down alleys, until he finally reached Market Row. The street leading directly from the main gates to the castle. It was lined with stalls that carried all assortments of wares, ranging from weapons to silverware, from fabrics to food. He paused, taking a quick breath, before moving to his favourite stall, his silver eyes never leaving the sight of the sizzling meat on the grill, the bustle of the market lost on him as he licked his lips, hunger gnawing at his stomach, the intoxicating smell of getting stronger with each step.

"Ah if it ain't young Master Avlin," came a gruff voice from behind the grill. "I wondered if I would see ya today."

"Hello Dal," he replied as he wiped his face, the sweat running into his eyes, his medium length, messy black hair was damp and clung to his temples. "I would like to get double my usual order, I am famished."

"Famished you say?" The dwarf laughed. "Don't they feed ya up in dat castle?"

"Oh they do but I skipped lunch and i do so love the grilled venison you make."

Dal, short for Dalidar, shook his head and laughed again as he began to package the venison, his thick red hair soaked with sweat from the heat of the grill.

"Here ya are," he said as he handed the young elf his order. "And don't worry about da cost, consider it my birthday gift to ya."

"My thanks Dal," he replied as he put the coin pouch he was carrying back on the black leather belt he wore.

The young elf looked at Dal, the dwarf was wearing his usual blood stained apron over the same old brown sleeveless tunic, his thick burly arms coated in a mix of charcoal and sweat. Hair tied back in a ponytail, a short beard and round face.

"Do say hello to yer parents for me," Dal said as he turned back to his work.

"I will," he replied with a wave as he walked away.

As he began to eat the tender grilled meat his mind wandered.

I wonder if Dal would treat me differently if he knew who i was, he thought.

The elf that Dal knew as Avlin was actually Ryuvin Ashgrove, the Crowned Prince of Avantharia and descendant of the great King Avanthar. According to legends, Avanthar was a mighty warrior, Commander of the legendary Knights of Medusal and had lead the united forces of Therago against the greatest evil the world had ever seen, the mordian.

Ryuvin always wondered how much of the legends were true as he looked around at the many different stalls while eating the tender grilled meat. When Avanthar first founded Avalon it was nothing more than a small fortress, with his guidance that fortress became the great city it was today. Fairly wealthy, Avalon was a lively cosmopolitan in central Avantharia, the country was nestled north of the Gosmara Plains and far to the south east of the Donmala Forest.

Once the grilled meat was done, Ryuvin wiped his chin with the cotton sleeve of his green tunic and rubbed his hands on his dark brown leggings. His black leather boots clicking on the stone stone as he looked from stall to stall, a stall of jewellery catching his eye.

"Well hello handsome," came a sultry feminine voice. "Is there something I can help you with?"

"Oh, no I am just browsing," Ryuvin replied, he could see the woman looking him up and down with lust filled eyes.

"Perhaps I can be of assistance," she continued. "Are you shopping for someone special perhaps? Everything here is of the finest quality. Even Queen Amilia shops here"

I highly doubt that, Ryuvin thought as he quickly glanced at the woman, it was clear she was trying to learn of his love life.

"Well if that be the case," Ryuvin replied. "Then I doubt I would be able to afford anything here."

"I'm sure we can come to some sort of....arrangement," the vendor replied and licked her lips, tracing her fingers over her voluptuous breasts. "I always enjoy helping handsome young men such as yourself."

Ryuvin was indeed handsome and he had figured that

many of the servant girls had fantasies of him taking them to his bed. In fact he would not have been surprised if there was already such a rumour spreading around.

"Well I am flattered," Ryuvin replied. "But i really must be going, I am sure my mother is waiting for me back home."

"Come find me when you are free," the woman said with a wink as she crossed her arms under her breasts and pressed them together.

With a smile and a polite bow, Ryuvin continued on his way. He always enjoyed the market district the most, though he was not entirely sure why. Perhaps it was how alive it felt as opposed to how lifeless the castle was.

I best be getting back, he thought, *it has been too long already.*

Glancing back behind him, Ryuvin quietly slipped into a narrow alley nestled between a blacksmith and a general goods store. It was not difficult to skirt between the buildings and did not take take long for him to reach the castle walls.

The sheer granite towered about fifty feet above him. The hand holds few and far between. Having climbed the wall countless times, it never failed to make Ryuvin nervous, the height would leave him seriously injured should he fall. Taking a deep breath, Ryuvin began the slow treacherous climb, each hand hold never the same.

Perhaps next time I should bring a rope, he thought.

It was something that came to mind for him each time he made the climb, he knew he would not be capable of this as a guard or servant could find the rope. Which means the castle is put on high alert as the guards search for the intruder.

Twenty minutes later, Ryuvin finally reached the top of the wall. Looking back over his shoulder he took in the breathtaking view of Avalon. The sun glittered over the many white stone buildings of the city. He then quickly pulled himself over the ramparts, onto the walkway and down the stairs. Reaching the ground, he brushed his hands together and looked up to the top.

As Ryuvin was about to turn, he felt the sharp tip of a sword press against his back. Cursing under his breathe, he raised his hands up.

"What have we here?" Came the silvery voice of a woman. "Thief or assassin?"

"Well," Ryuvin answered with a smile. "I will have to say thief, since I have already stolen your heart."

Spinning, he knocked the blade to the side and pulled the woman to him, his lips hungrily finding hers as they kissed passionately. A moan escaped her as she dropped her sword and wrapped her arms around Ryuvin's neck.

Finally breaking apart, she looked up to him, her emerald green eyes meeting his silver. Her face flushed as she tried to steady her breathing. Brushing aside her auburn hair, Ryuvin gazed upon her angelic face and smiled at her.

"My heart skips a beat each time I lay eyes on you Serina."

"I feel the same about you," Serina replied with a wistful sigh as she pushed him back. "But we can never be together, you know this. I'm just a scout, and you, you are the Crowned Prince of Avantharia."

"And you are the most beautiful wood elf I have ever laid eyes on," he said, eyes trailing over her lithe athletic body, she was a few inches shorter than Ryuvin.

"Is that so?" She laughed softly, picking up and sheathing her sword. "I'm fairly certain I am the only wood elf you have ever seen. And don't say that you have in the market, wood elves don't venture into high elf cities."

He could see the sorrow in her eyes, it made him hurt. But he knew it was true, wood elves rarely left the Donmala Forest.

In fact, no one even knew why Serina was taken from the forest and left in Avalon. She was but a baby at the time and it was assumed her parents were dead. She was raised by Torvan Althara, an old veteran that has been in the military since before King Tharndal, nearly four hundred years ago.

"Serina," Ryuvin began as he cupped her cheek. "I love you. I always will."

Serina smiled and nuzzled his hand slightly before kissing him again.

"Come on," she said as she pulled back and began to walk towards the garden entrance. "Your mother has been looking for you."

With a sigh he followed. Ryuvin knew exactly why his mother was searching for him. His father, King Tarin, expected him to marry Valeria, the Princess of Amenthur, the kingdom that neighboured Avantharia.

"Don't sigh, you know that the marriage is a good idea. Plus I hear that Princess Valeria is quiet beautiful."

"So i have heard," Ryuvin said and glanced at Serina. "But I have two reasons that make her not appealing to me. First, I have you. Second, from what I have heard, she has a terrible attitude and is a complete spoiled bitch."

Ryuvin heard Serina sigh softly, he guessed that she had heard the stories about Valeria as well. Turning back to her, Ryuvin brushed a tear from her cheek and kissed her one more time.

"No matter what happens, no one will ever change how I feel for you Serina."

***

From the third floor balcony, a man watched the young couple. Letting out a sigh, he turned to look at his wife and crossed his arms.

"Well you were right," he began, his voice husky. "I must admit, I am not happy about our son having this affair with a scout."

"Well what did you expect dear?" Queen Amilia asked, her voice regal and captivating. "They have known each other since they were infants, and were pretty much inseparable as the grew up. We were the same when we were young."

"True, although you were a princess," King Tarin replied.

He leaned on the raid of the stone balcony, watching as carriages of nobles entered the palace grounds. His crystal blue eyes reflecting the wisdom of his years, he stood and turned, walking inside. His shoulder length black hair was combed back and held with a dark blue ribbon.

"What are you planning?" The Queen asked, her soft silver eyes alive with curiosity.

"The only thing I can do," he answered as he strode down the hall.

Amilia watched her husband walk down the hall before looking back at the young couple as the exited the garden.

"Well Ryuvin," she said to herself with a soft smile. "What shall you choose? Love or duty?"

With that Amilia turned and followed Tarin.

CHAPTER 2

Evening had fallen over Avalon, the setting sun set the sky ablaze with a beautiful array of red and yellow. Ryuvin was standing on the balcony of his chambers, a crisp breeze brushing against his face, as he looked out over the city. The houses sparkling from the lanterns that lined the streets.

He wondered what was going on down in the city, even though the market had closed the city night life was as alive as ever. The inns and taverns giving music to the night. His thoughts drifted back to when he visited one of the many taverns, the performing bard had played a lute as a few of the tavern serving girls danced on a table. He remembered the night fondly, as it was the night he told Serina that he was in love with her for the first time.

A knock at his door startled him slightly, and as he turned he saw his mother, Queen Amilia, enter his chambers.

"Are you prepared sweety?" She asked, her voice as soothing to him as always.

Her tussled black hair, that framed her elegant face, was held back in a bun with a purple silk ribbon. Her slender frame covered by her favourite purple ball gown.

"I was just about to come down," Ryuvin answered as he strapped a ceremonial cavalry sabre to his waist. The white leather belt and scabbard created a stark contrast from the midnight blue regal jacket and dark leggings he wore.

His mother sighed softly as she stepped closer and adjusted the collar buttons then smoothed the gold tassels on the shoulders.

"Before we proceed, I wanted to wish you a happy birthday," she said and smiled warmly at him. "And that your father and I have a very special gift for you."

"Oh? And what might that be?"

"Well," she replied as she turned. "It would not be a surprise if I were to tell you now would it?"

Amilia began to walk away, stopping at the door and looking back at her son, dressed in his full regal attire.

"Before I forget, your Father is expecting you to choose your bride and future queen tonight. Though I wonder, will you go through with choosing Valeria?"

"It is my duty as Crowned Prince," Ryuvin replied sternly, though his eyes betrayed his true feelings.

"And if you did not have to choose her?" Amilia asked before turning back to the door.

The door closed behind her and with that, Ryuvin was alone again. He knew full well that his life was about to change forever, but what exactly did his Mother mean. Why ask if he did not have to choose Valeria? Ryuvin looked back towards the balcony and the city, letting out a sigh, he walked towards his bedroom door and opened it, nearly colliding with his younger sister.

"Oh!" He exclaimed. "Hello Titania, what are you doing here?"

Several inches shorter than Ryuvin, she wore a dress of similar design to their Mother's, only a light blue in colour. Her raven hair was held in a bun, her bangs dangled over her temples. Her slim face was flushed slightly, her crystal blue eyes narrow.

"Please do not tell me you are going to marry her?" She stated, her sweet voice made it difficult to take her anger seriously.

"By her, do you mean Valeria?"

"Yes, that bi-"

"Ah, language," Ryuvin said, interrupting Titania. "And it is not like I want to."

"Good, than choose someone else," she spat as she began

pacing back and forth. "I hate her. Did you know she had the gall to refer to me as a mere child?!"

Ryuvin only sighed as Titania ranted.

"I mean me; Princess Titania of Avantharia. Daughter of Queen Amilia and King Tarin!"

"Okay, okay, calm down sis," Ryuvin said calmly. "We all know you are not a child. Now deep breathe and give your brother a hug."

She let out a sigh and nodded as she hugged Ryuvin.

"Thank you for listening," she said looking up at him. "You always know what to say, you are the best."

Ryuvin smiled and fixed her silver tiara.

"Hey, I am your big brother, of course I am the best."

"You should not push your luck," she giggled then ran down the hall.

Ryuvin watched her go. Alone once more he glanced back over his shoulder before closing the door.

***

Several minutes later, Ryuvin approached the grand ballroom. Standing in front of the massive ornate oak door, stood Titania.

"Is everything okay?"

"Hmm?" She asked as she was brought out of whatever thoughts she was having. "Oh, yes. I was merely waiting for you."

"Are you sure?" Ryuvin inquired, slight concern in his eyes.

"I mean, is it weird that I am really nervous and all of this is for you?"

"I would think it is justified for you," Ryuvin replied thoughtfully. "I mean today you will be getting an older sister."

Titania merely nodded as she looked down at the stone floor.

"Well then, shall we make our grand entrance?" Ryuvin asked and held up his hand with a smile.

"We shall," Titania replied with a smile and took his hand.

With a nod to the guards, the siblings watched the ornate doors open. The herald announced the pair as they entered.

"Now presenting Ryuvin, the Silver Blade, Ashgrove, Crowned Prince of Avantharia. And Lady Titania Ashgrove, Princess of Avantharia."

The siblings strode down the oak steps that lead to the marble floor of the massive ballroom. To their left, arching glass doors leads to a balcony that stretched the length of the room. Against a portion of the wall to their right was a small orchestra, each instrument playing a soft harmonic melody in tune with the others. Several jade columns with gold trim lined each wall leading to a domed ceiling, upon which a map of Therago was depicted.

Nobles would stop and congratulate Ryuvin, wishing him a happy birthday and congratulating him on his future marriage, as they walked through the hall. Ryuvin and Titania would make polite small talk with the nobles as they moved slowly their parents at the far side of the hall. After several minutes, Titania and Ryuvin finally made their way to the raised dais where the King and Queen awaited them.

"Ah," Queen Amilia exclaimed happily as they approached. "There are my two precious children."

"Mother!" Titania began as she hugged Amilia. "Sorry to keep you waiting, how is the celebration so far?"

"Well enough," she answered, watching Ryuvin and Tarin from the corner of her eye.

"There you are son," Tarin said as he clasped Ryuvin's forearm in a firm grip. "We have been waiting for you."

With a quick gesture, a nearby servant bearing a pillow topped with a silver tiara, much like the one Titania wore, approached.

"Right," Ryuvin said with a sigh, then looked over his shoulder at Princess Valeria of Amenthur. "I am to choose my future wife tonight."

"Indeed," Tarin replied and gestured to another servant. "Though first, a special gift from your Mother and I."

As Ryuvin opened his mouth to speak, the doors of the ballroom opened causing him to turn.

"Now presenting," the herald began. "The Lady Serina of House Althara."

There, standing at the top of the stairs, stood Serina. Dressed in a flattering forest green gown, her auburn hair hair away from her face with a silver ribbon. She looked every bit a princess.

"We know you love her," his Mother whispered to him.

"I have already spoken to Allandar," Tarin added. "He is aware that you will not being choosing Valeria."

"Now go my son," Amilia said with a soft smile. "Choose the woman you love to rule beside you."

Stepping away from his parents, Ryuvin moved towards Serina at a brisk pace, his heart racing. He dared not blink for fear of losing sight of her. He watched her slowly descend the steps to the ballroom and met her at the base of the stairs.

"I-I think," Serina began nervously, her cheeks turning scarlet as she blushed. "Your parents know about us."

Ryuvin was at a lose for words and could only stare, which caused Serina to blush more. He then offered his hand, which she took, with a gentle squeeze Ryuvin then lead her back towards the raised dais and his parents.

"Are you sure about this Ryuvin?" Serina whispered to him as she glanced at the nobles.

Ryuvin looked at several of the nobles, hearing the whispers, then back to Serina.

"More than anything," he whispered back to her. "Your family has always been close to mine. You will be an excellent Queen."

"Attention," King Tarin commanded, his voice echoing over the crowd. "My son shall now present his future wife with this tiara, to symbolize their future union together."

The elf servant stepped forwards and knelt down, bowing his head, as he lifted the ornate royal purple pillow. Atop sat the silver tiara. Ryuvin picked up the tiara in both hands, Serina watched and could feel herself beginning to panic, she felt the need to flee when she felt someone take hold of her hand. She was not sure when Queen Amilia had moved beside her but looking at her soft smile eased Serina's fears. She took a breath and lowered herself, her head tilted forward as Ryuvin gently placed the tiara on her head.

"Lords and Ladies of Therago," the King boomed. "I present to you, Lady Serina, Crowned Princess of Avantharia."

There was a moment of silence, an applause began, slowly at first, leading into a crescendo. Ryuvin did not care as he leaned into and kissed Serina passionately, she was shocked at first but threw her arms around his neck kissing him back just as passionately.

"I am glad we no longer have to hide this," Ryuvin whispered to her, his forehead pressed against hers.

"I am too," she replied, smiling, her cheeks flushed.

"As is tradition," Tarin announced. "The Crowned Prince and Princess shall begin the first dance."

Hand in hand, Ryuvin lead Serina to the centre of the ballroom. A harp began to play a soft melody as Ryuvin lifted Serina's hand, his right on her lower back. Serina then placed her free hand on right shoulder and they began to dance to the angelic sound of the harp. More instruments joined in, as they waltzed, creating a beautiful harmonic song. After several minutes, Tarin and Amilia joined the couple on the dance floor, followed by a couple of nobles until most were dancing.

***

The party was in full swing as Ryuvin leaned on the stone railing of the balcony, a glass of dwarven wine in his hand. Several groups on nobles dotted the balcony, but that did not bother him, he was lost in his own thoughts which made him fail to notice the clicking of shoes coming onto the balcony behind him.

"Everything okay?" Titania asked him.

"Hmm?" Ryuvin replied as he was snapped back to reality. "Yes, I just wanted to enjoy some fresh air. What about you?"

"I just needed to get away from all the men wanting to

dance with me. Can you believe them? I can barely get a moments rest."

Ryuvin thought back for a moment, not recalling seeing his sister dancing with anyone.

"Are you just upset that Jassin never asked you to dance with him?"

"No!" Titania exclaimed and turned away from Ryuvin, clearly trying to hide the fact she was blushing.

Jassin was Count Vamir Venharice's youngest son and Ryuvin's closest friend. Fairly handsome with midnight black hair and sapphire blue eyes, Ryuvin was not surprised that his sister had a crush on him.

Vamir and Tarin were almost like brothers growing up; though the Venharice House was not of noble blood it changed nothing for the boys. It was not until Vamir nearly gave his life to protect Queen Amilia from a band of ogres, sacrificing his right arm in the process, did he become a Count.

"Really?" Ryuvin chuckled as he watched Titania's reaction.

"Why would I want to dance with him?!"

"Well he is handsome, smart and every time you are with him you are too nervous to speak. Plus he is coming this way."

Titania spun with such haste that it had caused her to lose her balance and fall into Jassin's arms.

"Well I have been told girls fall head over heels for me, but this is the first that I have seen it," he said, his deep voice almost turned Titania's face completely red.

"Um...I. Uh..." she managed to stutter.

"Are you not feeling well?" Jassin asked, concern showing in his eyes.

"She is fine," Ryuvin answered as he took a step forwards.

"Y-yes," Titania stated, finally regaining her voice as she took a step back while looking down.

"Well that is good to hear," Jassin replied with a smile then extended his hand to Ryuvin. "I wanted to congratulate you and wish you a happy birthday.

"Thank you," Ryuvin replied as he pulled Jassin in and hugged him. "It has been long but there is no need to stand on formalities with me my friend."

"That is has," Jassin said as the two pulled away.

They, like their fathers, were friends since childhood.

"Back when you told Serina you loved her, in the tavern. What was that? Two years ago now?"

"Three," Ryuvin answered as he thought about that night.

It had been Jassin's birthday, and he was able to convince Ryuvin and Serina to sneak out of the palace. He remembered how intoxicating Serina was when she had joined the serving girls as they danced.

"Your welcome, by the way," Jassin said with a smirk.

"What for?"

"Well think about it," he replied with a cocky grin. "If it was not for me, you and Serina would not be together now."

"Hey I would have told her," Ryuvin said defensively.

"When? Next century?"

"What are you boy arguing about?" Serina asked as she strode out onto the balcony.

"Well if it is not the future Queen herself," Jassin said as he hugged Serina. "Just reminiscing my birthday three years ago. Your welcome by the way."

"For what exactly?"

"He thinks that if it was not for him we would not be together now," Ryuvin answered.

Serina raised her eyebrow at Jassin then smirked before turning her attention to Ryuvin.

"I mean in a way he's right, how long would it have taken you to tell me you loved me?"

"Oh come on, why are you both ganging up on me?" Ryuvin said as he threw his hands up. "If this is how you treat me as the Crowned Prince, I worry about how it will be as King."

"Some one has to keep your ego in check," Serina laughed and took his hand in hers. "We do it because we love you."

"Crowned Princess and military, I think you are perfect to

be his Queen."

"I can only hope to live up to the expectation," Serina said as she leaned in to give Ryuvin a kiss noticing Titania for the first time. "Oh Titania, I didn't see you there."

Titania, still blushing, curtsied to Serina.

"Are you ill?" Serina asked as she felt Titania's forehead. "If you are you should go rest."

"She is fine," Ryuvin chimed in. "I believe she was hoping Jassin would ask her to dance with him."

"Ryuvin!" Titania gasped then hid her face in her hands. "Why are you embarrassing me?!"

"Well if it is a dance with the most beautiful girl here, who am I to refuse?" Jassin said with a smile as he held out his hand to Titania. "No offence Serina."

"None taken," she replied with a giggle as she waved her hand.

Her embarrassment immediately forgotten, Titania took Jassin's hand as he lead her back into the ballroom.

"You think Titania knows that Jassin like her?" Serina asked as she watch the pair begin to dance.

"And how do you know that exactly?"

"I have my ways," she replied with a smirk.

"Well it is hard to say," Ryuvin replied, leaning against the railing. "I know that she likes him."

"I'm sure everything will work out for the two of them," Serina said with a smile and took Ryuvin's hand as she gently pulled him towards the ballroom. "Now come on, I have to give you my gift."

Smirking, Ryuvin followed Serina back inside, unbeknownst to him, the red flash of light in the garden and the figure that followed.

***

Back inside, Ryuvin and Serina made their way towards the King and Queen. As they approached, the doors to the ballroom burst open from a gust of wind. Standing at the top of the stairs was a hooded. Dark blue robes were visible beneath the tattered and frayed cloak. With a staff in hand, the figure descended the stairs.

"Who dares to intrude in my palace?" King Tarin boomed as soldiers flooded through the doors and servant entrances.

The figure was almost half way across the room by the time the soldiers had them surrounded.

"It has been some time since I last laid eyes upon the Golden Tree of the House of Avanthar," she said with a wistful sigh as she looked around at the mithril armoured soldiers, each adorned with a golden tree, their shields raised and swords drawn. "We need to talk Tarin."

"You dare to enter our presence uninvited," Queen Amilia began as she stepped forwards, cold fury edging into her voice. "Then you proceed to make demands, you shall remove your hood at once and tell me who you are."

Ryuvin glanced quickly at his mother, it was rare for her become as angry as she was now and he knew full well to tread carefully when she was like this. Though he was curious about this new comer, whoever she was she acted as if she knows the kingdom yet she addressed his father instead of his mother, who is the descendant of Avanthar and ruler of Avantharia. So her knowledge of Avantharia was not as keen as she may have believed.

"Very well," she said as she pulled back her hood. "My name is Seleena Arrowsong."

Murmurs began throughout the hall from the announcement. Her emerald green eyes scanned the room as if she expected to see a familiar face. Ryuvin noticed the slight pained smile as her eyes landed on Serina, it was then that he noticed just how similar they were in appearance. He strode forwards and without hesitation, stepping passed the soldiers surrounding her.

"Hello Ryuvin," she said wistfully as he approached. "You know you look just like Avanthar."

He was unsure if that was a question or a statement.

"And you look just like Serina," Ryuvin replied as he

stopped in front of her. "Can I make the assumption?"

Seleena merely nodded and looked back to Serina.

"She will have questions for you."

"Of that I have no doubts."

"I believe proper introductions are in order Mother," Ryuvin said as he turned back towards his parents.

"Oh?" Amilia said, her eyes narrowing on Seleena. "Very well, tell us who she is."

"This is Serina's mother, and if I am correct, she is the same Seleena Arrowsong that was second in command of the Knights of Medusal and the High Queen of the Damaska Forest."

"Your son is correct," Seleena stated.

"Legends say that after your return to the forest you were never heard from again, but that was thousands of years ago."

"I did return, though it was only to find my kingdom had been stolen from me while I was away. Being pregnant at the time forced me to flee and not allow me to reclaim my throne," Seleena said and looked over at Serina. "I could not risk Serina's future."

"But..." Serina began as she stepped forwards. "How is that even possible? This was thousands of years ago, as you said."

"Hello Seleena," came a sinister voice from the entry way. "It has been far far too long."

Turning, Seleena looked towards the voice. There, at the top of the stairs, holding a blood covered sword, stood a man. A man in a hooded black cloak.

Chapter 3

Ryuvin lay in his bed staring at the ceiling. Serina lay naked next to him, asleep, her head resting on his bandaged shoulder, body pressed against his. As his limb burned with pain, he replayed the previous night's events through him mind over again.

***

"I see you haven't changed much since the last time we met," the black cloaked stranger said as he slowly descended the stairs. "Tell me though, how did you manage to survive my curse?"

"Time can be a fickle thing," Seleena retorted in an icy tone. "You seem to have forgotten that, have you not?"

"Ah yes," he laughed a reply and gave a mocking bow as he reached the base of the stairs. "The Great Chronomancer Seleena Arrowsong, High Queen of Damaska, Right Hand of Avanthar, Commander of the legendary Knights of Medusal."

Ryuvin saw Seleena's jaw clench.

"Well," he looked up with a grin. "At least you used to be."

"Remember Arondath, with a betrayal like yours, well, there is a special place in Nessus for that," Seleena responded through gritted teeth. "I was unprepared last time. I will not be this time."

Before anyone could react, Seleena launched a flurry of magical missiles at Arondath. Though he was able to dodge them with minimal effort and charged Seleena. Guards had rushed in but Arondath dispatched them with practised ease. Nobles had begun to panic and run for exits. Without even a second thought, Ryuvin had drawn his own sword and intercepted Arondath; who had lunged at Seleena again.

"Interesting," Arondath sneered as his sword clashed with Ryuvin's. "Now I get to kill you as well."

"You are welcome to try," Ryuvin retorted and pushed against Arondath's blade.

Arondath smirked and charged at Ryuvin, immediately taking the offensive. The clash of steel echoed throughout the ballroom. Arondath pushed hard, his blade a blur, Ryuvin was barely able to keep up when Arondath overstepped. His footing lost, Arondath stumbled back as Ryuvin pressed his advantage.

He is baiting you, came a voice barely more than a whisper, *disengage now.*

Heeding the voice, Ryuvin jumped back just in time, had he not Arondath's trap would have worked. The thrust meant for Ryuvin's throat instead hit deep into his left shoulder.

"How unfortunate," Arondath taunted as he licked the blood off his blade. "You made me miss my feint, well no matter. After I finish you, I will deal with that cocky bitch Seleena. I always did enjoy a good game of hide and seek."

The pain had caused Ryuvin to stagger and drop to his knee, blood running down his chest and over his abs. Seleena had disappeared when the nobles panicked, Ryuvin looked back towards the dais and saw the eagle helms of several of the royal guard, paladins known as the Silver Eagles, had created a shield wall around his family, while more were coming. Forcing himself to stand, Ryuvin turned his attention back towards Arondath.

Just have to hold for a little bit longer, he thought.

Arondath had finally removed his hood, revealing his face. He was a drow, a dark elf from Subterra; a massive underground country in western Therago. His white hair was cut short, face narrow with a pointed chin. He had a crazed look in his red eyes, and a smile that had made him all the more unsettling. He advanced forwards slowly, swaying as he did, like a snake. He made to lunge at Ryuvin but was stopped before he took a step by three throwing daggers. Caught off guard, Arondath retreated back a few paces as he deflected them.

"My apologies for my tardiness Ryuvin-sama," came the smokey voice of a woman from behind him, easing his pain slightly. "I had been held up do to the chaos this…..thing created."

"There is no need to apologize Kimiko," Ryuvin replied.

Kimiko was also a drow, at least he thought she was; his mother had saved her life years prior, in return, Kimiko swore a life debt. Her long white hair was tied up in a high ponytail, the sides hanging down over her temples, her left eye was always covered by the red headband she wore. Although, unlike other drow, Kimiko had purple eyes. She had a narrow face with a round chin and full lips. She wore tight black leather clothing with calf high boots and bracers.

"I shall deal with this filth Ryuvin-sama," she began, Ryuvin never could figure out why she called him that. "Return to the Silver Eagles and get your wound tended to."

"Aw come now," Arondath said maniacally as Ryuvin retreated. "Is that any way to speak about your big brother?"

"You are no brother of mine," Kimiko answered calmly.

By the time Ryuvin made it back to the dais, his jacket was soaked with blood. His adrenaline now fading, coupled with the blood loss, he blacked out.

***

Ryuvin shifted slightly, easing himself out from under Serina, she let out a soft whimper as he did, as if she did not want him to leave. Standing, Ryuvin moved to the window and threw open the curtains, sunlight poured over his thin muscular form. A whisper of movement caught his attention.

"Is everything alright Kimiko?" He asked as he turned to face the kneeling drow.

"I just wanted to make sure you were well, Ryuvin-sama," she replied as she turned her gaze away. "If you would please cover yourself."

"It is not like you have not seen a naked man before," Ryuvin said as he walked over to a nearby chair and picked up his robe. "I am a bit sore, but I will live."

"Shall I call for a healer?"

Before he could answer, Serina stirred. She yawned and stretched as she sat up, the blanket falling from her supple breasts. She looked at Ryuvin and smiled sleepily, it was a smile she only gave him; enchanting and sweet. She then noticed Kimiko, still kneeling, their eyes meeting, her face turning red as grabbed the blanket and covered herself again.

"Oh, I didn't realize you were here Kimiko," Serina said, avoiding Kimiko's gaze. "How are you this morning?"

"I am well Serina-sama," Kimiko replied, seemingly ignoring Serina's embarrassment. "I was about to leave and fetch a healer for Ryuvin-sama."

Kimiko stood and bowed, then turned and walked towards the door. Stopping, she looked back over her right shoulder towards Serina.

"You know this would not be the first time I have seen you naked."

With that, Kimiko left. Ryuvin looked at Serina, her face even more red than before.

"So you and Kimiko huh?" He asked as he raised an eyebrow.

"I-it was nothing like that," came Serina's stammered reply. "We simply shared a room in the barracks years back, that's all."

"Shared a room? Perhaps the same bed at times?" Ryuvin said with a smirk.

"By the gods, you are such a pervert," Serina gasped and threw a pillow at him. "Want me to check the dressing? You were pretty...rough with me last night."

"Do not act like you did not enjoy it," Ryuvin said and kissed her passionately.

Her lips were soft, always reminding him of the first time he had kissed her. Pulling away reluctantly, he sat on the edge of the bed and nodded."

"It is sore but I do not think it is anything that cannot be fixed."

"Okay," Serina said as she positioned herself behind him. "Can I ask you something?"

"Serina you do not need my permission, you can ask me anything."

She took a breath and nodded.

"What do you make of her story?"

Ryuvin sat in silence for a moment as he pondered the question. He figured that Serina was referring to Seleena and the revelations from last night.

"Well," he began. "If she really is your mother, and what she said is the truth, it does explain a few things."

"Such as?" Serina asked. "Also lift your arm."

"Well," Ryuvin began as he lifted his arm, wincing a bit, to allow Serina to continue to remove the bandage. "Such as why the wood elves became so reclusive, to start with."

"I guess that makes sense."

"As for Seleena being your mother, even you cannot deny it. You look almost exactly like her."

"I guess that is true, maybe I'm just overwhelmed with all of this. I finally know who my parents are. Or at least who my mother is."

Ryuvin flinched as Serina pulled the bandage from his shoulder, fresh blood slowly leaking from the wound.

"I'm sorry," Serina gasped. "I didn't mean to make it bleed again."

"It is okay," Ryuvin said to her with a smile then kissed her cheek. "I know you did not mean to do it intentionally."

"Am I interrupting something?" Asked a man from the door.

"Hello Ninthalor," Ryuvin said to the high elf that had just entered the room. "I trust you are well."

Ninthalor stood in the doorway, his hands folded in the sleeves of his cotton forest green robes. His face stoic as ever, the wisdom of his age reflected in his brown eyes.

"Kimiko has informed me that your wound is in need of attention," he said, his voice calm as he strode towards the bed. "Visual observation show my magic has healed most of the wound. Although...."

Ninthalor glanced at Serina, she was blushing again as she held the blanket tighter around her body.

"It still takes time for wounds to fully heal, even with magic."

Ryuvin nodded and shifted his position as to allow Ninthalor access to better inspect the wound.

"Thank you Ninthalor," Ryuvin began. "It there-"

"Now I will hear none of that," Ninthalor said, interrupting Ryuvin as he began healing his shoulder.

Ryuvin could feel the magic flow into his shoulder, the flesh slowly beginning to knit itself back together. Healing magic was always fascinating to watch. The caster, in most cases a cleric or priest, would draw in the magic from the natural world and focus on increasing the speed at which the body would naturally recover. And Ninthalor's family were the most adapt healers to ever grace the kingdom.

"My family," Ninthalor continued. "Has served the House of Ashgrove since before Avanthar became King and founded this nation."

Ryuvin nodded then turned a bit to kiss Serina softly on the lips. Ninthalor watched and smiled to himself.

"It does warm the heart, to see our future King and Queen as such."

"Well, Ryuvin always did enjoy having Serina around," Kimiko said as she approached Ninthalor. "Even as a young boy."

"How are your children Ninthalor?" Serina asked as she lay her hand on Ryuvin's. "I haven't seen them for some time."

"The last letter i received said they were well," Ninthalor replied. "They travelled to Sandara and should be home by tomorrow eve."

"Oh I can't wait to see Lelitha again," Serina said gleefully.

"Well sire," Ninthalor said as he straightened and folded

his hands back into the sleeves of his robe. "My magic shall take care of the rest and your wound will be fully healed in a short while. I shall take my leave now."

"Thank you Ninthalor," Ryuvin said as he rubbed his shoulder. "For everything."

Ninthalor did not respond. He simply smiled to the young prince and bowed before leaving with Kimiko.

"So," Serina began as she knelt on the bed. "Now that your shoulder has been taken care of, what ever shall we do today?"

"Hmm I am not sure, what would you like to do?"
"I can think of several things," she replied with a mischievous smirk as she let the blanket fall from her body.

Ryuvin watched, with hungry eyes, as she crawled slowly away from him, swaying her hips enticingly as she did. Ryuvin shifted closer, his hand reaching out, as he traced his fingers over her rear and down between her thighs. She let out a soft moan as she pressed back against his fingers and lay her chest against the bed.

"I need you now," Serina panted, her face flushed.

"Who am I to deny my Princess," Ryuvin replied as he pulled off his robe and knelt behind her.

A sudden knock on the door caused the two to jump slightly.

"Apologies your Highness," came the voice of a guard. "King Tarin has summoned you."

"Can it wait?" Ryuvin called out as Serina pressed back against him. "I am preoccupied at the moment."

"My apologies sire but it cannot, the King said it was urgent."

"Very well, tell him I am on my way," Ryuvin replied with a sigh. "Rain check?"

Serina pouted but nodded before sliding from the bed to dress.

CHAPTER 4

Wind rushed passed her ears, the sound was deafening. She opened her eyes, tears stinging her cheeks in the cold. She was falling, flames burning around her. She looked to the ground below, rapidly approaching, she did not recognize it.

Where am I? What happened to me?

The thoughts screamed in her head. She flexed her wings but they refused to work. The chains on her arms weighing her down.

Why do my wings fail me?

She was close to the ground now, she could make out the trees.

Is this where I die?

The ground was close, oh so close, there was nothing she could do as she watched her death approach.

***

Serina gasped as she awoke. She steadied her breathing and rolled over to cuddle Ryuvin, only the spot next to her was empty.

"That's right," she said to herself. "Ryuvin left for Sandara."

She sighed and slipped out of the bed, donned a robe before she walked onto the small balcony and looked over the city.

"What a strange dream," she said and looked up into the starry night. "No, not a dream. A memory. But who's?"

***

She sat, back pressed against the cool stone window of the temple dedicated to the Sandara's patron Goddess' Athena, Goddess of Peace and Wisdom, and Ares, Goddess of War and Valor.

"There you are child," an elderly said to the girl. "Must you sit in the window?"

"Oh, sorry Mother Partha," the girl replied as she looked at the elderly priestess. "I was just thinking."

"Come, your parents are looking for you."

"The girl nodded as she shifted and stepped back to the floor, the wood creaking slightly.

"Still dreaming of joining one of the Warrior clans?" Mother Partha asked as the two walked through the temple.

The girl merely nodded her response.

"Is that wise child?" Mother Partha asked. "With your eyes-"

"You always did say I was meant for greatness," the girl interrupted. "Ever since the day I was born."

"Yes that is true," the elderly priestess replied with a soft sigh and smiled at her. "The life of a weapon forger is never going to be enough for you."

"The Grand Tournament is starting soon," the girl said as the pair passed two warriors cloaked in grey. "And I intend to win."

"She sounds a lot like you do sister," the one warrior said as she watched the young girl and priestess.

"Do not mock me by comparing me to a mortal," the other warrior replied. "Worry about how they mock you."

The first warrior looked to her sister then to the statue of Athena, her golden eyes ablaze with fury.

***

Ryuvin leaned against the rail of the ship as it sailed towards the island nation of Sandara. It had been a month since he and Kimiko had left Avantharia with Lorewind, he was not sure what to make of her. She was a mage from a race of people calling themselves the Drothak; a mixed blooded race of mortals, half devil half elf, that had been living on the plane of Aventus, or at least that is what she claimed. Her flawless skin was a lovely shade of crimson, eyes glowed green, her long silky reddish black hair broken by horns that swept back. She wore dark grey robes that clung to the curves of her elegant body, she seemed more like a succubus. He glanced over at her then back over the ocean, his thoughts drifting back to when they had met.

The guard had brought Serina and him to the Great Hall of the castle, there they found Lorewind kneeling before his mother and spoke, her soft sweet voice filled with sorrow, of her ordeal. She told of how five years previously, a small group of her people had ventured from Aventus, their plan was to establish cross planar relations with the races of Therago. They were able to construct a small settlement in the forest along the edge of the Ecthar Mountains far to the south east of Avantharia. She then told of the monsters had destroyed her home; blood thirsty beast with greyish brown skin and black eyes. They had swarmed the town, killing everyone they found; women, children, all were butchered. Many were saved because of the Magus, as he was able to erect a magical barrier and create a portal back to Aventus, but still many more had been slaughtered.

Lorewind had claimed, that while the rest of her people fled, she refused to leave and allow what had happened to her people happen to others. She used her magic to escape and spent days hiding from the monsters, though eventually they found her. Wounded badly, and with what little magic she had left, she was able to escape through a portal, which had brought her to Ysegarde, there a young gnome had found her and saved her life.

She spent the next several days recovering, during which, she had a vision of a silver eyed elf alongside a drow with a single purple eye. She had inquired of the beings she saw in her vision and had learned of the bloodline of Avanthar, elves with silver eyes. Once she was sufficiently recovered, Lorewind thanked the family for saving her and opened a portal, stepping through, she found herself in the gardens of the palace where she collapsed. She was later found the next morning and, when questioned, had told her story to Torvan. After which she was brought before the Queen and King, here Seleena was able to confirm Lorewind's story, telling them that the mordian had returned. It was here that Lorewind had another vision; a warrior kneeling before two women with golden eyes. And so, Ryuvin, Kimiko and Lorewind had set out on their journey back to Ysegarde and then by ship to Sandara.

"What do you think of her Kimiko?" Ryuvin whispered.

"I think she is beautiful," Kimiko replied flatly as she leaned her back against the rail of the ship while staring at Lorewind.

"That is not what I meant and you know it."

"With everything that had happened on your birthday," Kimiko said and looked at Ryuvin. "Seleena reappearing after several hundreds years, that filth Arondath arriving in Avalon, and now her."

"I see what you mean," Ryuvin replied with a sigh then looked back to Lorewind and called. "Still nothing?"

"No," she replied and opened her eyes. "I can no longer feel the same power that fueled my magic."

"Perhaps," Kimiko interjected. "It is because your Magus is what powered your magic."

Lorewind shook her head as she stood and joined them at the rail of the ship. She sighed as she watched the ship sail into the crescent shaped bay of Sandara.

"Not possible," her soft voice contained a hint of fear. "When the first of my people came here, they had used magic. The Magus didn't arrive until after. What I feel now is…alien to me, almost li-"

"Miss Lorewind!" Came a young girl's voice.

A young gnome came bounding across the deck, her red braided hair streaming out behind her.

"Hello Rose," Lorewind said with a smile as the girl stopped before her. "Is there something wrong?"

Rose shook her head and looked up at her, blue eyes filled with excitement.

"Just eager to see Sandara for the first time. Father always promised he would take me when I was old enough."

"Well I'm glad you are here," Lorewind replied happily.

With a gleeful smile, Rose ran to the prow of the ship.

"I am told the view of Sandra is quiet beautiful from the harbour," Ryuvin said as he watched Rose. "Shall we join her?"

Lorewind and Kimiko nodded and the three of them followed after Rose. The ship slowly sailed passed the Gates of Athena; giant pillars of stone that held a massive interlocking metal chain, which could be raised to block entrance to the entire nation as the only other way onto the island would be to scale the massive sheer cliffs that encircled Sandara. Upon reaching the prow, the group found Rose, wide eyed with wonder, a smile plastered to her face as she stared up at the island nation of Sandara.

"It's so beautiful," Rose exclaimed.

Ryuvin, Lorewind and Kimiko gazed up at the city, stone and wood buildings, with sloped roofs of red clay tiles, had lined the mountain slope within the natural rock walls of the island. At the top, stood The Grand Temple, home of the Twin Gods Ares and Athena.

"You're right Rose," Lorewind said in awe "It's beautiful."

"Aye that it is," came a gruff voice with a slight squeak. "Sandara is said to rival the beauty of Ymitor in Jotunhiem."

"Will you take me there too some day Father?" Rose asked expectantly to the male gnome.

The balding gnome smiled as he pat Rose's head.

"One day," he said, his black beard ruffling in the breeze. "But not until we've seen Sandara together."

Rose beamed happily as she hugged her father tight.

"I wanted to tank you again," Lorewind said as she bowed to Rose's father. "Not just for taking my companions and I to Sandara, but for everything your family has done for me."

"Think nothing of it lass," he replied with a wave of his hand. "I may not know the pain of lose like you do, but that doesn't mean people should turn their backs on those in need. There is already enough suffering in this world without me adding to it."

**

Approximately an hour later, with the ship docked at the

port, Ryuvin, Lorewind, now fully cloaked to hide her appearance, and Kimiko bid farewell to Rose and her father before making their way through the streets towards the temple.

"Are you sure the temple is the best place to start?" Lorewind asked as she cast nervous glances at the people, many of which were human.

"You said your vision was of a warrior kneeling before two women with golden eyes," Ryuvin answered as he looked back at her. "Well, according to the legends, the Twins of Sandara were the only gods with golden eyes."

"Stay close to me," Kimiko said as she took Lorewind's hand in hers. "I will keep you safe."

Lorewind smiles slightly and looked down as if to hide her face, for a fleeting moment, Ryuvin thought she may have been blushing.

Ryuvin led Lorewind and Kimiko through the streets of the harbour district, most of the citizens here wore basic functional work clothing, a few wore more fanciful robes or gowns; Ryuvin had guessed they were the owners of the businesses. Several patrols of guards, each carrying large round shields marched through the port. The bronze tips of their spears glimmered in the sunlight. Full face bronze helms, a blue and white plume was affixed to the lead soldier's helm. Their chest armour, bracers and greaves, also made of bronze, bore an engraving of a serpent, and leather sandals. Beneath the armour, each hoplite wore light tunics and a leather ptergues to protect their thighs, with a blue and white sash hanging over their right thigh, also depicting the same serpent that was engraved on their armour. Ryuvin assumed that the sash was to represent which warrior clan they belonged to.

"Is every port this busy?" Lorewind asked as she watch the citizens with fascination.

"More or less," Ryuvin replied, watching a few hoplites as they chatted amongst themselves while they watched the three.

Several minutes later, the three of them made their way through a somewhat small public square. The sound of hammers clanging echoed from the many craftsmen shops, a stone entryway, consisting of two pillars and a crossbeam, stood at the north and south entrances to the square, jade dragons coiled around each pillar, looking into the square. At the centre of the square stood an ornate fountain, a statue of a Sandaran hoplite, carrying a spear and shield, full faced helm and armour, stood affixed a central column as water poured from ports on all four sides.

A commotion on the northern side of the fountain had gathered a crowed.

"Hear me brothers and sisters!" A man with a nasally voice yelled to the crowd as he stood on the edge of the fountain.

Dressed in a vibrant purple robe with only a single sleeve, adorned with gold trim. His curly jet black hair was damp with sweat, as his oil tanned lanky body seemed to buckle under the weight of the jewellery he wore. In front of him stood two hoplites, clad in the same armour as the others, the only difference was that the engraving was of a boar and their sash colours were red and black.

"Our once great nation has been weakened by those that look to us as allies!" The man continued, there were several murmurs of agreement within the crowd. "Even as I speak, these weak countries send spies and assassins to our shores in petty attempts to weaken us further."

"Cowards!" Yelled one of the men from the crowd.

"Purge the infiltrators!" Yelled a woman.

"Let us keep moving," Ryuvin whispered to Lorewind and Kimiko. "He staged those in the crowd to agree with his statements, he is trying to push the crowd into doing something dangerous."

"See my fellow countrymen! One of our *allies* already sent agents to silence me!" The man yelled as he pointed to Ryuvin and Kimiko. "But fear not, for they have been exposed for what they truly are. Liars and murderers!"

Suddenly, several more hoplites appeared and fanned out in front of them, speared levelled and ready to strike. Kimiko moved, protectively in front of Lorewind and put her right arm out across Ryuvin's chest. Her eye scanning every inch of the situation.

"Stay behind me, Ryuvin-sama," she whispered.

"Protect Lorewind," Ryuvin replied. "I can handle a few myself."

Kimiko nodded and shifted her left foot back slightly, placing her hand on Lorewind's hip.

"Actually my good sir," Ryuvin began as he took a single step forwards. "My companions and I are simply here to visit the Grand Temple."

"We are not here to listen to your lies," the man sneered. "Elven scum should never come to our shores."

"I have no reason to lie," Ryuvin replied, his voice calm. "In fact, perhaps a member of the great Kephelia clan would kindly point the way?"

"Enough lies knife ear filth," one of the hoplites said as he brandished his spear at Ryuvin.

"You best watch your tongue when you speak to Ryuvin-sama," Kimiko said, a calm anger edged into her voice, purple eye ablaze with cold fury.

The hoplites tensed up, raising their shields and readying their spears. Kimiko, also responding, her fingers of her right brushing across the concealed throwing daggers on her hip.

"This confrontation is hardly necessary," Ryuvin said, his voice hard, hand resting on his sword. "If I may-"

Suddenly, an object crashed into the ground, several feet from the group, kicking up a cloud of dust. The hoplites wheeled on the cloud, spears levelled and ready for battle. More hoplites, their sash orange and black with a wolf, had already entered the square and began herding the citizen away.

"So much power," Lorewind said in fear as she tried to hide herself behind Kimiko even more than she already was. "Not even the Magus wielded this amount of strength."

Ryuvin looked from Lorewind to the cloud as is swirled in the light breeze, drawing his sword he stood ready. When the dust finally settled, a warrior stood in the small crater left from her landing.

Chapter 5

The warrior stood, surveying the square as if she were looking for something. More hoplites of the Kephelia clan surrounded her. The grey cloak she wore fluttered in the breeze, long black hair spilled from beneath the hood. In her right hand she held a large two handed sword; the double edged blade, engraved with what appeared to be eagles, was easily just shy of four feet in length, a silver cross guard separated the blade from the black leather wrapped hilt and silver pommel, the entire length of the sword being roughly five feet.

"Look my fellow Sandarans!" The nasally man yelled at pointed at the warrior. "They have finally-"

"Be silent!" The warrior boomed as a wave of power radiated off of her. "Your voice is grating my nerves. I suggest you hold your tongue before you lose it."

"Easy dear sister," said another warrior as she approached the first, seemingly from nowhere.

She wore the same style cloak, a large two-handed sword, with a simple black leather hilt, hung from her back; the scabbard was made from red leather laced with gold filigree.

"I am sure this fool just does not recognize you and spoke out of turn."

"You telling me to calm down is rich," the first chided.

As the two women bickered amongst themselves, Lorewind had shifted slightly closer to Ryuvin.

"They are not from this world," she whispered to him.

"I gathered as much," he replied, sweat dripping down his temple. "The sheer amount of power they each wield just resonates off of them."

"Enough!" Yelled the nasally man from behind the Kephelia hoplites. "I will not listen to a pair of harlots argue!"

The sound of metal scrapping was heard as the second warrior drew her blade from its scabbard.

"You dare insult me?" She said, unlike her sister, the rage in her voice was clear.

"I dare," the man replied with a sneer. "You best show respect, for I am of the Kephelia clan, the greatest of all the clans of the Sandaran nation."

"Ha!" The warrior mocked as she pointed her nodachi at him, the engraved flames that ran along the blade's length danced like real fire. "Kephelia hoplites are weak, the only reason they have a clan is by the grace of the Twins."

Fury filled the man's face as it turned red, the insult clearly hitting a nerve, as the hoplites tensed with anger.

"You spew on about respect," she continued. "Respect from your betters is earned in combat. I challenge you to ritual combat. If you win then you have my respect. When you lose, your life will be mine to do with as I please, as is the Sandaran way."

"Very well," the man half sneered and half smirked, as if this was his plan all along. "I accept your challenge. I also choose to have a champion fight on my behalf."

"It matters not who you choose," she replied dismissively. "You will still lose to my champion."

"Afraid to die, harlot?" The man asked with a condescending tone.

Ignoring him, the warrior turned towards the crowd.

"You there, girl," she said as she pointed at one of the bystanders. "Come here."

A younger girl, no more than nineteen years of age, stepped out of the crowd and walked towards the warriors before bowing. She wore a blue haori with a red floral pattern held closed with a dark sash around her waist and a dark blue momohiki, her purplish black hair was held out of her face in a warrior's braid, a blue blindfold covered her eyes.

"You know who we are?" The warrior asked her.

"Yes," the girl replied, still bowed, with a calm voice.

"Good, follow me," the warrior said as she turned and they both walked towards Ryuvin, Lorewind and Kimiko.

"Ryuvin Ashgrove," the first warrior said with a nod as the reached the group.

"You have me at a disadvantage," Ryuvin replied cautiously. "You know me but I do not know you."

"All in good time mortal," said the second warrior then turned to the girl. "Prepare yourself."

"Of course," she replied.

She then loosened the sash around her waist and let it fall to the ground, her haori opening. She then shrugged it off, revealing her extremely well toned body, coated with a thin layer of sweat. Several scars along her chiselled forearms and abs were the only marks on her otherwise flawless olive skin.

"You know if you are going to stare," she said as she adjusted the wrappings around her average sized breasts, while tilting her head towards Kimiko and Lorewind. "I'm told my ass is my best feature. I believe it's 'so fine and tight that you can bounce a gold piece off it.' Though I haven't seen it myself."

Ryuvin laughed as both, Lorewind and Kimiko, blushed and looked away, clearly embarrassed.

"Are you ready child?" The first warrior asked.

"I am," she answered as she stretched her arms above her head a bit.

"Good," the second warrior said. "choose your sword."

The girl nodded and looked over to the first warrior.

"Very well," she replied and looked to her sister. "Your weapon."

"Are you not going to remove your eye wraps?" Lorewind asked, concern edging into her voice.

The girl tested the balance of the blade in her hand then gave it a few practice swings.

"I would," she replied as she turned towards the combat

area. "But being blind doesn't change if it stays on or not."

With that, the girl walked towards her opponent. He was a massive man, about two feet taller than her and extremely muscular. Like the girl, he was bare chested; but did keep the rest of his armour on. His brown hair was cut short and his beard clean. Carrying a shield, bearing the emblem of Kephelia, in his left hand and a spear, easily around eleven feet in length, in his right. Both warriors stopped a few feet from each other.

"I see you carry no shield," he said, his voice deep and calm. "I shall do the same."

The warrior shrugged off his shield, caught it and then tossed it several feet to his left, a dull thud sounded as it hit the ground.

"Very well," the girl said as she tilted her held and raid her sword. "Shall we begin?"

"We shall," he replied as he touched his spear to her blade.

Turning, both walked back several steps then turned and faced each other again.

"What are they doing?" Lorewind asked.

"It is a duel," Ryuvin answered. "For Sandarans, each part will state their names and rewards upon victory."

He then gestured to the two.

"Since they fight as champions, they will state who they fight for and that part will then state the rewards of victory. In most cases for Sandaran duels, the victor enslaves the loser."

"That's barbaric."

"That is the Sandaran way," Kimiko replied.

"I, Patridale, son of the General Particus," the warrior called out as he lifted his spear. "Fight as champion for Snakerius of the Kephelia clan."

The crowd began to cheer for Patridale.

"I, Snakerius, son of Thacrius," the nasally man sneered. "Shall claim upon victory, both the lives of my opponent and her champion, to become my slaves."

Next, the girl lifted her sword.

"I, Athanasia, daughter of the smith Haphesto," Athanasia

replied. "Fight as champion for our Goddess, Ares."

"I, Ares," the goddess began ignoring the shocked crowd. "Shall claim upon victory, the lives of both my opponent and his champion, to do as I see fit. As is the Sandaran way."

Both warriors had removed their cloaks. Each wore ornate armour consisting of bracers, greaves, a leather ptergues, pauldrons and a chest guard that left their mid section exposed. The difference was that Ares wore red armour with gold filigree, whereas Athena's was black with silver. Had it not been for the armour, Ryuvin would not be able to tell the twins apart. Both had perfectly toned bodies, just enough muscle to be seen, like Athanasia. Their pale skin, flawless, not a single scar. Slightly larger than average breasts and supple rears, they could easily be mistake for goddesses of beautiful; it if were not for the fire burning in their golden eyes.

It was only then did Ryuvin realize, Patridale had been kneeling before Athanasia, the colour drained from his face. Ryuvin looked around and saw that even the crowd had knelt down. Feeling Athena's gaze fall upon him, he began to kneel as well.

"There is no need for that young Heroes," she said to them, her voice now calm and sweet, unlike earlier.

Bewildered, Ryuvin, Kimiko and Lorewind stood and looked back to Athanasia as she stood over the kneeling Patridale.

"I yield to you Lady Athanasia," he said, keeping his head bowed. "I have no wish to fight one of the greatest weapon forgers of this era, nor a champion to our Goddess."

"What are you doing Patridale?!" Snakerius screamed, his nasally voice making it almost sound like a squeak. "She is nothing more than a blind skank! Kill her now!"

"Finish the duel," Patridale said as he looked up at Athanasia. "As is the Sandaran way."

She nodded and pressed her foot to his chest, pushing him to his back. Then she stood over him, sword raised above her head before swinging it downwards. Blood splattered across the stones and the crowd gasped.

"My blade has tasted the blood of my opponent," Athanasia declared as she held Athena's sword in the air, the blade tipped with crimson. "I claim victory in Ares' name."

"Your life is mine Snakerius," Ares called out. "As per the terms, your life is also mine, Patridale."

Patridale nodded and moved back to the other hoplites to have his wound tended to, blood streaming down his chest from the cut Athanasia left over his right pectoral.

"I will not accept this!" Snakerius scream as he grabbed Patridale's sword from next to his armour and rushed Athanasia from behind. "In Oa's name, I shall end you!"

"Athanasia!" Ryuvin cried and charged forwards, drawing his own blade.

I will not make it in time, he thought as he watched Snakerius swing the sword.

In a single fluid motion, Athanasia ducked the wild swing, spun on her left foot and thrust Athena's sword through Snakerius' midsection. Blood exploded out his back as the spear severed his spine. Shock registered on Snakerius' face as his body went limp. With a spin, Athanasia pushed him away from her and withdrew the sword in an arc, nearly severing his body in half as he hit the ground, Snakerius gasped and coughed up blood.

"This is the beginning of the end," Snakerius gave a gurgled laugh as Ryuvin reached Athanasia. "Oa has sent his cursed army to destroy this world."

Ryuvin watched as the blood pooled underneath Snakerius, death coming as he drowned in his own blood, a strange black serpent amulet slipping out from his robes.

"Forgive me Lady Ares," Athanasia said as she knelt before the twins. "His life was not mine to take."

"It matters not," Ares said as Athena took back her sword. "I would have executed him for his disregard for our traditions as it was."

Ares stepped forwards and cupped Athanasia's chin,

gently tilting her head up, and smiled at her, for a brief moment, Ryuvin thought he saw, what he could only interpret as a look of motherly affection. She walked passed Athanasia, towards Patridale, who was now seated as one of the other hoplites wiped the blood from the stitches of his wound.

"Lady Ares!" He gasped as he began to stand but was waved off.

"I have a task for you Patridale."

"My life is yours to command, Milady."

"You will go to your father, General Particus. He will assemble the heads of the clans and have them come to our temple."

"Of course," Patridale replied and bowed as best he could. "May I ask as to why?"

"There is an infection on our island," Ares began.

"And we intend to destroy it," Athena finished.

Ryuvin watched as the twins walked towards the Grand Temple then looked at the onyx pendant that Snakerius had.

What exactly is going on? He thought.

You will learn soon son of Avanthar, a voice whispered in his mind, *now follow them.*

Who are you? He asked the voice, only there was no reply.

"We best follow," he said to Kimiko and Lorewind before following the twins.

CHAPTER 6

The sun had begun to set, the shadows of the stone columns in the Grand Temple lengthened. Ares and Athena stood on the raised dais in silent conversation. The statue of Athena had been shattered, debris scattered across the ground.

"They know something about the mordians," Kimiko whispered to Ryuvin, keeping her eye fixed on the twins. "And who is Oa? I have never heard of that god before."

"That is because Oa is not a god," Athena said as she walked down the steps of the dais.

"Then what is he?" Ryuvin asked.

"*She* is the Primordial Dragon of Shadow, Death and Destruction."

"Primordial Dragon?" Kimiko asked. "I have never heard of such a thing."

"Ha!" Ares laughed from the dais. "Did you honestly think that the gods were the absolute power in the planarverse?"

"Mocking them does not help the situation sister," Athena chided. "It would appear a history lesson is in order."

"That would be most welcome," Lorewind said.

"I shall try to keep this brief," Athena began. "In the beginning, there was nothing save the Primordials. Oa, together with her siblings; Ao, Primordial Dragon of Light, Creation and Life, Gaia, the Earth Mother, Kossathia, the Eternal Flame, Aremto, the Great Tempest, Watroth, the Leviathan of the Depths, Skard, the Frozen Tundra, Temra, the Lightning's Fury, Entalia, the Guardian of the Living Wood, and Jarn, the Iron Soul, created the planarverse. Light, darkness, earth, fire, wind, water, ice, lightning, nature and iron. Each of these dragons holds dominion over one of the very aspects of the cosmos. They need no worshippers whereas the gods do."

"So how exactly is Oa connected to the mordians?" Kimiko asked. "Why send a force to destroy what she helped to create?"

"That is because she is not, none of the gods know where they came from," Ares chimed in. "When last the appeared, a group of fanatics, seeking to destroy the world, believed that Oa created them. And thus, created a cult called Vyizm Arvyr, or Death's Order."

"Ever since then," Athena continued. "They have been destroying cities, overthrowing thrones and instigating wars. And no matter how many times the gods have tried, the cult always returns."

"So what do-" Ryuvin began but was interrupted by Ares with a wave of her hand.

"The clan rulers are here," she said.

The sun had set when the sound of chatter reached Ryuvin's ears causing him to look towards the temple's entrance. A large group of Sandarans had begun to enter the temple, at the head of the group were the King and Queen. They both wore jade green single sleeved robes with a black sash. There was a standard bearer following holding a white banner with a jade dragon, similar to the dragons on the pillars in the town squares. Upon reaching the group they stopped and bowed.

"I am Shingen, King of Sandara," the king said. "And this is my Queen, Yukia."

Yukia was roughly a foot shorter than Shingen, her pale skin stood in stark contrast to his olive. The robes she wore did little to hide the curves of her shapely rear and large breasts. Her plump figure was matched by her round face. Her calming brown eyes and sweet smile made Ryuvin's heart ache for his future bride, Serina.

Shingen was younger than Ryuvin had originally thought. Roughly in his late twenties. He had shoulder length, reddish black hair that was tied back in a warrior's braid with the sides shaved short. Clean shaven and strong jaw, his hazel eyes locked with Ryuvin's silver.

"I have heard of you before," Shingen said to Ryuvin, his gaze refusing to waver. "You are Ryuvin Ashgrove, the Silver Blade and Crowned Prince of Avantharia. I will admit, I expected you to be...taller."

"And if I recall correctly Shingen," Ryuvin replied. "Were you not beaten in the first round of Sandara's Grand Tournament last year?"

Shingen kept a calm composure but Kimiko saw his jaw clench slightly.

"Ryuvin-sama," Kimiko interjected. "I believe Athena and Ares are ready to begin."

An older man, that was near identical to Patridale, aside from the grey in his hair and beard, as well a long jagged scar on his right cheek going down his neck, approached Shingen and Yukia.

"The drow is correct sire," he said, voice slightly deeper than Patridale.

"Of course Particus," Yukia said, her voice soft and sweet like honey. "Come my love."

Shingen finally broke eye contact with Ryuvin and looked at Yukia, a loving smile on his face. When the clan leaders formed a semi-circle in front of the dais around the twins, Athena finally spoke.

"As you should have been made aware," she began. "There is a fanatical cult in Sandara."

Before anyone could respond, a pillar of golden light descended upon the dais. And near the entrance, opened a black portal. From the light, a warrior, in golden armour, hovered slightly on outstretched wings as white as fresh fallen snow flecked, with gold. From the portal, several beings, cloaked in black, emerged.

"Good," Ares said as she addressed the cloaked beings. "It would seem Oa is finally taking this cult issue seriously."

With the mention of Oa's name, the hoplites of the clans reached for their weapons.

"Calm yourselves," Athena commanded. "These are the Valkyrie, Oa has tasked them to find and destroy this cult."

"Be grateful," hissed the Valkyrie leader, her voice as cold as death. "Our duty is not to clean up the mess of mortal fools."

"Yes, we are well aware of your duties, Freya," the golden warrior said, face hidden beneath a navy blue hood. "You shepherd the souls of the dead to the realms of the god they worship."

"Watch your tone with me angel," Freya snapped before turning her attention to Shingen, standing an easy two feet taller than him. "You will not impede our search, we shall deal with this annoyance in our own way."

"And what, pray tell, is your own way?" Shingen asked.

Freya did not answer, instead she merely shrugged off her cloak. She wore a tight black unadorned leather cuirass, that only covered her breasts, tight fitting black leggings and knee high leather books. On her back hung a bladed weapon, with a gnarled dark wooden shaft affixed with a metallic skull, between a pair of black feathered wings. She turned, her silver white hair framed her pale, hauntingly beautiful face. Black eyes, devoid of light and emotion, scanned the room. She closed her eyes and inhaled deeply, head turning slightly, as she searched for a scent. Ryuvin had then noticed the other Valkyrie had cast of their cloaks and did the same. Without opening her eyes, Freya had taken the weapon from her back and tapped it to the stone floor. The blade snapping out, revealing a wickedly curved scythe.

"Ah," she said as her eyes opened. "I have found you."

Scythe in hand, she advanced towards the man bearing the standard of the Royal Family. Two of the other Valkyrie had also moved, one now stood behind a clan leader wearing an orange silk robe, the other behind a hoplite standing near Athanasia.

"You chose the wrong monster to serve," Freya said coldly to the standard bearer.

In mere seconds, the scythes of the Valkyrie descended

upon their victims. In a spray of blood, the three bodies crumpled to the floor. Silence filled the temple as Freya knelt down and picked up the severed head of the now dead standard bearer. The clan leader had been sliced nearly in half vertically, her blood soaking her nearby handmaiden and pooling at her feet. The hoplite near Athanasia had been killed in a way that left him in pieces, diagonal slice that severed both his arms from his torso as well as his body in half. Several handmaidens screamed, while a few of the merchant clan members fainted or vomited. Even members of the warrior clans faces blanched at the sheer brutality of the Valkyrie.

"All those of the cult share the same fate," Freya declared as she threw the severed head at Shingen's feet.

Shingen looked down at the severed head, then back to Freya, her upper body and face covered with blood, her scythe dripping with gore. The Valkyrie flexed their wings, and in a flurry of black feathers, took off into the night.

Death had come to Sandara.

"Now, the other reason we have gathered you," Athena said as she returned her attention to the group. "Come forth, Athanasia."

Athanasia stepped forwards towards Ares and Athena, ignoring the few murmurs from a couple of the hoplites.

"Kneel," Ares commanded.

Athanasia did so, dropping to one knee and bowing her head.

"Nineteen years ago, on the day of your birth, the clan of Himikori would forever change."

"Blind and near death," Athena continued. "Your father prayed to us, so that your life would be spared."

"We named you," Ares said. "Athanasia, the Immortal Flame."

"Over the years we tested you," Athena continued. "We needed to see if you were worthy. Never once did you waver."

"Worthy?" Athanasia asked in confusion as she looked up.

"To wield our power," Ares answered. "Mortal legends are filled with stories of heroes that wield the power of gods."

"Mjolnir," Ryuvin said aloud, causing everyone to look at him. "To whomsoever seeks the Hammer, they must prove worthy in the eyes of the God of Thunder, only then shall they wield the power of Thor."

"That is correct," Athena replied. "Though simplistic. Mortals only wield the power of gods so long as we allow them. So long as the prove worthy."

"Mortals can wield the power gods through our weapons," Ares continued. "Weapons such as Mjolnir, the Storm Hammer of Thor, or Excalibur, the Righteous Blade of Justice, wielded by Dovaria."

At the mention of Dovaria's name, the angel tensed slightly, although no one seemed to notice.

"Wait," Shingen interrupted. "You mean to tell me that Excalibur actually exists?!"

"Forged upon the anvils of Himinsla, within the realm of Creation," Athena said. "Blessed by Ao and given to Dovaria, the Archangel of Justice. To protect the weak and punish the wicked."

"I am familiar with Dovaria," Kimiko said as she glanced at the angel. "Though is she not the goddess of righteous fury and retribution?"

"That is because she was cast out of Yggdrasil," the angel said as she pulled back her hood, her golden blonde hair flowing free from her face, ice blue eyes filled with sorrow and anger. "Eons ago, when the planarverse was young, Dovaria was the Archangel of Justice. Her purpose was to be the anchor that held justice across all of existence. For millennia, she did just that. While justice may not be apparent, Dovaria began drifting, her deeds more akin to vengeance than justice. Eventually, one of these acts ignited a war upon the mortal realm. This war nearly destroyed Therago; the end result gave birth to the gods and the Dread Knights."

A murmur arose with the mention of the Dread Knights, the angel looked over to Athena and Ares.

"The Twins know the war of which I speak."

"True leadership," the angel began without even glancing at Shingen. "Is not measured by the experiences of a single person-"

"It is measured by their capability to bring hope and inspire others," Ryuvin finished.

The angel nodded.

"Like all those of the Ashgrove bloodline," the angel continued. "You were born to lead."

Ryuvin looked back at Kimiko, uncertainty clear in his silver eyes. He was torn, part of him knew he had the capabilities of leading, he had been leading for as long as he could remember; from when he was a child with the few friends he had to his own command of a cavalry unit. The other part of him whispered doubts of his abilities and his ability to lead anything more than a single unit of soldiers.

"Ryuvin," Lorewind said, her soft voice cutting through his thoughts. "I know we haven't known each other for very long but I believe in you, I know you are stronger than you give yourself credit for."

"There are going to be times where you falter," the angel continued. "But I, along with your friends, shall be there to aid you."

"Ashgrove," Particus said as he walked over to Ryuvin. "Are you ready to do what is required of you?"

"Is-" Ryuvin began but hesitated. "No, I am not ready."

Particus nodded and turned back to the Twins.

"He is ready," Particus said to them before looking back to Ryuvin. "No one is ever ready to become more than what they already are."

"I, Kayle," the angel boomed as she spread her wings and lifted herself higher into the air. "Protector of the Gates of Creation and She whom commands the Angelic Legions, give unto you, Ryuvin, my powers."

A pillar of light descended upon Ryuvin, not blinding but warm and comforting. When it vanished, Ryuvin's clothing had changed. He now wore an ornate plate cuirass under a leather long coat, that covered the back of his legs, studded leather vambracers and pauldrons. Like Athanasia, the armour was black with gold trim, the left pauldron depicting a roaring lion. A single angel wing was embossed, in gold, on the back of his long coat. A plain bastard sword in a black leather sheath hung from his left hip.

"It is very light," Ryuvin said as he inspected the armour.

It is crafted from dragon weave, Kayle responded. *A special thread gifted to us by Ao.*

"Strong enough to stop a sword?"

It will take much for a normal mortal blade to pierce through, magical blades on the other hand...

"Ryuvin-sama, who are you talking to?" Kimiko asked.

Confused, Ryuvin looked over his shoulder towards Kimiko then back to Kayle, only Kayle was no longer there. In her place was an orb of pale gold.

They can no longer hear me, Kayle's voice whispered.

You were the one that helped me during my fight with Arondath, Ryuvin said to her.

Yes, Kayle answered. *I have watched over you since the day you were born. But be warned, I am not the only immortal that has.*

What do you mean?

You are he who walks between the realms of angels and daemons, she replied. *Soon you will have to face him if you want to reach your full potential.*

Him? Ryuvin questioned.

Altareon, the Daemon King.

I understand why you were watching over me, Ryuvin said to Kayle, *but why would a daemon?*

While angels protect the gates to the realm of Yggdrasil, the daemons are the beings the protect the gate to Nessus, the realm of destruction.

I have heard so many stories of how daemons are evil and that they seek to corrupt the mortal realm, Ryuvin said, *are you saying that is not accurate?*

As angels are born of the light, so to are daemons born of the darkness. It is that darkness that corrupts the weak willed, not the daemons themselves.

Ryuvin pondered what Kayle had told him. If daemons are not evil like the world believes, then what other inaccuracies are there among the legends and stories he has heard.

"Ryuvin?" Athanasia said, pulling him from his thoughts.

He looked over his shoulder to her and realized that, while conversing with Kayle, the clan leaders had left the temple.

"Do not worry," Athena told him. "I had informed the others that you were conversing with Kayle."

"Your next task," Ares said. "Is to find the Child of Ice."

"Wait, what about Lorewind and Kimiko?" Athanasia asked as she looked to them. "Are they not Knights as well?"

"Now that the call has sounded," Athena replied. "Their immortals shall reveal themselves. How and when, I do not know."

"Now go heroes," Ares commanded. "The fate of Therago rests on your shoulders."

CHAPTER 7

Light surrounded her as she stood in the crystalline chamber, bound in chains. Her jaw clenched as she watched the hooded woman descend from her throne, striding with purpose down the steps.

"Do you have any idea what you have done?" She asked as she approached.

"I did what I was born to do," the chained woman replied. "I brought justice upon the wicked."

"Foolish child," the other said. "You brought war upon the mortal realm. You have overstepped for the last time."

The chained woman looked around to the other hooded figures in the room.

"You were all too weak to act," she yelled. "We are angels, immortal beings meant to protect the races of the planarverse. Yet none of you so much as moved to lift a finger to aid the mortals of Therago in their time of need."

"You have stepped out of your domain sister," one of the angels said as she stepped forwards and pointed a massive spear of silver fire at her. "You have no prevalence within the domain of War, for that is my dominion."

"Enough!" The first angel yelled.

The War angel huffed and stepped back lowering her blade.

"You have committed grave crimes within the mortal realm," the first angel continued as she addressed the one in chains. "You are beyond redemption and are forthwith exiled from Yggdrasil."

"You think you can pass judgment on me? Ha do not make me laugh, you cannot judge justice itself."

"I can," the first angel replied. "And I will."

The first angel returned to her throne, picked up her spear and pointed a spear at the chained angel.

"I, Fyrir, Queen of the Angels, do hereby render judgment upon you," Fyrir began. "For the crimes of stepping from your path and igniting war upon the realm of Therago, you are stripped of your powers and banished to the mortal realm. Never shall you return to the Realm of Creation."

Fyrir and the convent of angels watched as the angel in chains was lifted in the air, light enveloping her being. If she tried to scream there was no sound. They watched as the angel was shot from the hall, a light streaking across the sky.

"And so Justice falls from the heavens," Fyrir said, tears filling her eyes. "The prophecy has begun. May the Dragons watch over the mortal realm."

Wind rushed passed her ears, the sound was deafening. She opened her eyes, tears stinging her cheeks in the cold. She was falling, flames burning around her. She looked to the ground below, rapidly approaching, she did not recognize it.

***

Serina awoke from her slumber with a start.

Again, she thought, *why do I keep seeing these memories?*

She rolled onto her side and gazed at Ryuvin, then to the orb that was Kayle.

Whoever she was, she was an angel. I wish I could ask Kayle, but I can't put more burden on Ryuvin.

Serina sighed and pressed her naked body closer to Ryuvin, sleep coming back to her slowly.

***

She stood alone. The small area of light was all that kept the darkness at bay. She stood alone. Shapes could be seen just outside the edge of the light, circling her. She stood alone.

"What is it you fear most?" Came the deafening whisper of a sinister voice.

"Show yourself!" She yelled, purple eye scanning for the source.

She stood alone.

"Do you fear death?" The voice asked from behind her.

Spinning, she reached for her daggers. They were not there. Her heartbeat quickened.

"I do not fear anything!" She screamed into the darkness.

She stood alone.

"All creatures fear something, Kimiko," the voice said, almost as if to taunt her. "Do you fear being alone?"

The hairs on the back of her neck stood. A cold sweat ran down her spine. The voice was directly behind her. Slowly she turned to face it. Inches from her face was the featureless face of a creature with empty pale blue eyes. She froze, unable to move, in fear. The creature smiled, then opened its mouth, a maw of needle like teeth descended upon her.

***

Kimiko let out a gurgled gasp as she sat bolt upright, cold sweat covered her naked body. Panting heavily, she felt movement to her right. Looking over to Lorewind, she let out a sigh of relief.

Just a dream, she though as she closed her eyes and placed her hand over her right eye.

Or was it? Came the sinister voice.

She froze, eyes shooting open. Something was wrong. She could now see out her left eye.

What have you done to me? She screamed at the voice, noticing the purplish black orb floating lazily above her head.

I restored your vision, the voice answered.

There was something in the creature's voice that Kimiko could not quite place, was it regret?

But why? Kimiko asked.

A token, of good faith, the creature said, *you are the Knight I've chosen to wield my powers. Like how Kayle chose Ryuvin.*

Who are you?

I am rokshara, the creature answered, *an embodiment of mortal emotion. I am fear made flesh.*

Do you have a name?

*My name....*the creature hesitated, *is Vigil.*

Why does everything I see from my left eye have this blueish tinge?

You can now see the world as I do, Vigil said, *the only way to restore sight in your eye was to effectively give you a magical eye, the Eye of Fear. Though it will be more sensitive to light.*

I may just keep it covered, she replied, *as I normally do.*

The may be for the best, my power will always run through your veins and can reach out into your world.

Meaning what exactly?

That, unconsciously, my power will affect those around. Fear is a powerful tool.

I understand, Kimiko replied as she lay back down, *and thank you*

What for? Vigil asked.

For trusting me with your powers, she answered before closing her eyes and falling back to sleep.

***

It had been a few days since Ryuvin, Kimiko, Lorewind and Athanasia had returned to Avalon, briefing King Tarin on the unfolding events.

"The Child of Ice?" He asked. "And the legends of Excalibur?"

"Yes," Ryuvin answered. "Yet we have no idea where to even begin."

"My first thoughts," Torvan replied. "Would be Jotunheim."

"That seems the most logical, though Jotunheim is a huge country and Ymitor is the only real city there."

"Hmm...you are correct about that son," King Tarin said thoughtfully. "The nomadic tribes will also complicate your search for this 'Child of Ice'."

"Perhaps we should search for Excalibur instead," Torvan said. "Having the mythical blade would be something to get the other nations to rally behind us."

"As much as I would like to," Ryuvin said, as he leaned on a table staring at the map of Therago. "Athena and Ares were clear on the next course of action."

"Why should we listen to Sandaran gods?" Torvan asked, a slight edge to his otherwise even tone.

"I will not sit by as you disrespect my gods," Athanasia said, anger creeping into her voice.

The tension in the air was thick as both, Athanasia and Torvan, squared off.

"Enough!" Ryuvin boomed, fist slamming down against the table. "This is not the time to fight amongst ourselves, there is too much at stake."

"Forgive me, my Prince."

"Yes, I apologize as well."

"Alright," Queen Amilia said, as she stood and smoothed her gown. "We have been here for a few hours. Let us take a moment to get some air and regather our thoughts."

King Tarin sighed as he glanced around the small study. Tall shelves of books and scrolls filled the north and west walls. A window, closed, on the south looked out over the castle gardens. The room was fairly plane and benefited more to one or two people rather than the seven people in the room.

"You are right my Queen," he said. "Let us step away from this for now. We shall meet back in the war room once we have sufficiently recuperated."

"Kimiko?"

"Yes Amilia-sama?"

"Why not give Lorewind a tour of the gardens on the northern side of the palace?"

"Of course," Kimiko answered, a small hint of glee in her voice, before turning to Lorewind. "Shall we?"

Lorewind smiled and nodded as she took Kimiko's hand before following her out of the study, a quick giggle echoing behind her as they left.

"Ryuvin, there is something I wish to speak with you about."

"Of course Mother."

Queen Amilia waited until the others had left and the door closed. Now alone with Ryuvin, she walked to the window and watched the servants tending to the garden.

"You did not tell your father everything," she began without looking at him. "Why?"

"I know not what you mean," he answered.

"Ryuvin," she replied, turning and facing him. "I am your mother, I know when you are troubled and when you are hiding something. What is it?"

Ryuvin sighed and sat in one of the few chairs that surrounded the table.

"All of this, it is overwhelming," he said, resting his head in his hands. "I am supposed to unite the world and fight the greatest evil it has ever known. I am supposed to protect it and yet I can barely keep Athanasia and Torvan from ripping each other's throats out."

"And you only fear it will just keep getting worse?"

"Yes...and what if I am not strong enough? What if I am unable to face him?"

"Him?"

Do you mean Altareon? Kayle asked?

I do, Ryuvin answered, *what if-*

Ryuvin," his Mother said, interrupting his mental conversation with Kayle. "Who is Altareon?"

Ryuvin looked up at his Mother in shock.

She...she can hear me? Kayle said, shock registering in her voice.

"Why would I not be able to?" She asked, head tilted slightly to the side.

Only Ryuvin should be able to, Kayle answered, *the blood of Avanthar flows through his veins.*

"Ah well I understand now," Amilia said. "You are connected to the bloodline of Avanthar. His descendants are capable of hearing your voice."

You are of the Ashgrove bloodline? Kayle asked.

"I am," Amilia replied.

Kayle's orb floated closer to Amilia, hovering in front of her at eye level.

I see, Kayle said, *you are more attuned with Avanthar's bloodline than i originally believed.*

"It is the eyes that give it away, is it not?" Amilia asked jokingly.

You have Avanthar's eyes, Kayle answered, her tone more serious than usual, *but how?*

"My Mother was a spirit shaman," Amilia-sama replied. "Perhaps that is what gave me the connection that I have, why it has manifested in me more than any other than came before me."

I see, that would make sense.

"So who is Altareon?" Amilia asked again.

"He..." Ryuvin began hesitantly. "Is the Daemon King."

He is the other half of Ryuvin's power, Kayle finished.

"Meaning what exactly?"

In order for Ryuvin to reach his full potential he must accept the powers that Altareon will give him.

"But why would anyone willingly accept evil into their soul?"

"Altareon, daemons in general, are not evil," Ryuvin said, as he leaned back in the chair. "Angels and daemons are simply two sides to the exact same coin."

"I do not understand," she replied as she looked at her son.

A daemon is not evil, Kayle said, *no more than that a sword is evil. Those that summon a daemon for the purpose of killing are evil. There are those that summon daemons and become corrupt because they lack the will to resist.*

"So daemons just corrupt people?" Amilia asked.

Daemons are dark by nature, Kayle continued, *but they are guardians by design. Those that have the strength to resist their dark nature are unaffected. Angels are the same, the light can corrupt those that are weak of mind.*

"I understand now," Amilia said and sat down across from her son. "You are afraid of what might happen?"

"What if I am not strong enough? What if the darkness is too much to handle? What if I lose myself?"

Amilia looked at Ryuvin, her heart ached as he struggled to keep from crumbling.

"I am the descendant of Avanthar," Ryuvin continued. "I should be better than this."

"Ryuvin," Amilia said, her voice stern yet comforting. "It is our actions that define who us, we become great not because who we are."

Ryuvin, caught off guard by his Mother's serious tone, looked up at her in silence.

"Avanthar was not a king, nor was he he a ruler. He was a simple farmer," she continued. "It was his actions that lead him to become the King we know him as today. He felt fear, just as you do now, but he did not allow that to hold him back, because without fear there cannot be courage."

What is it that Particus said? Kayle asked.

"He said that," Ryuvin answered. "No one is every ready to be more than they already are."

Good you remembered, Kayle said, *now it is time you prepare yourself. He is coming.*

Before Amilia or Ryuvin could respond, the room became devoid of light. It only lasted for mere seconds. When the darkness vanished, a man cloaked in black stood at the end of the table.

"Hello Ryuvin," he said, voice deep voice surprisingly calm.

"Altareon?" Ryuvin asked him, gritting his teeth.

"In the flesh," Altareon answered as he did a graceful bow before looking to Kayle. "Shall I assume you told him of me Kayle?"

"She did," Ryuvin answered as he watched the Daemon King.

"Good," Altareon replied as he straightened and stretched out his wings. "Then the process should be simple."

Ryuvin was surprised to see that Altareon looked more

human than he originally believed. Almost as tall as Kayle, he was handsome with horns like Lorewind, short white hair, a slightly narrow face. His skin was reddish purple with well defined muscles, his arms were completely black from the elbows and down, he wore black loose fitted pants and grey greaves engraved with skulls. His wings, that Ryuvin originally thought to be a cloak, resembled those of a bat.

"Shall we?" He asked.

"Wait," Amilia said as she stepped forward. "I want you to promise you will not harm my son."

"I will try," Altareon replied. "Though I can promise nothing."

"I am ready," Ryuvin said after taking a breath.

"I, Altareon," he began. "King of the Daemons. He who stands guards upon the Gates of Nessus, give unto you my powers."

The darkness flooded into the room once more, this time surrounding Ryuvin, as Altareon's power flowed into him. It was much different than the sensation of Kayle's light, it was not warm nor comforting, instead only pain flared through his body. Ryuvin cried out, his mouth open but no sound came.

Fight it, came a whisper from Kayle.

Do not let my nature over take your soul, whispered Altareon.

It hurts, Ryuvin screamed, *I was not prepared for this degree of pain.*

You have to fight through it, Altareon replied.

Think of what you hold closest to your heart, Kayle said.

Serina, Ryuvin answered as he pictured her face.

Yes, Altareon said, *now hold onto that and fight through the pain for her.*

After a few moments, though it felt like an eternity for Ryuvin, the pain stopped, the darkness gone. Ryuvin, doubled over and was panting, looked around the study in a daze.

You have done well, Altareon whispered.

Along side the orb that was Kayle was another, only reddish black.

"Are you alright?" Amilia asked.

Ryuvin turned to her, straightened up then collapsed.

***

It had been several hours since Ryuvin had accepted Altareon's powers. Still unconscious, he know lay in a bed in the royal medical wing. King Tarin paced back and forth at the foot of the bed. Serina sat on the bed, next to Ryuvin, clutching his hand, her eyes red from crying. Lorewind stood a few feet from the bed feeling helpless and fidgeting with her dress. Kimiko stood near the door, her back turned, to avoid looking at the family she was supposed to protect, guilt gnawing at her focus. Athanasia knelt in quiet meditation in the corner of the room. Queen Amilia sat in a chair opposite of Serina, her eyes closed.

What is happening to my son? She asked Altareon, her tone edged with tempered fury.

He is fighting, Altareon replied calmly, *it would seem that he did not fully bend the darkness to his will.*

Speak plainly daemon.

Not all battles are in the material world, Your Majesty, Altareon continued, *his battle now, it is fought within his soul.*

You promised you would not hurt him.

I said I would try, I made no promises.

He is fighting your nature, Amilia seethed, her composure starting to crumble.

Yes, Altareon answered flatly, *it is a struggle all creatures face. To fight against the darkness within themselves.*

There must be something you can do.

There is something that can be done, Altareon replied.

Are you sure that is wise Altareon? Kayle questioned, *in Ryuvin's current state...*

What is it? Amilia asked

*I can merge with Ryuvin and unleash his power, but...*Altareon hesitated.

But what?

If he fails, he will be lost forever.

What do you mean?

Our essences are already a part of Ryuvin, Kayle answered, *while Ryuvin can already use our powers to an extent.*

He can unleash the full extent of the powers we gave him, Altareon finished.

So it is a way for him to become stronger? By merging your orbs into his soul? Amilia asked.

Yes, Kayle answered, *but as I was saying, in his current state there is a high chance he will fall.*

But if he succeeds he will recover?

Yes, Altareon answered.

Do it.

Amilia opened her eyes and stood.

"Be strong my son," she whispered as she leaned over Ryuvin and kissed his forehead, then looked at Tarin. "Do you trust me?"

"With my life, My Queen," he answered in confusion.

With a nod she reached out and took Altareon's orb in her hand.

Please work, she thought.

She then pressed the orb against Ryuvin's chest and watched as it sunk into his body. Darkness once again enveloped him, vanishing moments later. Ryuvin's eyes opened and he sat up. Everyone had pulled away from him, fear and shock on their faces. He had changed, he no longer looked like an elf, instead he looked more like Altareon, only he still had his facial features.

Ryuvin, look at me, Kayle said as her orb floated in front of him.

Ryuvin looked at the orb, tilting his head slightly then let out a low animal like growl.

Amilia, we are losing him, Kayle exclaimed.

"Serina," Amilia said calmly. "He needs you now."

Serina nodded and sat back on the bed beside Ryuvin.

"Ryuvin? Can you hear me?" She asked as she took hold of his hand again. "It's me, Serina."

Ryuvin looked down at her hand then back to her face,

fear filling her emerald eyes.

Serina? What is wrong? He asked.

She cannot hear you, Altareon answered.

Ryuvin looked back at Altareon, now realizing they were in a dark room.

What is going on? Ryuvin asked him.

We are merged, Altareon said, *you and I are now one*

Why does she look afraid of me? Ryuvin asked as he looked at Serina as if through a window.

From the merge, Altareon replied, *you look like a daemon.*

"Ryuvin, if you can hear me," Serina said, tears welling in her eyes, her voice echoing around him. "Please come back to me."

How do I? He asked.

Allow me to answer your question with a question of my own, Altareon replied, *who are you?*

*I...*Ryuvin began but hesitated, *I am Ryuvin Ashgrove, Crowned Prince of Avantharia, Son of Queen Amilia and King Tarin. Commander of the Knights of Medusal.*

Good, Altareon said.

"Se-Serina," Ryuvin struggled as he lifted his free hand and cupped her cheek.

"Yes Ryuvin," she said with a smile, the smile that she gave only him.

"I am sorry," he said. "I am sorry that you were crying because of me."

"It's okay Ryuvin," she answered as she placed her hand on his and pressed her cheek against it.

I am going to release the merge, Altareon said.

The darkness enveloped Ryuvin again and, once it dissipated, he was back to his normal self.

What happened to him? Kimiko asked Vigil as she watched Ryuvin holding Serina.

He merged his soul with Altareon's, Vigil replied flatly.

Why did he change?

A side effect of the merging, Vigil answered, *and no, the change is different for any mortal merging their souls with that of an immortal.*

So what would I look like?

I'm not sure, Vigil said as his orb floated lazily into Kimiko's vision, *the rokshara have never been bound to a mortal before.*

***

"Ryuvin-sama," Kimiko said. "Are you sure you are well enough?"

It had only been a little over an hour since Ryuvin had merged with Altareon. They had all moved to the war room. A large circular room, roughly thirty feet in diameter, with a domed ceiling and wooden floor made of oak. In the centre of the room was a small set of steps that encircled a scaled map of Therago, about 10 feet in diameter, large enough for someone to walk on. Four marble pillars, each at a compass point, were the only ornamentation within the room.

"I will be fine," Ryuvin replied. "Right now, we need to figure out who to find this Child of Ice and who it even is."

"Well how did you know where to find me?" Athanasia asked as she crossed her arms, staring at the island depiction of Sandara.

"I had a vision that lead us to Sandara," Lorewind answered. "But I'm afraid I no longer feel the magic as I once did, it's changed."

"Changed how exactly?" Athanasia inquired as she tilted her head towards Lorewind.

"I can only describe it as it's there but it isn't. I can feel the magic, sense its flow, but I can no longer draw on its power."

"Perhaps-" Queen Amilia began but was interrupted as the heavy oak doors burst open.

A messenger, flanked by two royal guards, came rushing in.

"Sire," the messenger said as he knelt down. "Urgent news from the outpost in the Gosmara Plains!"

"From Captain Hendrick?" Torvan asked.

"Yes sir," the messenger said, his plain brown linen pants

and green tunic had a light layer of dirt and dust, he obviously rode hard from the outpost.

"Speak," King Tarin said to the messenger.

"It's Falcion, Sire," the messenger said as he looked up. "It's been destroyed."

Silence followed, the news of the felian city's destruction struck hard.

"What happened?" Tarin asked. "Why was there no request for aid? Did Falcion withdraw from our alliance?"

"There was no request, Sire."

"We had no warning of the attack," came a weary feminine voice from the door.

Standing in the doorway was a female felian hunter, she wore a black, hardened leather jerkin, with gold trim, over her lithe frame, tight fitting black leggings and knee high leather boots that covered the top of her foot paws. A single pauldron on her left shoulder, engraved with the golden lion of the Knights of Medusal. She had long onyx black hair, like all female felians, her face was more human than cat, her feline eyes were sapphire blue, a trait that was extremely rare amongst the felian. She bore white fur with black spots, her black tipped tail swished out behind her. On her back, an ornate silver bow and sword, a black leather quiver hung on her right hip.

"I am Kallindra," the huntress said. "Princess of Falcion."

"And Knight of Medusal," Ryuvin said with a nod.

"Yes, forgive me," Kallindra replied as she looked at the pauldron. "So much has happened recently, I am still trying to process it all."

"Start from the beginning," Torvan said. "Who attacked Falcion?"

"I wish I knew," Kallindra answered, returning her attention back to them. "By the time we had even realized we were under attack it was already too late."

"Greyish brown creatures? Demonic looking?" Lorewind asked. "Mindlessly attacking and killing everything in sight?"

"Yes," Kallindra replied as she looked at Lorewind skeptically. "But how-"

"It's them," Lorewind said before Kallindra could question her. "It's the mordians."

"Then we best get moving," Ryuvin said then turned back to Kallindra. "I am Ryuvin Ashgrove, Crowned Prince of Avantharia and Commander of the Knights of Medusal."

"Yes, Artemis told me as much," Kallindra replied. "I have but a single request. Will you give my people refuge?"

"You need not ask that of us," King Tarin answered. "Falcion has always been our ally. Your people are welcome in Avalon."

"Thank you, Your Majesty," Kallindra said as she bowed.

"Torvan, send out messengers to all our outposts. I want them to have the watch doubled and be vigilant."

"Yes Sire," Torvan said. "Shall I also have a refugee camp established for Kallindra's people?"

"Yes, make sure it is up to your standards and have it prepared for the first of the refugees."

"I shall see to it personally," Torvan replied then looked to Kallindra. "We shall make sure your people are taken care of."

Tears welled in Kallindra's eyes, she let out a ragged breath as she tried to hold herself together but could no longer. Breaking down, she fell to her knees, tears streaming down her face. Queen Amilia rushed to her side and knelt down beside her, doing what she could to comfort Kallindra.

"There there child," Amilia said in a soothing voice, her maternal instincts clearly showing. "Everything is going to be alright."

"I s-saw so m-m-many people d-die," Kallindra managed while struggling through sobs, attempting to wipe away tears with the heel of her hands. "P-p-people I gr-grew up w-with."

"It hurts, I know," Amilia said as she hugged Kallindra to her. "Be strong for your people. Show them that you are their rock in these trying times."

All Kallindra could do was nod as she cried into Amilia's shoulder.

"Now come, let us get you cleaned up and some food in you."

Kallindra nodded again and let Amilia help you to her feet and guide her from the room, followed by Lorewind and Serina.

"You best go get some food and rest as well," Tarin said to the messenger.

"Yes Sire, thank you," the messenger said then stood and bowed before also leaving the room, leaving only Ryuvin, Tarin, Torvan, Athanasia and Kimiko in the room.

"This changes things, Father," Ryuvin said as he walked around the city depictions on the map, stopping at Falcion. "If the mordians truly destroyed Falcion then they are moving faster than we anticipated."

"Perhaps, or maybe it was random," Tarin replied as he crossed his arms, staring at the map. "Aside from the attack on Lorewind's people, this is the only report we have of the mordians."

"This was strategic," Torvan said, examining the map and pointing out the roads through the plains. "The Gosmara Plains is central to all major trade routes to Western Therago."

"And Falcion is the centre of the Kingdom," Ryuvin replied. "Without it, the trade routes are unprotected."

"Letting an army slip through unnoticed," Tarin finished.

Everyone in the room looked to one another, the realization of what King Tarin had said suddenly sinking in.

"Torvan," the King began. "Reinforce every outpost we have, my forces must be ready to march at a moments notice, and send a force to Gosmara. Send word to all our allies, suggest that they do the same."

"Yes Sire," Torvan said then ran from the room.

Turning to Athanasia, Ryuvin was about to speak when she held up her hand and began the evocation of a spell.

I call upon the, Icarus, Messenger of War.
Come forth and bare upon your wings,
The summons of Ares.

A small ball of fire appeared then shot up from her hand, quickly morphing into a fiery red eagle. The eagle flew in a quick circle around the room before returning to Athanasia and landing on her outstretched forearm.

"Take this message to King Shingen of Sandara," she said. "The mordians have struck. Falcion has fallen and western Therago is vulnerable. Send a force to assist our allies. Kensei Athanasia."

The eagle cawed then pushed off her arm and flew out the window.

"Can we trust King Shingen to help?" Ryuvin asked her as he watched Icarus fly away.

"He is an honourable man," Athanasia replied. "I do not see him blatantly ignoring a request for aid, more so from me."

"In this war," Ryuvin said as they strode towards the door. "We are going to need all the help we can get."

***

A day had passed since Kallindra had arrived with the news of Falcion. Night had fallen over Avalon, not much seemed to have changed in the city, but the news of Falcion spread like a wild fire. Soldiers had been coming and going all throughout the day and into the evening. Torvan had been personally supervising the operations, making sure each outpost had been given the additional supplies and forces they would need. All of this, in addition to the refugee camp he had promised Kallindra, her people steadily trickling in.

"He is a force of nature," Kallindra said as she wandered through the camp with Ryuvin and Serina. "Has he gotten any rest?"

Ryuvin had, once again, donned the armour of the Knights, a daemon wing now on the back with the angel wing, while Serina wore her usual scouting gear.

"If I know Torvan," Ryuvin began with a laugh. "The answer will be no."

"Prince Ryuvin," Kallindra said as she stopped and bowed

to him again. "I want to thank you again for aiding my people."

Before Ryuvin could answer, a young felian boy charged out from between a couple of tents, running straight into Ryuvin, followed by a couple other children.

"Ouch!" The boy exclaimed from the ground, then snapped. "Hey, watch where you're going!"

Fear filled the boys eyes when he looked up to see Ryuvin and Kallindra. Ryuvin could only imagine what the perspective might have been for the young boy.

"I'm so sorry," the boy said as he scrambled to his knees and bowed his head. "Please forgive me!"

"Look at me," Ryuvin commanded to the boy.

"Ryuvin, they are just-" Serina began but stopped when Ryuvin waved his hand to silence her.

"What were you doing?"

"We were just playing a game of chase," the boy said as he looked up. "Please I didn't see you and I'm sorry I snapped at you."

Were you having fun?" Ryuvin asked as he knelt in front of the boy.

The children all nodded but said nothing.

"Good," Ryuvin said, his face softening. "Go back to your game. Just be mindful of where you are running, the last thing anyone needs is for you to hurt yourself."

The boy nodded as relief washed over his face before getting up and running off with his friends.

"They are still afraid," Serina said as she watched the children run off.

"They are in a new country, their home is gone and they probably lost loved ones," Kallindra replied with a sigh. "That fear is understandable."

The three continued on through the camp, stopping every so often to talk with refugees. True to his word, Torvan had the camp set up to his standards. The tents had been set meticulously in small sections consisting of a campfire and four tents set two by two, this would allow ease of movement throughout the camp, especially with the recent events, even with how organized Torvan was, the camp was still chaotic as many refugees wandered looking for missing loved ones. There was a fairly large open central area, to be used for gatherings, and two larger tents, one for refugees needing medical attention, the other for food. The group decided to check the medical tent first.

The tent was roughly fifty feet in length and about twenty feet wide, easily capable of holding around two hundred wounded.

"Ninthalor?" Ryuvin asked upon entering the tent. "What are you doing here?"

"Well, these people need our help," the stoic elf replied as he looked up from the small desk that was covered with papers. "So I volunteered, as did the medical staff from the infirmaries."

Ryuvin looked at the beds within the tent, well over half were occupied.

It could have been much worse, Kayle said to him.

Yes, but these are the ones that survived, Altareon replied.

Why must you be so pessimistic? She asked.

The same reason as to why you are so optimistic, he answered.

Forget I asked, she scoffed.

"How man volunteered?" Ryuvin asked Ninthalor, ignoring the two bickering immortals.

"Including myself, twenty-five," Ninthalor replied. "But there have also been many felians that have come to assist us wherever they could."

"And for that I am truly grateful," a female felian said as she walked up to Ninthalor, a plate of food in her hands.

She wore a plain green cotton dress, there were a few blood stains on the apron that covered her front. Her long black hair was tied back in a ponytail, and she had white fur with black spots like Kallindra.

"Mother?" Kallindra gasped when she saw the older woman.

"Yes," Ninthalor said. "Queen Koriana has be a great help."

"You give me too much credit," she said to Ninthalor as she placed the plate of food on his desk. "The other healers and yourself have done all the work."

"You are being too modest, if not for you, my people would be having a much more difficult time working their magic. You people are more at ease with your presence."

The two looked at each other fondly, they almost looked like love struck teenagers.

"Oh just get a room you two," Serina said jokingly.

"You know, we just might," the Queen replied with a smirk as she winked at Ninthalor.

"Gods ew!" Kallindra exclaimed as she covered her face with her hand. "Too much information, Mother, I did not need that mental image."

"What?" Koriana asked. "Because I am a Queen I am not allowed to have a sex life?"

"Please," Kallindra replied. "Just stop, I do not need to be hearing this."

Ninthalor gave a small chuckle and shook his head.

"If you need anything," Ryuvin said to Koriana. "Do not hesitate to ask. We will do what we can to help."

"My thanks," she replied, finally looking at Ryuvin. Looking him up and down, she gave him a flirtatious smirk. "If there is anything I can think of, I will be sure to let you know."

"Alright," Kallindra said as she clapped her hands together. "Ryuvin, I believe your wife wanted to also inspect the mess tent."

"Oh, forgive me for taking up your time," Koriana said, giving Serina the same smirk she gave Ryuvin.

"Oh it's no issue at all," Serina replied with a polite smile.

"We shall leave you to your work," Kallindra said before turning and hastily exiting the tent.

Once outside, she turned back to Ryuvin and Serina.

"I apologize on behalf of my Mother," she said. "She has never shied away from that type of...behaviour."

"Don't worry about it Kalli," Serina said with a soft smile

causing Kallindra to blush furiously. "I've gotten used to women flirting with Ryuvin."

"Well I will admit he is very attractive," Kallindra replied then quickly covered her mouth. "I am so sorry, I spoke without thinking."

Ryuvin and Serina laughed as Kallindra stumbled over her words.

"It's quite alright," Serina said as the made their way to the mess tent.

"My Mother is really open about her...entertainment," Kallindra replied, clearing taking care of her wording as she moved slightly ahead of them. "It is very common among felian culture to have more than one mate."

"Hence why she was flirting with both Ninthalor and Ryuvin."

"She was flirting with you as well," Ryuvin whispered to Serina before kissing her cheek causing her to blush.

"Yes well," Kallindra continued, unaware of what Ryuvin just told Serina. "My Mother enjoys the company of both men and women."

"Oh," Serina said, looking down so people would not notice her blushing.

"Yes, there have been several times she has brought couples to her chambers and bed."

"H-how interesting," Serina stammered. "What about you?"

"To be honest," Kallindra answered plainly. "I have yet to bed anyone, Mother says my first time should be with a female wood elf because, and I quote, they taste like honey."

"That I can agree with," Ryuvin laughed as Serina gave him a glare that could melt ice.

"Did I miss something?" Kallindra asked, looking back as the approached the mess tent.

"Nothing important," Serina quickly answered, her face beet red. "Come, let's go inside."

Quickly moving passed Kallindra, Serina entered the tent.

Kallindra gave Ryuvin a confused look before following her with Ryuvin. The tent was larger than the medical tent, with several tables running the length, there were a few people spread sporadically throughout. The food was served at the far end of the tent to any refugee that came in, at the opposite side to that was a bar.

"Mother?" Serina gasped as she stopped suddenly.

"Hmm?" Seleena said as she looked over to Serina then smiled. She was wearing a plain blue cotton dress and a brown apron.

"What are you doing here?"

"Well I could not sit by and do nothing," Seleena answered as she carried a tray of dishes. "These people needed help, so here I am."

"Ah if it ain't young Master Avlin," Dal called from over near the entrance of the tent. "Come ta help da refugees?"

"Sorry Dal," Ryuvin answered as the dwarf approached. "I have another mission to see to."

"Ah I see, off to scout da plains?" He asked, then noticed Serina and bowed. "Your Highness, my apologies, I didn't know ya were with Avlin. How is Prince Ryuvin?"

"Oh," Serina said and looked at Ryuvin, her eyes narrow. "Well I might not allow him to share our bed tonight."

"Do not be like that Serina," Ryuvin said with mock annoyance. "You and I both know that you would have difficulties sleeping without me next to you."

"I hate that you are right," she replied with a smile then leaned in and kissed him.

Dal gave the two a confused look, then was hit with the sudden realization of who exactly 'Avlin' was.

"My sincerest apologies," Dal said as he bowed. "Had I known-"

"There really is no need for that Dal," Ryuvin said, interrupting the dwarf. "You have been a good friend to me these past couple years and I wish that to remain the same."

"So this is the famous Dal I have heard so much about,"

Queen Amilia said as she approached the group, Titania and Jassin alongside her.

"Mother? Titania?" Ryuvin said as he turned and looked at them. "What are you doing here?"

Amilia and Titania were both dressed similar to Seleena, the only difference were the colours of their dresses. Titania wore a grey dress, while Queen Amilia's was a dark red.

"Like Seleena had said," Titania replied plainly. "These people need our help, so here we are."

"You don't have ta, Yer Majesty," Dal replied as he bowed to the Queen and Princess.

"Nonsense," Queen Amilia said. "One thing my Father taught me was that a nation is only as strong as its people and a ruler must care for them. So if that means working in a mess tent to aid refugees, then so be it."

Serina glanced at Kallindra and, seeing that she was on the verge of tears again, took hold of her hand.

"There is enough grief and sorrow in this world," Jassin added, he was wearing the armour of the royal guard.

"Now Dal," Amilia said to the dwarf.

"Yes, Your Majesty?" He asked as he looked up at her.

"I have heard a lot about you," she continued. "My Son has told me what kind of man you are. He told me about how you gave a young child food without a second thought. And how welcoming you were towards him the day you befriended him. And for that, I thank you."

"My Queen," Dal said, clearly awestruck as Amilia gave him a graceful bow.

"My Brother says you make the best grilled venison in the kingdom," Titania said. "What can we do to help?"

"Well," he began as he turned towards the cooking area in the back. "Follow me, we have a lot ta do and a short amount of time ta do it."

"Jassin," Ryuvin said as he watched his Mother and Sister following Dal. "Make sure they are protected."

"Have some faith in me," Jassin replied jokingly. "You kn-"

Jassin stopped when he saw the look in Ryuvin's eyes.

"Yes," Jassin said, now serious as he saluted Ryuvin. "You have my word, Your Highness. So long as I draw breathe, no harm shall befall the Queen and Princess. By my life, I will protect them."

"Thank you," Ryuvin said as he held out his hand. "Brother."

"Anything for you," Jassin replied, clasping Ryuvin's forearm. "You can count on me, Brother."

"What was all that about?" Kallindra asked Serina as she watched Jassin follow Amilia and Titania.

"I'll tell you about it later," she replied as they followed Ryuvin from the tent.

The three walked towards the city gates, stopping at the edge of the camp, Ryuvin turned towards Kallindra.

"Be prepared," he said to her. "We leave at dawn."

"Very well," Kallindra replied. "Where are we going?"

"Jotunheim."

"I may not be a Knight," Serina said to them. "But I'm coming with you, and you won't stop me."

Before either of them could answer, she walked away into the city.

"Sir?" Kallindra asked. "What is in Jotunheim?"

"The Child of Ice," Ryuvin answered and followed Serina.

Chapter 8

"Are you sure this is wise?" Kallindra whispered to Kimiko as she watched Ryuvin and Serina.

"Probably not," Kimiko replied with a shrug. "But she refused to remain behind, no matter what Ryuvin told her."

It was already noon as the party continued on their mission. Leaving at dawn, the previous day, the Knights set off on the four day journey northwest to the city of Rinhorn, a trade city near the border of Jotunheim. The plan was to procure suitable mounts that can traverse the tundra during their search.

The day was beautiful, the sky clear, a slight breeze kept them cool in the midday heat as they walked the road. Winding through rolling fields of grass, occasionally passing small farms and villages. A few hours later, they came upon a stream, about six feet wide, along side the road.

"Let us stop here a moment," Ryuvin said as he stepped off the road.

Pulling out a map, he sat beneath one of the trees near the river back while Lorewind, Kallindra and Serina moved over to the stream to refill the water skins.

"Kimiko," Athanasia said, barely more than a whisper. "A moment if you will."

"Yes?" She asked as she moved closer to her, also in a hushed tone.

"Something is wrong here," Athanasia answered. "it's too quiet."

"I know," she replied, her eyes darting around, from the trees near the bank to the wheat fields across from them, not a single animal could be heard anywhere.

"I don't like this," Athanasia said.

"Keep ready, there is something here."

With that, Kimiko moved away from Athanasia, casually walked over to Ryuvin.

"Pretend you are discussing the route with me," he said as she knelt beside him.

"You sense it as well?"

Ryuvin nodded and flicked his eyes to the right quickly. Keeping her head down, as if to look at the map, Kimiko looked towards where Ryuvin had indicated. There, in a small grove of bushes, was a creature of sorts. Kimiko's jaw clenched as she looked behind her towards Serina, Lorewind and Kallindra. Kallindra suddenly looked up from the stream, her ears flicking around. She stared, for a moment, at the cluster of cattails on the far side of the stream before standing and walking over to Ryuvin and Kimiko. Confused at her sudden behaviour, Lorewind and Serina followed.

"There is something across the stream," Kallindra whispered, holding out a water skin.

"That makes two," Ryuvin answered as he took the water skin. "The other is in the small grove just up the road."

"Four," Athanasia said as she joined the group. "There are two in the wheat field."

"We are being hunted," Ryuvin said as he stood up. "There are probably more."

"So what is the plan?" Athanasia asked as she laced her fingers behind her head.

Strike hard and fast, Kayle said.

Show no mercy, Altareon finished.

"Athanasia, take the two in the field," Ryuvin began.

Athanasia nodded but did not change her posture.

"Kimiko, you assist her," he continued.

"Yes, Ryuvin-sama," she replied as she stretched her arms

above her head.

"Serina, you and Kallindra will take the one across the stream."

"Of course," Serina replied and nodded to Kallindra. "Want to bet which one of us gets the kill?"

Kallindra rolled her eyes and shook her head, a slight smile on her face.

"I will take the last one in the bushes," he continued. "On three."

Looking around quickly one last time, Ryuvin began to count.

"One," he said as Kallindra and Serina unslung their bows.

"Two," Athanasia continued as she and Kimiko flexed their hands.

"Three!" Ryuvin finished.

Athanasia and Kimiko bolted towards the wheat field, drawing their weapons. Serina and Kallindra spun and fired several arrows across the stream and Ryuvin charged towards the last creature. Crashing out from the bushes came a monstrously large dog like creature. Furless, black leather skin stretched tautly over its muscular body, wickedly sharp claws of obsidian, its head was just a bleach white skull, the blazing fury of hellfire instead of eyes. Ryuvin cursed under his breathe as he reached for Kayle.

"hellhounds!" He yelled as he took hold of the pale golden orb.

Gold light enveloped Ryuvin as he and Kayle merged. When the light dissipated he was now wearing gold plate armour with white feathered wings, that fanned out from his back, crystal blue eyes and long blonde hair. Drawing his now angelic sword, Ryuvin flexed his wings and launched himself at the beast with incredible speed. The hellhound reared up just as Ryuvin thrust the silver blade deep into its side, dark blue blood spewing from the wound. Howling in pain, the beast swung its massive paw, causing Ryuvin to his grip on the blade and sent him tumbling towards the stream, feet sliding across the ground, his left hand digging into the dirt to slow him.

The hellhound that Kallindra and Serina were fighting had charged at them. Serina evaded with a roll, firing off two more arrows from a kneeling position, while Kallindra hopped back several feet, firing several arrows as she did. The hellhound howled and surged after Kallindra. Turning, she sprinted towards a tree several yards away, with the hellhound almost upon her as it leapt at her. Kallindra pressed her foot against the tree taking a step and continued to keep her stride, as she ran up the trunk of the tree, before pushing off into an elegant back flip. As she reached the pinnacle of her flip, she aimed at the hellhound.

I invoke thee Artemis, Huntress of the Moon.
Infuse my arrow with your silver light,
Let me vanquish the dark before me,
Moonlight's burst.

As she finished the evocation, an arrow of pure silver moonlight formed on her bow. She released the arrow, the twang of the bow string echoed, the whistle of air being cut by the arrow, the tearing of flesh as it embedded into the base of the hellhound's skull. The hound howled in pain as silver light filled its eyes and mouth before its head exploded.

The two hounds in the field had also charged out. Though between Kimiko and Athanasia, they did not survive long. Kimiko, with practised ease and daggers drawn, slid under the hound. One dagger slicing its throat, while the other, she thrust into its underbelly. The forward moment of the hound doing most of the work as the blade cut down its entire length, its dark blue blood spraying out and innards spilling to the dirt. Athanasia threw her claymore to impale the hound, as the beast staggered during its charge she spun to the right, nodachi in hand, and used the beasts forward moment to cut deep into its side and down its body.

Steadying himself, Ryuvin saw the hound had turned its attention to Lorewind. Ryuvin pushed off of the ground and flew at the hound. Grabbing the sword, he flew above the hound and pulled the blade with him. The blade shifted and followed, cutting thew the beast and severing its spine in a spray of blood.

"Is everyone alright?" Ryuvin called out as he flicked the blood from his blade.

Before anyone could respond, another creature burst from the trees, across the stream. It was massive, easily ten feet tall, with short back legs, the creature hunched forwards supporting it weight with its arms; which were a few feet in diameter. A black tendril like mane covered its back and upper arms, the rest of its body was hairless, it had a bear skull for a head, and a red glow that emanated from its otherwise empty eye sockets. Lumbering into the stream, the creature kept looking in different directions and sniffing the air, as if searching for something.

"What in the name of Artemis is that?" Kallindra asked, taking a few steps back while notching another arrow.

Altareon? Ryuvin asked after hearing Altareon curse.

It's a dreadbeast, Altareon replied, *the apex predator of all the layers of Hell. Devil Lords like to keep them as pets.*

How do we fight it?

You do not, Altareon answered, *you run.*

Cursing, Ryuvin turned and grabbed Serina.

"Run!" He yelled.

The dreadbeast let out a deafening roar as it slammed its fists into the stream then charged after the Knights. Kallindra had let loose the arrow she had notched but turning and sprinting towards the road.

"Incoming!" Kimiko screamed.

Looking back, Ryuvin saw the beast had uprooted a tree and was about the throw it. Lorewind had yet to move from where she was standing.

"Get down!" Kimiko yelled as the tree sailed through the air, crashing into the field as the Knights dropped to the ground. "Lorewind!"

Lorewind had dropped to her knees, eyes glazed over as if in a trance, she mumbled. The sound was deep, as if the earth itself was rumbling. She traced her fingers through the dirt in front of her.

I need you Vigil, Kimiko said.

Let us show this creature the meaning of fear, Vigil replied gleefully.

Reaching up, Kimiko pull off her headband and opened her left eye. Light flooded her vision, the intensity making her wince slightly for a moment. Taking hold of the purplish black orb that was Vigil, she pressed it against her chest. Darkness enveloped her for a brief moment, when it dissipated, Kimiko opened her eyes, which were now pale blue, like Vigil's, her face featureless, hair now purplish black, her clothing remained unchanged and it almost seemed like a shadow kept passing over her almost wraith like form. Pulling out three throwing daggers, Kimiko took a running leap into the air and threw them at the dreadbeast. The first dagger landing in front of it, causing the beast to stop and look at Kimiko, the other two landing behind it.

Yami.
Kage.
Baindo.
Kyofu no tend.

As she chanted, she made several different hand gestures, before she opened her left palm, conjuring a dagger of black flames. Kimiko threw the dagger at the dreadbeast. When it landed a few feet in front of it, she clapped her hands together then quickly pressed them to the ground. A shadow shot out, from the conjured dagger, across the ground to the first dagger. When the shadow reached the dagger it split towards the other two daggers, until all three were connected. Once connected, shadowy tendrils erupted around the dreadbeast and began constricting its limbs. The beast roared and thrashed against the tendrils wildly, tearing them off as fear gripped its very being, only for them to quickly regenerate.

"Whatever you are doing, do it now!" Kimiko yelled, sweat beading on her brow. "I cannot hold this forever."

Ryuvin, Kayle said, *this beast is here from a summon.*
That means the summoner must be close, Altareon finished.

"Kallindra," Ryuvin called out as he staggered to his feet. "The summoner of this beast is nearby, find them."

Nodding, Kallindra closed her eyes and took a deep breathe.

"Come out, come out, wherever you are," she mumbled to herself as she focused on tuning out the sounds around her.

Ears flicking around, she searched for a sound that would give away her prey. She forced out the ambient sounds of the rustling leaves on the trees, the flowing water of the stream, the thrashing of the panicking dreadbeast. She focused until the only sounds she could hear were the heartbeats of the other Knights.

One, she thought as she began counting the heartbeats, her ears flicking towards Ryuvin.

Two, her ears flicked to Serina.

Three and four, ears flicking towards Kimiko and Lorewind.

Five, she counted as her ears picked up Athanasia.

Six, her ears flicking towards the stream.

"Found you," she said as she opened her eyes before she dashed towards the sixth heartbeat.

As Kallindra vaulted the stream, with a single leap, the earth began to rumble around Lorewind as she began the evocation of a spell.

Son of Gaia I beseech thee,
Come forth, oh protector of stone,
Grant me thine aid.
Verdag, I summon you.

The summoning circle, that Lorewind had drawn earlier, began to glow. Cracking at the centre, the ground pushed up, a clawed hand breaking though the surface, followed by a draconic humanoid. As tall as the dreadbeast, the draconic being had brown stone like scales and a white under body, several horns made a crown around his head, a short snout and glowing yellow eyes. Its arms were practically all muscle, black granite spikes running down the centre of its back to the tip of its tail, its claws were also black granite.

"You called for aid?" The draconic being asked, its voice a low deep rumble.

"Please, Verdag, we need your aid," Lorewind answered.

"You shall have it, Lady Lorewind," he answered and turned towards the dreadbeast.

There was a loud crack as the beast finally broke free of the shadowy tendrils, sending Kimiko flying and colliding with Athanasia, both crashing to the ground. The beast thrashed more, kicking up dirt and stone before noticing Verdag. Both roared and charged at each other. The collision caused a small shock wave as the two fought. Ryuvin, still merged with Kayle, flew in and caught Lorewind as she teetered and began to fall.

"Are you alright?" He asked as he held Lorewind.

"Just-" Lorewind panted. "Just a bit tired."

"Then we had best get a safe distance so you can rest."

Lorewind nodded and let Ryuvin carry her back towards the road. The sound of tearing flesh and muscle caused Ryuvin to look back over his shoulder. He watched as Verdag ripped one of the arms off the dreadbeast. The beast howled in pain as dark green, almost black, blood sprayed out of the wound. Verdag then slammed the beast to the ground, pinned it, grabbed its jaws and pulled, ripping the top half of its head from its body. Verdag roared in triumph, his stone like body scratched from the battle.

So much for apex predator, Ryuvin thought as he sat Lorewind against a nearby rock and released the merge with Kayle.

Having recovered, Kimiko sprinted over and knelt next to Lorewind.

Well, Altareon replied, *I did not expect Lorewind to be able to summon Verdag.*

Who is Verdag? Ryuvin asked.

He is the first elemental of the earth, the First Son of Gaia, Altareon answered, *though his summoning has taxed Lorewind heavily.*

It was true, Lorewind was visibly exhausted, sweat dripped down her face and slightly pale. And with his adrenaline wearing off, Ryuvin too felt the fatigue setting in.

As you grow stronger, Kayle said, *the physical demand of harnessing out powers will diminish.*

Lorewind, having finally succumb to exhaustion, had passed out as Kallindra returned to the group, dragging a man in a black robe behind her.

"Let me go you filthy beast!" He demanded.

"I got him," Kallindra said as she threw the man in front of Ryuvin.

"Who sent you?" Ryuvin asked calmly as he stood over the man.

"Your world has come to an end. Your kingdoms shall burn and we will usher in a new era to Therago."

"Allow me," Kimiko said as she stood and walked over.

The man trembled as she approached, her pale blue eyes boring into his.

"You feel it do you not?" She asked, her voice edged with a sinister tone as she slowly circled the man. "That chill running down your spine?"

Darkness suddenly enveloped the two of them.

"Where are you?!" The man screamed.

"That trembling in your knees?" Kimiko asked, ignoring the question, her whispers echoing in the dark as she continued to circle the terrified man. "That racing of your heartbeat?"

The man fell back as he turned to see Kimiko standing above him.

"That is fear," she smiled down at the man and grabbed his throat. "Show me what it is you fear."

Moments later, Kimiko let go of the man and he toppled over, dead. Releasing her merge with Vigil, Kimiko collapsed to her knees, pale face, drenched with sweat and panting.

"Kimiko," Serina began as she knelt next to her. "Are you alright? What happened?"

"I used his fear to break into his mind," she answered. "I saw his memories, or at least fragments of them."

"What did you learn?" Kallindra asked.

"Not enough," she replied as she struggled to stand. "I could not see the face of who hired him, only that it was a woman. More than likely someone from the cult."

"If we are lucky," Athanasia said. "This woman was in Sandara and the Valkyrie already found her."

"Unlikely but at least the immediate threat has been dealt with," Ryuvin said as he looked to Lorewind. "I think it best to rest now and regain our strength before pushing on."

"Time is not on our side right now Ryuvin," Serina said as she knelt beside Lorewind.

"Serina is right," Lorewind said, having regained consciousnesses and struggled to stand. "We have to press on."

"Lorewind," Kallindra said as she helped steady her. "You are in no condition to continue."

"I shall carry her," Verdag said, still standing over the spot where he killed the dreadbeast, its body gone now that the summoner was dead.

"It's settled then," Athanasia said as she finished cleaning her swords. "We continue to Rinhorn."

CHAPTER 9

The wind bit into his face from atop the hill; white tundra spanning miles in every direction. Leaning on his spear, he watched, with curiosity, the six travellers below.

What would drive these people to Jotunheim? He thought to himself.

Looking back behind him to his tribe, he pondered the though of guiding him to the nomadic village. With a sigh, he descended the hill towards the group as the snow swirled around him.

***

It had been almost a week since the Knights had left Rinhorn, riding dire wolves, and having finally made it to Jotunheim; the cold of the north having set in well before reaching the tundras of the region.

"How could anyone live in such a place?" Lorewind asked as she shivered and pulled the fur clothing she wore tighter to her body.

"Perhaps they do not feel the cold as we do," Athanasia replied.

"Why did I decide to come along?" Serina asked again, also pulling the furs tighter to her body.

"Because you are stubborn and would not listen to me," Ryuvin answered, the icy wind biting his face.

"You should've tried harder to stop me," she retorted.

"Let us find some shelter, or at least a way to get out of the wind."

He patted the side of the black dire wolf he rode. The wolf

turned and took a step towards the nearby hill but stopped. Looking towards the hill, Ryuvin could make out the shape of something descending towards them.

"Kallindra?" He called out.

"Yes, I see him," she replied as she pulled her white wolf next to Ryuvin's. "Looks like one of the tribesmen, I cannot see any markings as to indicate which tribe."

"How far off is he?"

"Best estimate? Approximately one hundred and twenty meters. He does appear to be alone."

"Come," Ryuvin said and gestured for the others to follow. "He is the first person we have seen since we arrived. Perhaps he may help us but be weary."

The Knights steered their wolves towards the man and rode closer. He had stopped and watched as the approached. He pressed his left gloved fist to then held out his hand, palm opened.

"Hail travellers," the man called, with the heavy accent of the north, as they neared. "What brings you so close to my tribe?"

"We apologize," Ryuvin answered as he made the same gesture in return to the man. "We were unaware that your tribe was so near."

"Then why are you in Jotunheim?"

"We search for the one known as 'The Child of Ice' and decided that Ymitor would be the most ideal place to start."

Ryuvin studied the man. He wore a grey and brown fur coat and pants with fur lined boots. He kept his hood up, but Ryuvin could see the lower half of his pale brown face. He carried a bone spear in his right hand, and, as Kallindra said, he bore no tribal markings on his clothing.

"I see you bear no tribal markings," Ryuvin continued. "To which tribe do you and your people belong?"

The man did not answer, instead he muttered something to himself and turned back towards the hill. He gestured for the Knights to follow, he then leaned forwards and propelled himself along the snow with magic.

"That is really amazing," Lorewind said as the Knights followed. "Can everyone do magic like that?"

"In theory," Kallindra answered. "I would assume the spell would change based off of the environment you wish to use it in."

Cresting the hill, the Knights looked down at the village, there was around forty fur tents. The tribe members milled around the village, several children could be seen running around and chasing each other, their laughter barely audible above the wind.

The man had lifted his spear and yelled down, in the native language of Jotunheim, to the village, causing everyone to look. Parents of the children could be seen ushering them into the tents, while several others moved towards the edge of the village. The Knights followed the man down the slope towards the village. The tribe members that waited at the edge of the village were clearly warriors, each holding a similar bone spear as the man that was leading the Knights. They parted, allowing an elderly man to pass, he was hunched over and leaning heavily on his staff as he shuffled over to meet them. Dismounting, the Knights met him halfway.

"This is our chief," the man said. "He speaks for the Isvandrere. I shall translate for you."

"Very well," Ryuvin said before turning to the chief and bowing. "My name is Ryuvin Ashgrove, Crowned Prince of Avantharia and Commander of the Knights of Medusal."

The man translated to the chief, who bowed then spoke to Ryuvin, the man continuing to translate.

"Greetings Prince Ryuvin, you are a long way from your home. Why have you come to our lands?"

"We are here searching for the one known as 'The Child of Ice'."

The chief looked over his shoulder and nodded. One of the warriors nodded and returned to the village. The chief returned his attention back to Ryuvin and continued.

"Why do you search for the child?"

"The goddesses Athena and Ares sent us," Ryuvin answered. "The call for the Knights has sounded."

"The Isvandrere have protected the knowledge of what you seek for thousands of years," the chief said.

"Is the child here?"

The chief shook his head and continued.

"What you seek is not of the mortal realm. If you truly wish to continue, be warned, none that ventured to seek the child has ever returned."

"We do not have a choice," Ryuvin said.

"All creatures have a choice," the chief replied. "We shall show you the way."

The chief bowed, turned back to the village and shuffled away.

"Whoever this child is," Kimiko said. "They must be extremely dangerous."

***

The Isvandrere chief, along with several of the tribal warriors, lead the Knights through the tundra. After a few hours of travel, a dark shape, almost like a tower, could be seen in the distance.

"What is that?" Ryuvin asked as he gestured to the structure.

"That is what you seek," the chief answered.

The terrain slowly began to change as they neared the structure. The ice began to turn black, the wind slowly died down and no sign of any living creature within the area.

"Can you feel it?" Athanasia asked.

The Knights gazed up at the ziggurat before them.

"There is something evil here," Kimiko answered. "Are you sure this is where the 'Child of Ice' is?"

The chief nodded.

"Only death awaits those that enter," the chief finally said.

Turning, the chief and tribesmen headed back towards their village.

"Well that doesn't sound ominous at all," Athanasia said as the Knights watched them leave before turning back to the ziggurat.

Made from ice blacker than night, the ziggurat stood about twenty feet above the ice, bones of the dead lay scattered before the only entrance. Hovering just above was a giant white crystal, smoke swirled inside it.

"So what's the plan?" Athanasia asked.

"Go in, find 'The Child of Ice' and get out as fast as possible," Ryuvin answered.

"So...we have no plan?"

"Not at all," Ryuvin said as he started towards the entrance.

"Good plan," Athanasia replied as she and the rest of the Knights followed Ryuvin.

***

The Knights followed a long winding passage that lead down into the frozen tundra. Ryuvin lead with Kayle lighting the way, via her orb. The ice suddenly changed to stone, clearly weathered with time.

"This is strange," Ryuvin said as he knelt and examined the stone. "This stone seems ancient."

"Perhaps," Serina said. "There was an outpost here at one point in history?"

"But at what point in history?" Kallindra countered.

"Whatever this was," Athanasia said as she tapped her foot on the stone stairs. "The stairs end in about twenty feet then opens into a big chamber."

"Then we find out what is ahead," Ryuvin replied as he lowered his voice to a whisper and pushed on.

As they reached the end of the stairs, they found a doorway and, as Athanasia had said, the area opened into some sort of large chamber. A bright, pale blue light flooded through the door. Pressing against the wall, Ryuvin peaked around the entryway. His eyes slowly adjusting to the light. The area was that of a castle courtyard, easily one hundred meters across, a high domed ceiling of ice enclosed the courtyard. At the centre, sitting upon a throne, crafted from bones and ice, was a man.

"There is no point in hiding," the man on the throne called, his calm voice echoing in the chamber. "Come out."

Ryuvin nodded to the Knights. They entered the courtyard and approached the throne. The man, an elf, sat relaxed, head resting on his fist, black eyes watching the Knights. His skin was pale, white hair tied back in a tight ponytail, he wore full plate black armour adorned with skulls.

"Now this is interesting," he said as the Knights stopped several feet away. "It is not everyday that immortals enter my domain."

He looked over the group again, as if to gauge which of the Knights was the strongest. It was then that Ryuvin noticed the massive sword resting against the throne, my like the elf's armour, the sword was black with skulls engraved along the blade, the edges were a pale blue with a strange black smoke swirling inside.

"So tell me," the elf continued. "What reason do gods and angels have to come here?"

"We seek 'The Child of Ice'," Ryuvin answered as calmly as possible.

"You are not the first," he replied and gestured to the bones that littered the courtyard. "To what purpose I wonder. Is it power you seek?"

The courtyard suddenly became much colder, power radiating off the elf, much like when Athena first appeared in Sandara, only this was much more intense.

"I am Ryuvin Ashgrove," Ryuvin said. "Crowned Prince of Avantharia and Commander of the Knights of Medusal."

"The Knights of Medusal?" The elf asked as he stood. "Who or what are the Knights of Medusal?"

"We were chosen to protect Therago from the mordians."

"And why should I give you the child?" The elf asked as he stepped forwards from the throne. "You have failed to answer that."

"I do not have an answer to that question," Ryuvin replied as he tensed up. "Athena and Ares sent us to find them, whoever this person is, clearly Athena and Ares believed they would help."

"Interesting," the elf replied and returned to his relaxed state. "I am 'The Child of Ice'."

He bowed slightly to the Knights.

"I am King Valtherol, Ruler of Ymithraldo and the last of the ice elves."

"Ymithraldo?" Serina asked.

"It would seem that time has forgotten me," Valtherol said. "Though the stories whisper of my other name, Isgrav, the Dread Knight of Ice."

Turning, Valtherol returned to his throne and sat down in the same position as before.

"I assume you want me to join you," Valtherol said. "I have no intention to do so."

"Even if that means the destruction of Therago?"

"This would not be the first time," Valtherol replied flatly to Serina. "Look around you. This is all that remains of my home. I have been cursed with this existence, and for what? One man's greed to take the power of creation. I care nothing for the mortal realm and if that means it would be destroyed, then so be it. Let the Dragons rebuild it if they wish."

"We were sent to you for a reason," Kimiko said.

"Will you at least aid us in some way?" Kallindra finished.

"Why should I?"

"Then if you do not wish to help so be it," Athanasia snapped, anger in her voice. "You can wallow in despair as time continues on and you remain a forgotten relic of a world that no longer exists."

The courtyard became tense. Valtherol watched as the Knights turned and began to walk away, letting out a sigh, he stood.

"Wait," he called to them and picked up a small box from behind the throne. "I will not join you, but you can take this."

He handed the box to Ryuvin. It was nothing more than a plain wooden box with a hinged lid.

"Inside is a tome containing a lost magic, something that a very select few can wield."

"You have our thanks," Ryuvin said as he tucked the box into his pack.

"There is also one among the Isvandrere that has an ancient power in his veins," Valtherol said. "Perhaps he will be willing to join you."

"Thank you again, Valtherol," Serina said as she and the Knights bowed before heading back towards the doorway.

"Be warned," Valtherol called after them. "Just because I care not what happens to the mortal realm, does not mean that Blood and Death are standing idly by."

With that, the Knights left behind the long forgotten King.

***

By the time the Knights had finally returned to the Isvandrere village, night had already fallen. The chief had waited, with the warrior they first met, at the edge of the village for them.

"I had wondered when you would return," the chief said, again the warrior translating for him. "The great Dragon God, Skard, gave me a vision. You have a tome from the child?"

Nodding, Lorewind handed the chief the ornate red book that had been in the wooden box. The chief opened it to a random page and read it before handing the book back.

"The tome contains the secrets of dragon magic," the chief said. "It would seem that you are in need of a dragon shaman."

"Where can we find one?" Ryuvin asked.

The chief only shrugged and gestured for them to follow, leading them to an empty tent with several fur cots.

"Rest here for the night, at dawn you shall continue your journey," the chief said. "We will provide you with some supplies, enough to reach your village."

"Thank you," Ryuvin said and bowed. "For everything."

"Do not thank me yet," the chief replied. "The fate of our world is in your hands."

"We will not fail," Kallindra said.

As the knights entered the tent, a young tribesman watched for behind one of the tents. The chief approached the young man eyeing his black and gold leather armour, bearing the emblem of the Knights, a pale green orb floating close to him.

"It seems your powers have awoken," the chief said to him.

"The spirits have shown me what I must do," the young man replied. "I know that I belong with them, I am not truly Isvandrere."

"Though you may not be of my blood," the chief began. "You are my son and this will always be your home."

"Thank you...father."

The young man hugged the chief.

CHAPTER 10

Having left Jotunheim, the Knights returned made their way towards the Monastery of Belhalus, the largest centre of knowledge in Therago. Their first stop was Rinhorn, there they procured more supplies and a mount for Ulrick, the Isvandrere chief's adopted son. He was young, only twenty years of age, tan skinned, with short brown hair and eyes, and a few inches taller than Ryuvin. He was extremely fit for someone who lived in Jotunheim, having cast of his shirt due to his body not being acclimatized to the warmer weather, he had little fat on his body and well defined muscles. His powers were gifted to him by the immortal Artio, the First Druid, who's forest green orb floated close by.

"So I understand that you draw your strength from nature," Lorewind said to him. "But I still don't understand what a druid is."

Lorewind now also donned the armour of the Knights, wearing flowing off the shoulder robes, thigh high slits on both legs, with fur around the neck and lined with chain mail, thigh high leather boots with iron shin guards, and elbow length gloves with iron bracers, all of which was black with gold trim. In her hand she held an elegant staff of polished black elm, a green crystal floating around the head.

"Druids are the guardians of nature," he replied, his voice soft. "We are meant to be the bridge between nature and mankind. It was Entalia who taught Artio this. Through the spirits of the animals and trees."

"And now she is guiding you?"

"Yes," Ulrick answered. "She has much to teach me."

"Are there more druids?" Kimiko asked.

"Perhaps," Ulrick answered, a sadness filling his eyes. "Though I think most are gone."

"I am sorry," Kimiko replied.

The Knights continued on in silence, each lost in their own thoughts. Four days since leaving Rinhorn, the Knights travelled an old road through a forest. There was a slight chill in the shade beneath the trees but the day was beautiful. The journey through the forest was uneventful, the Knights spent much of their time conversing and learning about each other.

It was after midday when they finally exited the forest and came upon a small town. The town seemed mostly farmland but there was a smaller than average tavern, a supply store and blacksmith.

The Knights followed the road through the gate of the wooden wall and dismounted at the edge of town as a middle aged orc approached them.

"Welcome to Morningside," he said, his voice deep and gruff. "The road to the Monastery is on the north side of town."

"What makes you assume that is our destination?" Ryuvin asked.

The orc, like most male orcs, was about seven feet tall, with broad shoulders, pale green skin, dark blue eyes and jet black hair, which was held out of his face with a brown bandana. He had stubble along his wide chin, a pair of short tusks protruded from his lower jaw. He wore a grey cotton shirt, with the sleeves rolled up, that barely fit over his chest and arms, along with a pair of black pants and brown shoes, he also wore a thick brown a thick brown leather apron with a layer of sweat and soot on his arms.

"Judging by your attire," he said as he crossed his arms. "You are some sort of order of warriors. Not really much reason to come here save for the Belhalus monks."

"That is why we are here."

"Barubar," the orc said and held out his hand. "I run the blacksmith."

"Ryuvin Ashgrove," Ryuvin replied as he clasped Barubar's forearm. "Commander of the Knights of Medusal."

"Can't say I've ever heard of your order before," Barubar replied as he looked at the others. "I would offer to do repairs on your equipment but unfortunately I only do farming tools."

"That is quiet alright," Ryuvin answered. "We are only in need of a few supplies before we continue on."

"Talk to Nusha, she runs the shop here in town."

After thanking Barubar, Ryuvin watched as he returned to his forge before turning to the others.

"Kallindra, take Kimiko and scout the road to the Monastery."

"Are we searching for anything in particular?" Kallindra asked.

"Anything out of the ordinary," Ryuvin answered. "Something feels off about the area."

The two nodded and, with a light jog, set off towards the road.

"Lorewind, you go with Serina and restock our supplies."

"Yes sir," Lorewind said then followed Serina to the store.

"The rest of us will see what information we can dig up."

"Any information in particular?" Athanasia asked.

"News on the mordian, however small the chances of that being, but be subtle about it."

"On it, let's go Ulrick."

But Ulrick was not listening, his focus was back towards the gate they had come through earlier.

"Ulrick!" Athanasia shouted and snapped her fingers in front of his face.

"Sorry," he said, having flinched but looked back towards the gate.

"What is it?" Ryuvin asked.

"It may be nothing," he answered. "But does that segment of wall seem…off to you?"

Ryuvin looked towards the wall where Ulrick pointed.

"Nothing looks out of the ordinary."

Ulrick walked towards the wall, Ryuvin and Athanasia following. The wall was roughly twelve feet high with thick posts roughly ten feet apart. Several logs reached between each post and was held together with large iron spikes.

At first glance the wall seemed like any normal wall that surrounded towns, although, upon careful inspection it became apparent that this particular segment had been hastily repaired. There were burn and claw marks on the either side of the post and one of the horizontal logs had been recently replaced.

"What happened to the wall?" Athanasia asked Barubar as he approached.

"It's not your concern," he answered roughly.

"This wall has been reinforced with magic," Ulrick said as he ran his hand along the replaced segment. "It's clear you are trying to keep something out."

"Or perhaps something in?" Athanasia asked.

Barubar glanced over his shoulder then leaded in.

"You're right," he whispered. "Lately, something has been stalking our town, but we don't know what."

The Knights exchanged glances.

"At first it seemed like it was nothing," Barubar continued. "Just some minor scratches and damage along different parts of the wall. Then livestock started to disappear. We thoughts wolves at first but found no evidence. Then last night, once of Zavabar's stable hands was attacked."

"What exactly happened? When the stable hand was attacked?" Ulrick asked.

"Well several days ago, that the town's hunters would do nightly patrols around the interior wall," Barubar began. "It had been Zana's turn, normally only one person would do the patrol, but Kaleg had volunteered to go with her."

"And Kaleg was the one injured?" Athanasia asked.

Barubar nodded.

"When they had reached here, there was a strange clicking sound outside the wall. Kaleg had come over and tried to see what could have been making the sound. That is when whatever it is had reached through the gap, bit into his arm and began to try and pull him through the fence. Zana reacted swiftly, using her hunting knife to attack the thing and free Kaleg. By the time Norig and I heard the commotion and got here, Zana had already driven the creature off, though Kaleg's arm was practically shredded. We rushed him to our village elder, Roshamrik."

"What happened next?" Ryuvin asked.

"Well Norig stayed behind, and a few others had volunteered to patrol the rest of the night," Barubar replied.

"And in the morning?"

"When we checked," Barubar continued. "The wall had large chucks torn out of two pieces and burned to the point where it had crystallized somehow."

"Where are Kaleg and Zana now?" Ryuvin asked.

"Both are at the tavern. The town has a small medical wing setup there."

"May I speak with them?"

Barubar nodded and gestured to follow before turning and walking towards the tavern.

"Athanasia," Ryuvin began as they followed Barubar. "Can you send Icarus to find Kallindra and Kimiko?

"You want them back immediately?" She asked.

"Yes."

"Only one of you should follow," Barubar said as they approached the tavern. "Zana is on edge after what happened and she might not take well to strangers."

Ryuvin nodded and stepped inside with Barubar. The interior of the tavern was quiet large, light filled the room from several windows, set high on the walls, several iron chandeliers hung from the thick ceiling beams, a large stone hearth sat at the far end of the room, and opposite, near the entrance, was the bar.

The tavern was empty, save for the female orc that was bent over and wiping down the table just ahead of them, her back turned towards the door.

"You going to keep gawking?" She asked without looking, her voice gruff yet sweet. "Or you plan on telling me what you want, Barubar?"

"Just admiring the view," Barubar replied, clearly staring at her backside. "Can't a guy – Oof!"

He was cut off as an empty wooden bowl hit him square in the face. Ryuvin had ducked as the bowl bounced off Barubar and flew at him.

"You are such a pig," the woman said in a huff.

She was several inches shorter than Barubar with pale brown skin and green eyes. She had a slim, muscular build with a plump figure, her short black hair was held away from her face with a grey ribbon, her tusks were much less noticeable, which was typical of female orcs. She wore a light blue shoulder-less blouse and a long black skirt with a brown cloth apron around her waist.

"What do you want elf?" She asked with a hostile tone as Ryuvin straightened.

"He is here about what happened last night, Zavabar," Barubar said as he rubbed the spot where the bowl hit him.

Zavabar narrowed her eyes at Ryuvin before turning and gesturing for them to follow.

She lead Ryuvin and Barubar to a door on the opposite side of the room, down a short hallway and stopped at another door.

"Medical wing is through here," she stated then turned and pushed passed them.

"Sorry about Zavabar," Barubar said, watching Zavabar saunter back to the tavern. "I think she blames herself for what happened to Kaleg."

"You can go and talk to her if needed," Ryuvin replied as he turned back to Barubar. "I can speak with Kaleg and Zana alone."

Barubar hesitated then shook his head and turned back to the door.

The medical wing was larger than Ryuvin had expected, with larger windows, letting light flood into the room. There were ten beds, each separated with curtains, in total, five on either side of the room. Like the tavern, there were also iron chandeliers hanging from the ceiling. A large supply cabinet was pressed up against the wall immediately left of the door and a small desk to the right.

An orc sat in a chair next to one of the beds, their back towards the door, at the far end of the room. An elderly orc, with long white hair and glasses, and wearing simple faded black robes, who was sitting at the desk, looked up from the notes he was reading as Barubar and Ryuvin entered.

"Ah, Barubar," the old orc said, a slight wheeze in his weary voice, as he sat back against his chair.

"Hello Roshamrik," Barubar said then gestured to Ryuvin. "This is Sir Ryuvin Ashgrove, he is the leader of an order of knights."

The elderly orc turned his attention to Ryuvin, his grey eyes examining him closely.

"An order of knights?" Roshamrik asked as he stood, a cane, that was leaning against the desk, supported the weight of his frail body. "Which order?"

"I command the Knights of Medusal," Ryuvin answered and bowed.

"It has been nearly three thousand years since the Knights had vanished," Roshamrik said as he bowed the best he could. "What business do the Knights have in our small town of Morningside?"

"Originally, we had only been passing through on our way to the Monastery of Belhalus," Ryuvin answered. "However it is my understanding that something plagues your town."

"You are here to help?" Came a woman's voice.

Turning, Ryuvin noticed that the woman was the one that had been sitting in the chair. She had braided, long dark hair, brown eyes, a narrow face and tan skin. Her figure was more muscular than Zavabar's and was slightly taller, sporting a brown leather tunic and dark green legging with knee high brown leather boots.

"We are," Ryuvin replied. "Are you Zana?"

"I am," she said and visibly relaxed.

Zana hesitated and looked at Roshamrik, who nodded.

"About a fortnight ago I had been returning from a rather successful hunt," Zana began. "That is when I had noticed some damage along the wall, nothing major really, a few scratches or bite marks. I decided to check along the entire perimeter and that's when I realized that the damage was more spread out."

"So it was not the type of damage you could expect from the normal behaviour of an animal marking its territory?" Ryuvin asked.

"Maybe at first it could have been," Zana continued. "But it was always low, as if it was trying to hide, and never in the same area of the wall. A few days later some she had disappeared, most of the town chalked it up to some wolves getting in."

"But not you?"

Zana shook her head.

"See the gate is always closed at sundown," she said. "And there was never any wolf tracks. I had been hunting when I stumbled upon the corpse of one of the missing sheep."

"Let me guess," Ryuvin began. "Blood drained and in a tree?"

"Yes," Zana answered. "How did you know?"

"Just a guess," Ryuvin answered. "Please continue."

"Well once that happened," Zana continued. "Myself and the other hunters decided to start doing patrols along the interior wall. Last night, Kaleg volunteered to join me."

"Tell me about the attack," Ryuvin said.

"As we patrolled, Kaleg and I heard this strange clicking sound. It wasn't anything I had ever heard before. We approached the wall to see what it could have been. Kaleg had rested his hand against it. That's when the thing grabbed his arm and tried to pull him through. It all became a blur after that, I must've wounded it because I remember hearing a shriek and when I looked at my knife, the blade was destroyed. When the other hunters check in the morning, they found nothing other than the damage to the wall."

"You said your knife was destroyed?" Ryuvin asked. "How?"

"The blade was all but gone," Zana answered. "Like it was melted away by acid, yet the end of it was crystallized."

Ryuvin thought for a moment as he crossed his arm, right hand on his mouth.

Altareon, Kayle? He asked, *does any of this sound familiar to you?*

Nothing I have seen in the Nine Layers, Altareon replied.

Apologies Ryuvin, Kayle answered, *but our knowledge of creatures of the mortal realms is severely lacking.*

No need for apologies, Ryuvin said, *I have a few theories.*

"What of Kaleg?" Ryuvin asked.

"He is stable for now," Roshamrik answered. "He has lost a lot of blood and my healing magic is working to pull all the muscles back together, but it will take time. The amount of damage to his arm is like nothing I have ever seen before. Whatever attacked him has a lot of teeth."

"Thank you for all the information," Ryuvin said and bowed. "I shall return to my companions and go from there."

***

Ryuvin stepped out of the tavern and walked to where the others had gathered near the stables.

"Report," Ryuvin said to Kallindra and Kimiko as he approached.

"Before Icarus found us," Kallindra began. "We had found a strange trail, something had been through the area, perhaps the size of a bristle boar."

"Whatever it was," Kimiko continued. "I believe it injured. Along the trail we had found tracks that seemed to put more weight to its right side."

"We also found strange crystallized burns," Kallindra said. "Not to mention a few trees with blood stains in some of branches."

Ryuvin nodded.

"You think vampires are hunting this town?" Serina asked.

"No something else," Ryuvin answered and filled in the

others of what he learned from Roshamrik. "Let us break it down, what do we know?"

"Its roughly the size of a bristle boar and its injured," Kallindra said.

"It has acidic blood that crystallizes when it dries," Kimiko added.

"It has a mouthful of teeth and claws," Ryuvin continued.

"It's strong," Serina said. "Strong enough to hold an orc in place."

"This thing makes a clicking sound right?" Lorewind asked. "Maybe it cannot see?"

"Some livestock has gone missing," Athanasia added. "So that means it has gotten in before."

"Zana told me there were no tracks," Ryuvin said. "Maybe this thing has wings that lets it fly short distances."

"Perhaps," Ulrick countered. "It could also be climbing the wall."

"Zana did say that any damage from this thing has always been low and hidden," Serina replied.

"So it is intelligent," Ulrick said. "Like it was testing the wall for weak points."

Athanasia suddenly jerked her head, and Kallindra's ears began to swivel in multiple directions.

"What is wrong?" Lorewind asked.

"Do you hear that?" Kallindra asked Athanasia.

"Yes," she answered.

"I do not hear anything," Lorewind replied.

"Exactly," Kallindra answered.

The others listened and, like Lorewind said, heard nothing. No birds, no insects, even the livestock made no sound. Just silence.

"It is watching us," Kimiko said and looked out the gate. "It can see during the day."

Just then, Barubar had stepped out of the tavern.

"This is bad," Ryuvin said then called to Barubar. "We need to close the gate."

"Wha-" Barubar began.

"Now Barubar!" Ryuvin commanded and sprinted to the gate.

Barubar and the Knights raced after Ryuvin. Reaching the gate, they began to pull doors shut. The heavy wood groaned as the slowly swung closed. A heavy beam was lowered into place to secure the gate, once in place, Ryuvin climbed to the top of the wall and focused his gaze towards the woods. His face paled.

"What is it?" Serina asked as she reach the top along side him.

She followed his gaze and roughly one hundred and fifty meters from the gate was a young girl picking flowers. But it was what was the creature in the woods, another two hundred meters beyond her that was the concern.

"Is that what I think it is?" Serina asked as the other Knights joined them.

Ryuvin nodded and reach for Kayle, then hesitated.

"Will you be fast enough?" Serina asked.

"I do not know," Ryuvin answered. "But I have to try."

Taking a breathe, Ryuvin took hold of the pale gold orb. As he merged with Kayle, he launched himself forwards from the wall and flew as fast as he could to reach the girl first. At the same time the creature burst out from the trees, also charging at the girl.

"Hurry Ryuvin!" Serina screamed.

Ryuvin gritted his teeth and pushed harder. The girl turned and saw the creature, eyes wide with terror as she screamed. With mere moments to spare, Ryuvin had grabbed the girl and dodged backwards, avoiding the creature's snapping jaws. It gave chase after Ryuvin as he flew back towards the wall. From their position at the top of the wall, Kallindra and Serina began to fire arrows at it. The creature did not relent as it chased Ryuvin, dodging the arrows with ease, until one of Kallindra's silver moonlight arrows had clipped its hind leg. Letting out a shriek of pain, the beast retreated back towards the forest and out of range.

"What is that thing?" Barubar asked as he peered through the wall at the creature.

It watched them as it paced back and forth. Dark brown bristle like fur covered its back, a leather like membrane stretched from its skeletal limbs to its body, it had a long muzzle full of razor sharp teeth, beady red eyes and large bat-like ears. It was quite large, about the size of a hellhound.

"It's called a camaborg," Ryuvin answered as he put the girl down. "And it is not alone."

Chapter 11

Later, as the sun began to set, Ryuvin and Serina stood in the tavern, listening to the chatter of the townsfolk. Ryuvin had been able to convince Roshamrik to call for an emergency meeting.

"They have no idea what is going on, nor the danger they are in," Serina whispered to him. "Are you sure it's a good idea to tell them?"

"We have no choice," Ryuvin replied, also whispering. "Many others saw it, it will not take long for rumours to spread."

Zavabar and Barubar approached and nodded to Ryuvin before turning to the crowd.

"Alright everyone," Barubar called out over the chatter, silencing everyone. "I'm sure most of you have heard about the events of this afternoon by now."

A small murmur spread through the crowd.

"I will give the floor to these two Knights to explain everything."

Barubar turned back to Ryuvin and nodded.

"This is not going to be news you want to hear," Ryuvin began as he stepped forwards. "But you town is square in the middle of the hunting grounds of a pack of camaborgs."

"What's a camaborg?" An orc in the back called out.

"It is a very old, very viscous and very territorial predator," Ryuvin answered. "Extremely intelligent, fast, nimble and strong. It can somewhat fly a decent distance, which is how it was able to get over your wall and take your livestock."

More murmurs arose from the crowd.

"Its blood is highly acidic and will crystallize when it dries," Ryuvin continued. "It primarily hunts at night using echolocation."

"Wait, if that is the case," Zavabar interrupted. "Why was it out during the day?"

"While not unheard of to hunt during the day," Ryuvin replied. "This one was not hunting, I assume it was here because Zana either injured or killed the one from last night. These things most likely view the town as a threat now, instead of rival hunters."

"So what do we do?" Another orc asked.

"There is nothing you can do," Ryuvin answered. "These things have been hunted to extinction by elves many times before, at least we thought."

The townsfolk had began chattering and arguing amongst themselves.

"Shut it!" Zavabar yelled over the crowd. "Obviously we wont do nothing!"

"Zavabar is right," Barubar said.

"While there is nothing you, yourselves, can do," Ryuvin continued. "The Knights of Medusal will deal with these creatures. I only ask that you remain within the town until it is safe. These things are a danger to more than just your home, if left unchecked, they will breed extremely quickly and become a threat to everything."

The crowd murmured more as Ulrick entered the tavern and walked over to Ryuvin.

"We have a problem," he whispered to Ryuvin and Serina. "Kimiko is gone."

"What do you mean 'gone'?" Serina asked.

"When I went to check on her, she was nowhere to be seen, no tracks either."

Ryuvin cursed as the three of them rushed out of the tavern and into the soundless night. They paused and looked at the roof of the general shop, a clicking sound reaching their ears. A camaborg sat perched on the roof. It screeched and launched itself at them.

***

It was a moonless night. Kimiko, having merged with Vigil, moved as a shadow through the trees. Her vision enhanced, she followed the trail of the wounded camaborg she and Kallindra discovered earlier that day.

Ryuvin said there would be a nest, she thought to herself, *let us see if my hunch is correct.*

The tracks were easy enough to follow, the beast seemed to want to get to safety, and injured creatures always run for home. She followed the tracks deeper into the forest, and after several minutes, came upon a clearing with a stone monastery. Keeping low, she moved closer, each step silent. She reached the stairs that lead to the main door. No torches were lit anywhere and she could see no light inside. She ascended the steps and, upon reaching the main door, she took hold of the large iron handle, giving it a gentle yet firm tug; the door refused to budge. Slowly, she returned the handle to its original position, careful not to make a sound. Taking a quiet breathe, Kimiko focused, allowing Vigil's power to flow through her. She stepped forwards and melded into the shadows of the monastery. Reemerging from the shadows, she scanned the entrance room of the monastery. Everything seemed normal, save for the coppery tinge of blood that filled the air. Submerging herself back into the shadows, Kimiko continued her search.

This must be the Monastery of Belhalus, she thought as she moved through the shadows from room to room, each filled with books.

A whisper of movement caught her attention as she moved up to the second floor. Remaining submerged, she watched as a few hooded figures silently moved amongst the bookshelves. She watched as they crept by her shadow and towards another set of stairs. After several minutes, Kimiko stepped out of the shadow she was submerged in. She contemplated following when a book caught her eye; it was ancient and out of place from the rest with black leather bindings. She pulled it free and flipped it open to a random page, the red text, standing in contrast on the black pages, was in a language she did not recognize.

Do you know what language this is Vigil? She asked.

It could be one of several, Vigil responded.

A sudden clicking sound made her freeze, she waited a moment and heard the clicking again, this time closer. Quickly and silently closing the book, Kimiko focused her powers again and melded back into the shadow. She waited a few moments and watched as a pair of camaborgs ascended the stairs, clicking and sniffing as they went. One had stopped and sniffed the shadow she was hiding in before continuing on.

What was it Serina had said? She thought to herself, *camaborgs make their nests in cold dark places?*

Moving through the shadows, Kimiko made her way back the way she came and through the silent halls of the monastery. Eventually she found a stairway leading down, a damp metallic smell wafted up to her. Slowly, she ventured down the worn cobblestone steps, the smell grew stronger the farther she went down the long winding stairway. Finally reaching the base of the stairwell, Kimiko was greeted by the carcass of some sort of animal, mutilated beyond recognition, and a wooden door that was broken and hanging on a single hinge. The smell of death, decay and filth flooded her nose as she peered inside the room.

Found you, she thought.

Inside the room, amidst the dozen half rotten corpses and piles of bones, was the camaborg nest; several dozen clusters of eggs, roughly two feet in height, several camaborgs moved around the nest, and, at the centre of the room, was a much larger one, presumably the queen.

Now I best get out of here, she thought.

Moving back the way she came, Kimiko eventually made it back towards the entrance. The sound of foot steps reaching her ears. Staying hidden, she watched as a group of bandits slowly moved around the entry room, weapons in hand.

Curious, she thought to herself, *do they not know about the camaborgs?*

"Are you sure this is a good idea?" One of the bandits whispered.

"Chief sent us here to find Sylas and his group," the lead bandit replied. "He has been gone far too long."

"Maybe the monks got 'em," another said.

"Monks ain't been seen or heard from for days," the leader replied.

These fools, Kimiko thought.

They are going to get themselves killed, Vigil said.

Before Kimiko could step from the shadows, an echoing click came from one of the two corridors.

"What was that?" A bandit asked, fear creeping into his voice.

"Split up," the leader said. "Flynn, you and Cal go left. Kurt, you come with me."

Kimiko cursed as the bandits split up.

Do not bother with those two, Vigil said to Kimiko as she watched the leader and Kurt head towards the clicking.

Moving swiftly, she caught up to Flynn and Cal with ease in the next room.

"You both need to get out of here," she raid to the bandits as she stepped out of the shadows.

The two bandits spun around, swords raised.

"Who are you?" Flynn asked, his voice shaking.

"I am the Shadow Knight," she answered. "There are-"

A scream cut her off.

"Run, now!" She said and turned, running towards the window at the far side of the room.

The two bandits hesitated for a moment then followed. Sprinting at full speed, Kimiko hurtled the window, smashing through the glass, ran towards the stair and leapt down them, landing gracefully at the base. Flynn and Cal scrambled after her, tripping and stumbling. Turning back, they saw Kurt get tackled by a camaborg, its jaws closing around his head, killing him instantly, before dragging his body back inside.

"W-w-what was that thing?" Cal asked in horror.

"A camaborg," Kimiko answered. "And there are more of them."

"Did those things get Sylas?" Flynn asked

"More than likely," Kimiko replied. "It is not safe here, go back to your camp. Tell your chief that if he wants help to come to Morningside."

"The orc town? Why?"

Kimiko did no answer, instead she turned and started to jog back towards the town.

"What do we do?" Flynn asked Cal.

"Well, we start by getting the hell away from here," Cal answered. "Then we report to the chief and let him decide."

Flynn nodded to Cal. A scream rang from inside the monastery causing the two bandits to scramble along the ground before they were able to get their footing and sprint off into the woods.

***

It took several minutes for Kimiko, no longer merged with Vigil, to get back to Morningside and reach the edge of the forest. Stopping, she watched the activity inside the wall. Moving silently, she circled the town towards the gate.

Why is the gate open? She thought.

She watched for a moment before noticing someone leaning against the gate, their arms crossed. She sighed and approached.

"Forgive me," she said as she knelt down, head bowed. "Ryuvin-sama."

Ryuvin looked at her, arms remaining crossed while leaning against the open gate.

"I trust you disappeared for good reason," he said.

"Yes sir."

"Well what do you have to report?" Ryuvin asked.

"I have found the nest," she said as she looked up at Ryuvin. "And you will not like where it is."

"It is in the Monastery of Belhalus, is it not?" He interrupted.

"It is," Kimiko replied as she pulled out the ancient tome. "I also found this."

Taking the tome, Ryuvin opened it to a random page.

This should not be here, Altareon stated.

What is it? Ryuvin asked.

This tome is written in the daemon tongue, Altareon answered, *if you are willing, I can give you the knowledge to read and speak the language, but it will take time.*

That would be most helpful, Altareon, Ryuvin said.

"Will it be of use?" Kimiko asked.

"It might be," Ryuvin answered. "In the meantime, you will inform the others what you have found."

They pulled the gates closed and made their way to the tavern, passing the charred remains of several camaborgs.

"Kimiko!" Lorewind yelled and ran over as she and Ryuvin entered the tavern, hugging her tight. "Where did you go? We were worried."

"I found the nest," Kimiko replied, after Lorewind let her go.

"Kimiko," Serina said as she approached. "You should have told us where you were going."

"Forgive me, Serina-sama."

As the Knights gathered around one of the tables, Kimiko began her report.

"The nest is in the Monastery of Belhalus," she said. "With at least several dozen eggs."

"What of the monks?" Kallindra asked. "Do they yet live?"

"Unknown," Kimiko replied. "I saw a few robed individuals but my main objective was to locate the nest."

"Then they may yet live," Ulrick said.

"There is also a group of bandits in the area," Kimiko continued. "They have already lost several to the camaborgs. I told them to come here, should they seek aid."

"Is that wise?" Athanasia asked.

"We will have to see," Serina answered. "If they left Morningside alone, they must of had good reason to do so."

"How many camaborgs?" Ryuvin asked.

"A single queen," Kimiko replied. "And about a dozen in the nest itself, though I cannot give an exact number."

"So how are we going to play this?" Kallindra asked.

"We need to deal with the smaller ones first," Athanasia began.

"Either way, the nest needs to be eradicated," Ryuvin finished.

"So we bait them out," Kallindra said.

"They will figure out our plan quickly," Ryuvin replied. "We will probably get a few before then."

"What about ambushing the ones not in the nest?" Ulrick asked.

"It is possible," Kimiko answered. "It would be extremely difficult, the traps would have to be different every time."

"Can you make traps?" Ryuvin asked Lorewind and Kimiko.

"Should be simple," Kimiko replied. "I can make several different kinds."

"I can try," Lorewind hesitantly answered, fiddling with her hands.

"We thing them out the best we can," Ryuvin said. "Take out as many as possible before we go after the nest. Serina, I need you to stay and protect the town."

Serina opened her mouth to protest, but a stern look from Ryuvin kept her from continuing.

"Get whatever rest you can, we leave in two hours."

**

Two hours later, the Knights had gathered at the gate.

"Ryuvin," Serina said as she stepped up to him. "Come back safe."

Ryuvin smiled and pulled her close, his lips brushing against hers as he gently kissed her.

"I will," he said, holding her close. "No matter what."

Serina hugged him tight for a moment longer before letting go. Stepping away, Ryuvin joined the rest of the Knights outside the gate, where the were confronted by a small group of human bandits. There were only six of them, each in basic leather armour and armed with short swords, two of the bandits were heavily injured, one more so than the other, and were being held up by the others. One of the wounded Kimiko recognized as Cal, though Flynn was not among the group.

"I am Mareck," the leader said as he stepped away from less wounded bandit. "I was told we could seek aid here."

"You must be the bandit clan I was informed about," Ryuvin replied.

"Aye we are," Mareck said. "I am Chief of the Raven's Talon, or at least what is left of it."

"How many did you lose?"

"Including the ones in the monastery? Twenty-six dead, eight missing," Mareck answered. "Flynn and Cal were reporting back when those beasts attacked. We managed to kill two."

"Serina," Ryuvin said as he looked to her. "Bring them to Roshamrik."

"Right away," she answered and gestured for the bandits to follow as she walked away.

Mareck watched his men follow Serina then looked back to Ryuvin.

"You are going to the monastery?" He asked

Ryuvin only nodded.

"I would come with you," Mareck said. "But my men need me so you make sure you kill them all."

Chapter 12

You are doing well, Verdag said to Lorewind as she cast the rune he taught her, *you have mastered this trap spell with ease.*

Thank you Verdag, she replied as she moved as silently as possible, *may I ask something?*

You need not hesitate to ask, he said to her.

Lorewind watched Verdag's crystal slowly floating around staff, a large prealescent gem affixed the top. The black and gold robes of the Knights of Medusal flowed over her body, a single pauldron on her right shoulder.

You said I can summon elementals and from that I can harness their strength as my own, she said, *so what I want to know is how does it affect you?*

You calling upon our power does not harm us if that is what your concern is, Verdag answered.

"All set?" Kallindra whispered.

Lorewind nodded to her.

Nodding back, Kallindra lifted one of the two heavy tomes she carried and, with a slight grunt, threw it down the corridor, the loud thud echoing through the halls. They waited. Eventually they heard the claws of a camaborg scrapping against the stone corridor. Kallindra threw the other tome, again the thud echoed through the corridors. In the moonlight, they watched as a camaborg stalked the dark shadows of the corner, sniffing the tomes. Lorewind shifted slightly, her boot scrapping against the stone of the corridor. The camaborg swivelled its head towards them, made several clicking sounds and, after a few moments, shrieked and charged at them with frightening speed. When it reached the runes of the trap, Lorewind had drawn into the stone, spikes erupted and impaled the camaborg, killing it instantly.

"That makes four," Kallindra said.

"I wish we had an exact number," Lorewind said as she dispelled the trap. "I hope the others are safe."

***

Ryuvin and Ulrick moved through the corridors of the upper floor,

"You really think we will find any survivors?" Ulrick asked with a whisper.

"Kimiko said she saw a few people come this way," Ryuvin replied as he peered around a corner. "I cannot imagine it being anyone other than the monks."

The two did their best to keep to the shadows.

Note to self, Ryuvin thought, *learn how Kimiko hides as she does in the shadows.*

Eventually they came upon several bodies of dead camaborgs in front of an ornate door at the end of the corridor.

"Well I guess we should check the door," Ulrick said as he stepped over a camaborg.

"Wait," Ryuvin said and grabbed his shoulder. "Something does not seem right."

"You think?" Ulrick replied and looked back to the door. "I don't sense any magic."

Not all magic can be sensed so easily, Artio whispered, *some require time to cast and therefore time to sense.*

Nodding, Ulrick took a breath and focused his mind. While he worked on his magic sense, Ryuvin began to study the floors and walls.

What are you looking for? Kayle asked.

I am not sure, Ryuvin answered, *I sense something but I am not sure what.*

"There is something here," Ulrick said, eyes closed. "It is... intricate, almost like it is layered on top of itself."

"Sounds powerful," Ryuvin replied as he ran his hand along the wall. "Can you dispel it?"

"Hard to say. I don't even know what 'it' is."

"Then it will have to wait," Ryuvin said as he pushed a brick of the wall. "I found what I was looking for."

A section of the wall shifted and depressed before sliding to the side, revealing a dark narrow corridor.

"Could be a trap," Ulrick said as the two peered down the secret corridor.

"Perhaps," Ryuvin said as he stepped through the doorway.

Ulrick, Artio whispered, *I sense something powerful behind that door.*

Ulrick nodded and followed Ryuvin. Once both had entered, the wall slide shut again, the pale gold light of Kayle's orb was all that illuminated the narrow passage. After a few sharp turns, Ryuvin could see the glow of a fire up ahead and a few figures milling about a room.

"Looks like the monks survived," Ulrick said.

"It looks that way," Ryuvin replied.

The two Knights proceeded and stepped into the chamber, it was not very large, probably about thirty feet in length and about twenty feet in width, a few small windows on the left side of the room.

"You are not of the Monastery," an old man said as the approached, face hidden by his hood. "Did you respond to our request for aid?"

"No we did not," Ryuvin replied.

"I see," the man said with a sigh. "Then it would seem Brother Resh did not make it."

"We are sorry for your lose," Ulrick said to him.

"My Brothers and Sisters around the room are all that remain."

There were only sixteen monks in the room, most of which lay injured in cots and in need of medical attention.

"If you did no receive a request for aid," the monk said.

"Then why are you here?"

"We are Knights of Medusal," Ryuvin answered. "I am Ryuvin Ashgrove and this is Ulrick of the Isvandrere."

"Abbot Mortimore," the monk said as he bowed.

Ryuvin and Ulrick bowed in turned then told the Abbot of their mission.

"I see," Mortimore said. "A Dragon Shaman is rare indeed. If you are in need of one perhaps you should turn your search to Mystaria. There is a student, by the name Argenta, who's magic is...different from the rest of the students."

"Different how?" Ulrick asked.

"According to what Headmaster Frandel told me," Abbot Mortimore said. "She doesn't draw magic in from the world around her. Instead, she seems to just innately have magic of her own.

That almost sounds like the magic of immortals and gods, Kayle whispered.

"Is something like that even possible?" Ryuvin asked. "I was under the impression that only gods and immortals wielded magic in such a way."

"I'm not sure, though she struggles with that and is afraid of what she is."

"Meaning what?" Ulrick asked.

"She fears she is a monster," Ryuvin answered.

"If you search for a Dragon Shaman," Mortimore said. "Then she may be who you are looking for."

"There is one other thing," Ulrick said. "What did you seal behind the door?"

"The Staff of Aos Si," the Abbot replied. "Though we did not seal the door."

"Then who did?" Ryuvin asked.

"We aren't sure, not long after we were attacked, Thunan; one of the younger novices, went to retrieve the staff. This was five days ago and he hasn't returned, the door has been seal ever since."

Ryuvin, Altareon whispered, *I have finished imparting the knowledge of the daemon tongue to you, as well as a spell that should be of use.*

Thank you, Altareon, Ryuvin replied.

Shall I open your mind to it? Altareon asked, *be warned, the process will be painful.*

Do it.

Pain flared in Ryuvin's head, almost as if someone had poured molten iron into his brain. Ryuvin did his best to fight through the pain but failed, he staggered and clutched his head.

"Sir, are you okay?" Ulrick asked.

"I will live," Ryuvin replied through gritted teeth.

It is done, Altareon said as the pain stopped, *the spell is called daemon fire.*

Ryuvin searched his mind feeling the knowledge and power of the spell.

I will use it with caution, Ryuvin said.

"You said that the Staff of Aos Si was sealed," Ryuvin said, his head still throbbing. "Is she not one of the Gods of Wind and Storms?"

"Goddess of the South Wind and Storms," Abbot Mortimore replied. "The Monks of Belhalus have trained for centuries in the way of the staff. The one who founded this monastery, Belhalus, was said to be Aos Si's chosen champion on Therago. When he passed, the staff remained and the monks slowly became keepers of knowledge."

"Perhaps the young monk, Thunan, is trying to prove his worth and wield the staff as Belhalus once did."

"That may explain the seal," Ulrick said as he contemplated Ryuvin's words. "It is very powerful. Perhaps Aos Si is testing him."

"It is not something we can be distracted with," Ryuvin answered. "If Aos Si did seal the door than so be it. Our focus right now is to eliminate the camaborgs."

"I will leave you to that task," the Abbot said as he bowed again. "I thank you for any aid you can provide."

Both Ryuvin and Ulrick bowed to Abbot Mortimore, then

turned and began heading back to the main corridor. They stopped at the sealed door for a moment.

"The seal hasn't changed at all," Ulrick said.

"Then it seems we will have to continue on without the aid of Aos Si's champion," Ryuvin replied.

If Aos Si even has a champion, Kayle whispered, *the gods can be fickle beings.*

The two began heading back the way they came towards the stairs.

"We should get to the nest and destroy it now," Ryuvin continued. "The others should have thinned out the pack enough."

***

Meanwhile, at the top of the stairs leading to the nest.

"Ryuvin and Ulrick are taking too long," Kallindra said, her arms crossed as she paced back and forth. "We need to destroy the nest."

"And how hard was it to kill just the few in Morningside?" Athanasia asked with an irritated tone. "We need all of the Knights for this."

"And the longer we sit here," Kallindra countered. "The harder it will be to destroy the nest."

"And if we go in there when we aren't at full strength it will get us killed," Athanasia argued.

"What do you even know about warfare?" Kallindra asked as she moved closer to Athanasia. "You are just a blacksmith."

"Says the pampered princess," Athanasia replied not moving from her spot. "You know nothing of war, my people breathe war."

"Do not make me laugh," Kallindra countered. "You have never even seen real battle. I know how Sandara is, ruled by the warrior clans. And you, always chasing after glory that you could never have."

"You know nothing about who I am," Athanasia said, rage building in her voice. "Athena and Ares-"

"You think you are special because you were chosen by

two gods?" Kallindra interrupted. "You are nothing but a blind girl pretending to be a warrior because, face it, you will never be accepted as anything else."

"That is enough," Kimiko interjected as she pushed the two apart. "We need to be working together, no mat-"

Kimiko gasped and spit up blood, looking down she saw the claws of a camaborg buried into her abdomen.

"Kimiko!" Athanasia screamed, claymore flashing into her hand.

***

Ryuvin and Ulrick made their way as quickly as possible to the first floor. They passed multiple corpses of camaborgs; either having been impaled by large spikes or arrows, others having fallen to Kimiko and Athanasia's blades.

"We best hurry," Ulrick said. "The queen will not be idle and will more than likely know of our intent here."

"Agreed," Ryuvin replied.

Ryuvin and Ulrick eventually met up with the rest of the Knights at the top of the top of the stairs that lead to the nest, dozens of dead camaborg littered the area. Lorewind was visibly exhausted, Kallindra was out of arrows, now relying on her short sword. Athanasia was coated in sweat and panting, her arms scratched up and bleeding as she guarded the top of the stairs. But it was Kimiko that was in danger. Sitting against the wall, face pale, holding a blood soaked bandage to her side. Lorewind and Kallindra were knelt beside her, doing what they could to help stem the bleeding.

"Kimiko!" Ryuvin cried and ran to her. "What happened?"

"I was careless," she replied and coughed, fresh blood dripping down her chin. "We were not expecting them to swarm from the nest."

"She is lying," Kallindra said, tears running down her cheeks.

"What are you talking about?" Ryuvin asked.

"Sort this out later," Ulrick said. "Let me look."

Ryuvin nodded then he and Kallindra moved aside. Ulrick

knelt beside Kimiko and slowly peeled away the bandage. Blood surged from the large hole in her side. Kimiko coughed up more blood. Lorewind pressed the bandage back against the wound as Ulrick cursed and reached for Artio.

"Artio taught me basic healing magic," Ulrick said. "I can stabilize her but we need to get her back to Morningside."

"Athanasia," Ryuvin began as he turned towards her. "What happened?"

"It my fault," she answered, her muscles tensing. "I let myself get distracted and Kimiko paid for it."

"Distracted how?"

"It was my fault," Kallindra answered. "You and Ulrick had not yet returned and I wanted to push ahead to the nest."

"I told her we needed to wait for you," Athanasia continued. "We needed to be at full strength before going in."

"And that is when the camaborg attack?" Ryuvin asked.

Both Kallindra and Athanasia refused to meet his eyes.

"Athanasia, get them to Morningside," Ryuvin commanded.

"What about you?" Athanasia asked.

"I will end this," he answered.

Ulrick, now merged with Artio, had begun to tend to Kimiko. His hair had become longer as antlers broke through his hairline, his armour almost seemed like bark, eyes seeming to shift between green and gold.

"Lorewind," Kallindra began as she gathered Kimiko's gear. "Are you well enough to summon Verdag?"

"Even if I'm not," Lorewind answered, determination burning in her eyes. "I won't let her die."

"Commander," Athanasia said. "You need help, I won't let you go in alone."

"He won't be alone," a man said as he entered the room, voice deep and modulated.

"You must be Thunan," Ryuvin replied as he and Athanasia turned to the young human monk.

Roughly five and a half feet tall, Thunan was easily in

his early twenties with an average build, head head shaved, strong jawed with deep green eyes and dark skin. He wore a gold trimmed, black silk sleeveless tunic that was long in the back and held closed with a gold sash, black leggings and dark knee high boots. The lower half of the tunic had gold cloud like patterns, along with the roaring lion on his back. His hands were also wrapped in a black cloth that reached halfway up his forearms. The Staff of Aos Si was a quarter staff about six feet in length, engraved with intricate patterns of wind and clouds, ornate metal caps on each end of the staff.

"The two of you won't be enough," Athanasia continued.

"Then it's a good thing I make three," came a gruff voice from the other corridor.

An orc, roughly seven and a half feet tall, with green skin, stepped into the moonlit room. He had the typical orc build, though he looked less fit than Barubar but his arms were clearly more muscular. Reddish brown hair in a mohawk and a noticeable stubble along his jaw, a long jagged scar along his neck, anger raging in his hazel coloured eyes. He wore simple black leggings and boots, his burly chest bare, save for the leather strap running across his chest, holding the single leather pauldron, on his left shoulder, engraved with the gold roaring lion of the Knights. Two double bladed axes hung from his back.

"Name's Waruk," the orc said with a slightly unsettling smirk.

"Ryuvin Ashgrove," Ryuvin replied. "Commander of-"

"The Knights of Medusal, blah blah blah," Waruk interrupted and gestured to a crimson orb floating near him. "Reidi already told me about you."

Interesting, Vigil whispered, *I did not expect the rokshara of rage to be an ally.*

"You best show respect when you speak to-" Kimiko began but was interrupted as she coughed up more blood, leaning heavily on Kallindra and Ulrick.

"Athanasia, you have your orders," Ryuvin said, ignoring Kimiko.

"Very well, Sir," Athanasia replied and begrudgingly followed the other Knights.

"So what's the plan boss?" Waruk asked nonchalantly.

"We eradicate the nest," Ryuvin answered as he reached for Altareon.

"Simple, I like it," Waruk answered as he merged with Reidi. "Doesn't need much strategy."

The three descended the stairs; Ryuvin leading in his daemon form, bare chested, black leggings with silver greaves engraved with skulls, wings folded back, daemon sword in hand. Waruk, skin now pale red, eyes blazing with blood lust and fury, taller and even more muscular, axe in each hand, hair reaching down his back, followed behind. Thunan, calm and focused, staff of Aos Si in hand, wind swirling around him.

"Here we go," Ryuvin said as they reached the base of the stairs.

The three charged in, the nest had been what appeared to be the store room for the monastery, tipped over and broken shelves, covered in filth, littered the area. The camaborg had worked to make the room much larger than it had originally been.

Ryuvin flexed his daemon wings, as they entered the room, and launched himself into the air, sword swinging in an arc as a few camaborgs leapt at him. His sword cutting through their bodies with ease. Waruk let out a roar and charged forwards, like a whirlwind of blades, he cut through dozens of young camaborgs and eggs as he went. Thunan swept through the nest like a storm, lightning cracked from the staff upon impact with the eggs and camaborgs that leapt at him.

The three had made quick work of the camaborg that were in the nest when a much larger one dropped from the ceiling at Waruk. He easily caught and threw the beast, Ryuvin followed in with a swing of his sword and cut off its front left leg, Thunan ended with a blast of lightning from his staff.

"Well that was easy," Waruk said as he prodded the charred corpse with his boot.

"Yes," Thunan replied. "Almost too easy."

No sooner did the words leave his mouth, the ground shifted and shook. Waruk and Thunan, both, struggling to maintain balance. A massive camaborg pushed itself out of the muck and dirt. The queen. It swung its head back and forth, then spotted Waruk and let out and ear piercing shriek. Waruk roared in response and charge at it, only to be batted aside, crashing heavily into a stack of shelves.

"Lucky hit bitch," he grunted as he stood and spit some blood from his mouth. "But you're going to need more than that."

He roared and charged again, this time ducking under the swing from the queen. Ryuvin dove in as well, spinning his blade and sliced open a deep wound on its back. Meanwhile, Thunan had leapt back and began the evocation of a spell.

I call upon thee, Thor,
God of the Northern Storm.
Let your power flow through me,
Let it take shape so I may smite my foe,
With the Fury of your wrath.
Storm God's Hammer!

A hammer, forged of pure lightning, formed above the camaborg queen and, with a downward swing of Thunan's hand, came crashing down upon the queen. Shrieking in pain, the queen lashed out towards Thunan, but Waruk charged in again, blades whirling as he let his rage and bloodlust take hold. Thunan joined in on the assault, lightning crackling along his staff. Ryuvin used this as his chance for a spell of his own and sheathed his sword.

Come forth, dark flames of Nessus.
Bend to my will.
Become the blade that calls forth the Valkyrie,
And deliver my enemy to your gates.

Scythe of the Reaper.

Black fire formed in his hand, quickly extending out into the form of a massive scythe. Diving towards the camaborg queen again, he swung the massive blade of black fire. The queen had not seen Ryuvin until it was too late, unable to avoid the attack, the blade faded into its body, a line of black flames following the blade. The queen reared its head back but made no sound as it crashed back to the ground. Waruk walked up to the body and swung his axe hard, the blade sinking several inches into its skull.

"Let's make sure this bitch stays down," he said as he grunted and pulled his axe from the queen's head.

"Fair enough," Ryuvin replied as he landed behind Waruk, both released their merges.

"There are still more eggs to deal with," Thunan said, exhaustion setting in on all three of them.

Altareon, Ryuvin whispered, *can daemon fire clear what remains in the nest?*

Yes, Altareon replied flatly, *though in your exhausted state, you will not be able to control the flames for long.*

How long?

Four seconds, Altareon answered, *any longer and the flames will consume you.*

"Waruk, Thunan," Ryuvin said as he walked to the centre of the room. "Wait upstairs while I finish the nest."

The two nodded and staggered for the stairs. Once they were clear, Ryuvin took a deep breath and began the evocation, cutting his hand as he did. Blood filled his fist.

Through blood,
I call upon the dark guardians.
Those that stand upon the Gates of Nessus.
Let your power flow into this world,
Unconstrained.
Let your fire consume and burn unhindered.

Daemon Fire.

The last line of the verse coming as a whisper. Ryuvin opened his eyes, glowing purplish black, arms outstretched as black and purple flames enveloped his body.

One.

He pushed the flames outwards and watched as they quickly enveloped the room.

Two.

The flames greedily consumed the corpses and eggs in the nest.

Three.

He could feel the last vestiges of life die to the hungry flames.

Four.

Time was up.

***

Serina paced back and forth at the gate of Morningside, constantly looking to the northern road for signs of Ryuvin and the Knights.

"You know pacing won't help at all," Mareck said, leaning against the gate.

"What else should I do?" She spat back angrily.

"Look I get it, the guy in command is your lover," he answered and stretched. "But be real for a minute, you are a commoner and he is royalty. He will never marry you."

"Is that so?" Serina countered as she crossed her arms and stared him down.

"That is so," Mareck replied and smirked as he looked her up and down. "So why don't we find a way to distract you."

"You have another thing coming if you think I'm going to sleep with you, I do have standards."

"Clearly," Mareck retorted. "You are sleeping with a Prince after all, how lucky for you."

"Don't pretend you know anything about me," Serina replied and turned away.

"I know your type," Mareck answered. "Orphaned at a young age, got adopted by servants of a Lord, was raised to be a maid but you wanted more. So instead you joined the military."

"Wow," Serina said and shook her head. "I was actually raised by a General, so from a young age I breathed military. And actually I will marry Ryuvin."

"Keep dreaming girl," Mareck laughed.

"My name is Serina Arrowsong, Daughter of Seleena Arrowsong, the rightful Queen of Damaska, and Crowned Princess of Avantharia."

"Fancy titles don't mean anything out here," Mareck said as he stepped behind her.

"Perhaps," Serina replied as she glanced over her shoulder. "But touch me and it will be the last thing you do."

Looking down, Mareck saw the tip of a dagger pressed against his groin.

"No need for that," he said and smiled. "I never had any intention of forcing you."

"How noble of you," Serina sneered.

"Believe it or not," Mareck replied. "I live by a code of honour."

"And that involves not forcing yourself upon another?" Serina asked.

"Amongst other things, yes."

"You were a soldier at some point," Serina said. "Weren't you?"

"For a time," Mareck said and stepped passed her. "But that was a long time ago."

Serina was about to question Mareck more when several orcs, armed with makeshift weapons, came running over to them.

"Something is coming!" One of the orcs said and pointed to the forest.

Sure enough, Serina could see trees sway from side to side, the sound of heavy footfalls reach her ears. Eventually a massive shape could be seen coming through the trees.

"Be ready," Mareck said to the orcs, drawing his sword. "Whatever it is, it's big."

"There is someone ahead of it," Serina said as she squinted to see who it was. "It's...Kallindra."

Sure enough, Kallindra leapt through the treeline, sprinting at her top speed and waving her arms.

"Hold!" Serina yelled as the orcs hefted their weapons. "It's the Knights."

"Serina!" Kallindra yelled as she neared the gates. "Roshamrik...attention...medical...Kimiko!"

"Slow down," Serina said as Kallindra stopped in front of her, panting. "What happened?"

"No time...Kimiko," Kallindra answered then turned and sprinted back the way she came.

"Get Roshamrik," Serina said as she watched Verdag emerge from the trees, Lorewind, Kimiko and Ulrick in his arms.

"What in the realms is that?" One of the orcs said.

"Now" Serina screamed and chased after Kallindra.

"Lady Serina," Verdag said calmly as she and Kallindra reached him. "We must act with haste. Kimiko is gravely wounded and Ulrick does not have must strength left to keep her stabilized."

Ulrick was pale with exhaustion, sweat coating his face, a green glow emanating from his hands, which were pressed to Kimiko's side. Both, Kimiko and Lorewind were passed out in Verdag's arms. Nodding, Serina turned and sprinted back to the gates as Roshamrik shuffled up.

"What is happening?" He asked then saw Verdag approaching. "By the gods, is that an elemental?"

"No time to explain," Serina answered. "Kimiko is severely wounded and if she doesn't get aid fast she will die."

"Of course," Roshamrik said as he snapped back to reality. "Bring her to the medical wing."

"Can't do...that," Ulrick panted as Verdag reached the gate. "Need to...maintain spell...otherwise..."

"I understand, you there," Roshamrik said, pointing to one

of the orcs. "Fetch a stretcher, and be quick about it."

The orc nodded and ran to the tavern. A few moments later, he returned with a stretcher, along with Barubar, Zana and Zavabar.

"Zana, Barubar, take the stretcher," Roshamrik ordered as he took Ulrick's place. "Zavabar, I need you to help keep everything steady."

Kallindra and Serina helped lay Kimiko onto the stretcher while Barubar and Zana took each end. Zavabar moved to the side opposite Roshamrik and did her best to keep the stretcher steady.

"Tend to your comrades," Roshamrik said to Serina. "There is nothing more you can do here."

Serina watched for a moment, as the orcs carried Kimiko slowly back to the tavern, then turned to the others. She moved to Ulrick, who had collapsed against the gate.

"What happened?" She asked. "Where are Ryuvin and Athanasia?"

"Ryuvin stayed behind," Kallindra answered as she took Lorewind from Verdag. "He ordered Athanasia to bring us back. Once we were in sight of Morningside though, she went back for him."

"You left him there alone?"

"No..." Ulrick said, exhaustion finally overtaking him.

"There were two others with him," Kallindra continued. "An orc warrior named Waruk and a monk named Thunan."

Serina barely registered what the two had said as she looked towards the monastery, fear filling her eyes.

CHAPTER 13

She opened her eyes slowly, pain shooting through her body as the light blinded her momentarily. Pushing through the pain she sat up and looked around the crater, next to her lay a sword, before looking at herself. Her wings heavy, the chains still clung to her arms, her body bruised and healing slower than what she was used to. Tentatively, she reached for the hilt, only to pull back as lighting sparked off it towards her hand.

"Tch, I cannot even hold my own sword," she started as she pushed herself to her feet. "Is this what you wanted, Fyrir?"

"Mother did not do that," a woman said from behind her. "Your lose of ability to wield Excalibur is of your own doing."

Spinning, she looked at the woman across from her. She was identical, the only difference was she did not have the chains around her arms.

"Who are you?" She asked the woman.

"I am you," the woman replied. "Or at least the version of you that you were meant to be."

"Speak plainly," she snapped. "I am in no mood for riddles."

The other woman sighed.

"I am Dovaria," she said. "I am She Who Holds Justice Across the Planarverse."

"You lie," she said, her rage building. "I am Dovaria."

"I never said you were not," the clone said calmly. "I am simply what you no longer are."

Dovaria watched her clone as she walked over and picked up Excalibur then turned back to her.

"You are no longer justice," the clone said. "That is why we are *separated now."*

"This is all just a trick," Dovaria replied. "An illusion conjured by that daemon Kiko and her black foxes."

"If that is what you want to believe," the clone said flatly. "But deep down, you know it is not true."

Dovaria looked away, eyes stinging slightly with tears, she knew what her clone said was true. She could feel a piece of herself was missing. She took a breathe and looked back to her clone.

"I shall make a place of my own here," Dovaria stated and knelt down. "I have two things to ask of you."

The clone nodded and stepped forwards.

***

Dovaria climbed out of the crater, looking back she watched as the fire consumed the last of her wings before slinging Excalibur, now wrapped in a red cloth, over her shoulder, blood running down her back.

"Miss?" Came a man's voice. "Were you in that crater? Are you alright?"

Dovaria looked at the man, he seemed nothing more than a farmer, she could sense his anger and sorrow.

"You have something burdening you mortal," she said to him. "Tell me."

"Uh…I…" the man stammered. "Bandits took my daughter and burned our home."

"Very well," Dovaria said as she began to walk away. "I shall find them and rain fury down upon them."

"Who are you?" The man asked.

Dovaria stopped then turned and looked back at him.

"I am Dovaria," she replied. "I am fury and retribution incarnate."

***

She woke up with a gasp. Breathing heavily, Serina wrapped her arms around herself.

"Dovaria," she whispered to herself. "Why do I see your memories?"

Swinging her legs off the bed, Serina donned her shirt,

moved across the small room and over to the window, looking up at the moon and stars.

"I don't understand," she continued. "Why stray from justice? I know justice is not perfect but it can never be black and white. You can't have the ends justify the means."

What is justice?

The thought suddenly came into her head.

"Justice is balance," she answered to herself. "Justice must counter those that are unjust, to strive to help make the world a better place."

And how is that possible?

Again the thought suddenly came to her.

"It is possible because if justice was to strike first than it is not justice," she again answered. "Instead it becomes injustice and therefore can never help to strive for a better world."

Turning away from the window, Serina returned to her bed and sat down.

"Therefore," she continued. "In order for justice to exist there must first be injustice. And thus, it creates balance."

Laying down, Serina stared at the ceiling.

"Justice without injustice," she whispered to herself. "Is that what drove you off your path Dovaria?"

Slowly, Serina fell back to sleep. Meanwhile, in the plane of Refsingu, a blade wrapped in red stirred.

***

Light filtered through the window causing Serina to stir from her slumber. Shifting from the bed she strode over to a bucket filled with water to wash her face, then dipped a cloth into the water before washing her neck and arms.

Fully dressed, Serina left her room and slowly walked towards the medical wing. She replayed the previous night over in her mind.

Seeing Ryuvin, half carried by an orc, stagger his way back to Morningside with Athanasia and a monk from the monastery. She remembered the minute he saw her, how he stumbled away from the orc towards her, she ran to him and embraced him tight. He kissed her tenderly then pulled away.

"See," he whispered through his exhaustion. "I...told you...that I would...come back."

Tears filled her eyes as he pressed his forehead against hers.

"Ryuvin," Athanasia said as the others approached. "You need to get some rest."

"Yeah," the orc continued. "You can be all lovely dovey later."

Now she stood in front of the door to his room the next morning, hand resting against the wood. She hesitated before pushing the door slightly open and peering inside. She could see Ryuvin, passed out on the bed, and wondered how long he will be in that state.

"Are you okay Serina?" Kallindra asked.

Startled slightly, Serina spun and collided with Kallindra. She felt Kallindra's arms slip around her waist and felt safe, like when Ryuvin held her tight.

What is this feeling? She thought to herself.

"I'm sorry," Serina said as she looked up at Kallindra. "It's just hard. Seeing Ryuvin like this."

"He just needs to rest," Kallindra answered. "But I think I know what you mean. Seeing someone I love like that."

They looked into the room again, the realization of what Kallindra said suddenly hitting her.

"I-I mean someone close to me, l-like a friend," she stammered. "Yeah, that is what I meant."

Serina giggled softly listening to Kallindra.

"It's okay Kalli," she said with a smile. "I knew that's what you meant."

But why does it hurt when she says that? She asked herself, do I secretly wish Kallindra loved Ryuvin?

Serina gasped suddenly as she felt Kallindra's hand slide down over her rear.

"Um...Kalli? What are you doing?"

Kallindra squeaked and let go of Serina as she jumped away, her face turning scarlet as she blushed hard.

"I am so sorry," she said. "I do not know why I did that."

Both women blushed hard, stealing quick glances at each other.

"I better go," Kallindra said before turning and rushing down the stairs and out of the tavern.

Gods what is wrong with me right now? I can't fall in love with Kallindra while still being in love with Ryuvin...can I?

"How scandalous," a man said causing Serina to spin around.

"What do you want this time Mareck?" She asked as she crossed her arms.

"Nothing at all," Mareck replied as he leaned against the wall. "I thought you were engaged to the Prince?"

"I am," Serina retorted.

"Then what was that?" He asked as he gestured towards the tavern door. "Sure looks like you were getting cozy with the cat girl."

"Her name is Kallindra," Serina answered.

"Apologies, but it still does not answer the question."

"I don't know," Serina sighed. "Everything I used to know is wrong."

"Why not start from where everything changed?"

"Remember how you guessed I was an orphan?" She asked.

Mareck nodded.

"You were half right," Serina began. "I was left in Avantharia as a baby and was adopted by Torvan Althara. I grew up in the palace and I was with Ryuvin since we were babies."

"Makes sense," Mareck replied. "The connection between you both is pretty easy to see."

"Well until only a two months ago," Serina continued. "Everyone, including myself, assumed my real parents were dead."

"Clearly that changed," Mareck answered. "I assume your real parents showed up."

"In a sense," Serina replied and leaned on the banister railing. "It was Ryuvin's birthday and he had just chosen me as his future Queen. My mother, Seleena, appeared not long after."

"Ah, so long lost mommy threw a wrench into everything?"

"No," Serina answered. "A warning about what was coming. Regardless, I had always believed my parents were either dead or didn't want me."

"Well did you asked her about it?"

"She was betrayed," Serina replied. "By someone close to her. She said she couldn't risk my safety so instead of trying to take back her kingdom, she fled while pregnant with me."

"Interesting," Mareck said as he pondered his next words. "So you do not know who you are supposed to be anymore, is that it?"

"It's just growing up," Serina sighed. "I always knew I was going to be in the army. I always knew Ryuvin and I would be close. We used to pretend we were married when we were young. As I grew older, I started to learn that we wouldn't have that chance. That it was all just a silly dream of a silly little girl, well until he picked me that is. I was afraid of what would happen. Was I being selfish? Should I have told Queen Amilia no? And then I learned I really was a princess and that Ryuvin would still marry royalty."

"And you do not want to be royalty?" Mareck asked.

"I want to be able to live a life without regrets," Serina answered.

"Ah yes," Mareck laughed. "A happy fairy tale life. No one gets a life like that. In the battle with life, no one walks away unscathed, life is undefeated in that manner"

"Well it has been so far," Serina retorted as she glared at Mareck. "Well at least it was..."

Serina trailed off and looked back towards the tavern door.

"Look kid," Mareck said with a sigh and leaned on the rail next to her. "Love is not an easy thing."

"Tell me about it," Serina answered wistfully.

"There is always that one person that will complete you," Mareck continued, seemingly ignoring Serina's comment. "That person that makes you feel safe, who you want to be vulnerable around."

"And for me that is Ryuvin," Serina answered.

"True," Mareck replied and looked at her. "Though I have been around long enough to know that sometimes, not always, there are others that do that for people."

"I know," Serina answered. "But not at the same time."

"Why not?" Mareck asked. "Are felians not known for having multiple partners at a single time?"

Before Serina could answer, Mareck pushed off the rail and descended the stairs.

"Think about it kid," he said as he reached the bottom then exited the tavern.

***

The next few days passed in a blur for Serina as she replayed her conversation with Mareck over and over again.

Can I really love both Kallindra and Ryuvin at the same time? She asked herself as she wandered around Morningside.

"Oh, hello Serina," Lorewind said as she exited the general store, a small pack in hand. "How are you feeling?"

"I'm well," Serina answered. "What's that?"

"Just some herbs," Lorewind answered. "Ulrick said they will help with Kimiko's wounds."

"Still no change?"

"No," Lorewind said sadly, tears welling in her eyes. "There is only so much Roshamrik and Ulrick can do. I feel so useless right now."

"Didn't Roshamrik start teaching you healing magic?" Serina asked.

"He said he would," Lorewind answered. "It is different for me than it is Ulrick."

"How so?" Serina asked.

"Ulrick already has some knowledge of healing because of Artio.," Lorewind answered. "Verdag can't help me at all with it."

"That is why you need to draw on a different element," Roshamrik said as he hobbled up to them.

"Which element would that even be?" Serina asked the elderly orc.

"Water," he replied as he leaned on his cane. "If you wish to tap into your potential you must learn to harness the element of water."

"I just wish I knew how," Lorewind said, her head down.

"Patience child," Roshamrik replied, resting his hand on her shoulder. "All things take time. You will learn how."

"You can do it Lorewind," Serina said with a smile. "I know you can."

"Thank you," Lorewind said with a nod. "Both of you."

Serina watched as Lorewind and Roshamrik meandered towards the tavern before she turned and walked in the opposite direction. It was not long before she found Ryuvin and Kallindra, they were in deep conversation and did not notice as she approached.

"I understand what you mean Kallindra," Ryuvin said, still a bit pale from the events at the monastery. "You do not need to worry about it."

"It is just that Serina and I are worried about you," Kallindra replied as she puffed out her cheeks and stamped her foot. "You are pushing yourself too hard."

"As I said," Ryuvin continued. "I am well enough to be able to do some scouting."

Before Kallindra could answer Ryuvin turned and headed towards the gate, leaving her to simmer as she watched him.

"Gods why must he be so thick headed?" Kallindra asked aloud as she rubbed her temples. "And why must I be attracted to him and Serina?"

"You are attracted to me?" Serina asked, hand clutched to her chest.

"S-Serina?!" Kallindra gasped and spun around. "It... I mean..."

Kallindra stammered, her face turning red as she blushed.

"Okay," Kallindra said as she avoided Serina's eyes. "Yes, I admit it. I think I am in love with you and Ryuvin."

"Oh...That's...I mean..." Serina stammered, her face also turning red.

"I know you both will never feel the same," Kallindra said as she fidgeted. "But I cannot help how I feel."

"For h-how long?" Serina asked.

"Since we left for Jotunheim," Kallindra replied. "When my Mother was flirting with you and Ryuvin. It made me start thinking about finding someone to be with. I know it is pretty naive of me to think I would ever be with you and him but-"

Kallindra was cut off as Serina pulled her close and kissed her lips passionately, Kallindra froze for a moment before deepening the kiss. Eventually pulling away, Serina panted slightly and looked into Kallindra's eyes.

"Truth be told," she said softly. "I have been conflicted lately with my feelings for you and Ryuvin."

"I wish we could be more," Kallindra said as she pulled away. "But I cannot do that to Ryuvin."

"Neither can I," Serina said as she hugged herself.

"We are pathetic," Kallindra laughed bitterly. "Both in love with the same man while in love with each other."

***

For the next several days, Kallindra and Serina avoided each other, Kimiko had finally regained consciousnesses and, although still weak, had begun to walk around Morningside.

"How are you feeling Kimiko?" Serina asked as she approached her and Lorewind near the blacksmith.

"Serina-sama," Kimiko panted and bowed, sweat coating her brow. "I am recovering, I was able to do several laps around the town."

"You need to rest," Serina said told her.

Serina glanced at Kimiko, she did not have her armour, instead she wore a simple cotton tunic, leggings and boots. Serina noticed a bit of blood seeping onto her shirt.

"Make sure she gets those bandages changed," Serina said to Lorewind.

"I will," Lorewind replied with a nod before turning to

Kimiko. "Okay, you've wandered enough for now, time for new bandages and rest."

Kimiko nodded and slowly made her way back to the tavern with Lorewind.

"She is pushing herself too hard," Ryuvin said as he walked up beside Serina. "She is not giving herself time to heal, even with Lorewind's new magic."

"It's not like you gave yourself time to recover either," Serina replied as they watched Lorewind and Kimiko.

"I did," Ryuvin answered. "I slept too long after what happened."

"Ryuvin," Serina said as she turned and cupped his cheek. "You don't need to shoulder all of this alone."

Ryuvin nodded and pulled away from her.

"I just need some time to sort this out," he said to her before walking towards the gates.

Turning, Serina began walking through Morningside when she saw Mareck approaching her.

"Mareck," she called out.

"Oh?" Mareck said with mock surprise. "You are coming to talk to me on your own? The nine hells must have frozen over."

"I'm already regretting this," Serina said with a sigh. "But did you mean what you said?"

"I usually do," he answered. "But you need to be more specific."

"About having more than one partner at the same time," Serina said, fidgeting slightly. "I don't want to hurt Ryuvin or Kallindra."

"Sure, why not?" Mareck replied. "As long as it is consensual for everyone involved."

Serina nodded and turned away, making her way towards the leather workshop that was in town.

***

Later that evening, all the Knights, except Kimiko and Lorewind, sat around the tavern. Athanasia and Waruk sat opposite each other as the arm wrestled, several orcs surrounded them as they cheered. Ulrick and Thunan chatted with each other while they ate and Kallindra sat at the bar, swirling a cup as she sat quietly in contemplation. Serina then saw Ryuvin, sitting alone in the corner of the tavern, his food barely touched. Ryuvin's eyes met hers and she smiled at him, it was the smile she only gave him, he smiled back, though it did not reach his eyes. She moved over towards the bar, sitting next to Kallindra.

"Does it seem like Ryuvin is acting different?" Serina asked her as she glance over her shoulder at Ryuvin.

"I do not know," Kallindra replied as she looked at Serina. "Maybe."

"You are not a very good liar," Serina giggled.

Kallindra sighed and looked over her shoulder at Ryuvin then blushed as she turned back to Serina.

"You have also been avoiding me," Serina continued. "Is it because of the kiss?"

"Yes," Kallindra said guiltily. "I cannot be in love with you and Ryuvin. You both are already together and I doubt he feels anything for me."

"You may be surprised," Serina answered as she put her hand over Kallindra's. "I've seen him steal a few glances at you."

"Do you think so?" Kallindra asked.

"I have a plan," Serina said as she leaned in and whispered to Kallindra.

Serina strode over to where Ryuvin was sitting, a mug in her hand.

"How long you plan to sit here and pretend nothing is wrong?" She asked him.

Ryuvin looked up at her and frowned.

"I am fine Serina," he answered.

"Ryuvin," Serina said. "You've barely touched your food."

A loud cheer echoed from where Athanasia and Waruk had been sitting, looking over they saw Athanasia triumphantly flaunting her win over Waruk.

"Okay girl," Waruk said over the cheering. "Round two,

this time we drink."

"Oh you are on," Athanasia replied confidently.

"She is going to lose that one," Ryuvin stated to Serina then noticed Kallindra striding up the stairs to the rooms.

"Did something happen with you and Kallindra?" Serina asked him.

"I could ask you the same thing," Ryuvin answered. "You both seem to be avoiding each other lately, save tonight."

"Just girl stuff," Serina replied and waved him off. "Nothing you need to worry about."

"Uh huh," Ryuvin replied as he raised his eyebrow. "And why do I not believe that?"

"Well forget about that," Serina said as she leaned in and whispered flirtatiously. "How about you follow me to my room tonight instead?"

Serina smirked as she walked away from Ryuvin, swaying her hips as she went.

CHAPTER 14

Grief and doubt weighed heavily in her mind as she ran out of the tavern.

What the hell is wrong with me? Kallindra thought to herself as she ran.

She did not bother to look around Morningside as she ran out the gates and into the woods. All she wanted to do was get away from it all. When she finally stopped to take in her surroundings, she found herself at the Monastery of Belhalus. She wanted to turn and run more but could not, she simply stood and stared at the silent building.

Everything that happened yesterday was my fault, she thought, *if Kimiko dies it is all my fault. All because I let my pride blind me and made me ignore Athanasia.*

Unable to hold in her rage anymore, Kallindra screamed as she fell to her knees, fists smashing into the dirt, tears burning her eyes.

"Is that what you want to believe?" A woman said from behind her.

Kallindra recognized the voice but did not turn to face the woman.

"Yes," she answered. "I am not worthy of being your champion, Artemis."

"Why?" Artemis asked as she strode towards Kallindra.

"Because I am not," Kallindra answered. "I let my pride blind me to what was happening. I should have known what was going to happen."

"I am not the Goddess of Foresight child," Artemis replied. "I am the Huntress."

Kallindra looked back over her shoulder. As with the first time she saw Artemis, her dark brown hair spilled from beneath the hood of her green cloak, a simple brown leather jerkin and bracers over a green tunic, brown cotton leggings and knee high dark leather boots.

"You are also of my kin," Artemis continued as she removed her hood, revealing black felian fur and features. "The call to hunt has always been in our blood but time seems to have made them forget that."

"Then what was the point of choosing me?" Kallindra asked as she dug her fingers into the dirt. "As you said, my people have forgotten what it means to be hunters."

"You are a huntress," Artemis answered. "You did not forget what it means to be one with the wild, I can feel it in your blood."

"That does not mean anything to me anymore," Kallindra spat angrily, fresh tears running down her cheeks. "I failed and because that, Kimiko is going to die."

"Nothing is certain," Artemis replied calmly as she crossed her arms. "Your comrade is stronger than you realize."

"Even if she survives," Kallindra spit back. "How can I ever face her again?"

"By doing better," Artemis answered.

"You make it sound so simple."

"Because it is," Artemis said with a shrug. "So stop wallowing in self pity, it is pathetic. Bad things happen, deal with it and come out stronger for it."

Kallindra gritted her teeth as she glared at Artemis.

"You are far from the first to have something bad happen to them," Artemis continued, ignoring Kallindra's glare. "And guess what? You are not going to be the last. Grow up and act like the Princess you claim to be. Or is that just the posturing of a scared little girl that used her title to make herself feel special?"

Kallindra was taken aback, no one had ever spoken to her

like this before and Artemis' words cut deep.

"Out here in the wild there are no titles," Artemis said as she stood at her full height. "In the wild you survive by making yourself the smartest and most dangerous. You feel fear? Good, you should be afraid because no matter how good you think you are, you are always a single step away from death. In the wild, nothing is certain except death."

"You think it is that easy?" Kallindra retorted as she pushed herself to her feet. "You know nothing about what it is like to be mortal."

"Please," Artemis growled. "You really believe that the gods just magically poofed into existence? I was mortal once, like you. I watched as my tribe was butchered. Did I sit and cry about it? No, I survived and became who I am today. I made any that tried to oppose me fear the wilds that I ruled."

"You have become detached from what mortals suffer," Kallindra growled back as she bared her fangs. "You are nothing but a cold hearted bitch."

"Ha," Artemis laughed. "I did what I had to in order to survive, as would anyone. Why do you think I chose you?"

Kallindra clenched her jaw and stared back at Artemis.

"You are a survivor," Artemis continued. "And your people need to be reminded of that. Now come on."

"Where?" Kallindra asked as she watched Artemis turn on her heel.

"To the Eternal Hunting Grounds," Artemis answered as she strode into the trees.

Kallindra jogged after Artemis, stepping through the trees as she followed the goddess. It was not long before she realized that the forest had changed, she was not sure when it happened. The trees seemed more crystalline in nature, the bark shimmering in the sunlight, the leaves upon the branches a vivid blueish green. The forest itself alive with the songs of birds. The pair reached the edge of the forest and Kallindra gasped. Before her sat rolling fields of grass filled with grazing beasts the likes of which she had never seen before. She could see mountains in the distance, reaching up to touch the clear blue sky.

"It is beautiful," Kallindra said in awe.

"Welcome to the Eternal Hunting Grounds," Artemis said with pride. "My home."

"Why bring me here?" Kallindra asked. "Many know you are not one to bring mortals here."

Artemis glanced over at Kallindra then gave a sharp piercing whistle. Kallindra watched as a beautiful falcon, with gold tips wings, landed on Artemis' outstretched arm.

"You must learn to tame the wilds," Artemis said as she stroked the breast feathers of the falcon. "Just like how I learned how to tame Ruby."

The falcon cooed softly before flexing its wings and flying away.

"You want me to tame animals?" Kallindra asked.

"Yes," Artemis replied. "The wilds are teeming with beasts that you can tame."

"How?"

"You must feel the bond with the beast," Artemis said as she crossed her arms. "Feel its strength, its desire, its hunger. Make it your own."

"So what must I do?" Kallindra asked.

"First you hunt," Artemis answered. "Start with something small, learn to tame a falcon or a hawk."

"Is that what you did?"

"Yes," Artemis replied with a soft smile, looking up to the sky. "Ruby has been with me since the beginning. She is...important to me."

"Alright," Kallindra said as she looked around then strode towards the open fields. "What should I expect?"

"They are wild animals," Artemis answered as she followed Kallindra. "They will act as such. Some might flee, others will defend their territory. Some will even try to kill you."

"That is a comforting thought," Kallindra said sarcastically.

"Just so you are aware," Artemis said as the pair approached a grove. "You are physically here, not spiritually, so do not die."

"That is your advice?" Kallindra asked. "Do not die?"

"Yes," Artemis answered and walked away with a wave. "Good luck."

"Wow," Kallindra said as she watched Artemis. "What a bitch."

Kallindra sighed and moved into the grove, eyes scanning the numerous branches and tree tops.

So many nests, she thought to herself, *here is hoping I find a hawk willing to let me tame it.*

She continued through the trees, the songs of birds filling the air. She smiled and brushed her hand against a nearby tree as she pressed on, feeling pulled towards something. After several minutes, Kallindra happened upon a large nest resting on a boulder roughly twenty feet tall. She listened carefully, her ears flicking around, the only sounds she could make out were the birds back the way she came.

Hmm, she thought, *why was I drawn here if there is nothing here?*

She placed a hand against the boulder and closed her eyes trying to focus her hearing.

Still nothing, she thought then looked up, *not even the sound of chick in the nest.*

She began to climb the boulder, the sheer face making it difficult but she persisted, digging her claws into the rock. She grit her teeth as the rock face cut into her hands. After several minutes of climbing sheer rock face, her palms bloody, she reached the large nest. Several broken eggs lay scattered amidst the near empty nest, the broken bloody carcass of the hawks, that made it their home, lay amongst the shells.

Always a single step away from death, Kallindra thought as she looked around.

Turning to step out of the nest, Kallindra noticed one egg still intact nestled against the side of the nest. Kneeling down, she reached into the branches of the nest and pulled the egg free.

It was fairly large, filling up both her hands as she held it up, and weighed several pounds. It blue scale like shell was speckled with black.

The only one to survive, she thought, *I wonder if I can hatch the egg myself.*

Kallindra cradled the egg close, using her body to keep it warm.

"Artemis!" Kallindra called out. "I know you are watching me! Come out!"

"Pretty presumptuous of you to assume I have been watching you," Artemis called from below the nest. "What do you want?"

"I was right though," Kallindra replied as she peered over the edge of the nest. "You said I have to form a bond with a hawk, what if I hatched it from an egg?"

"Well I cannot see why that would not work," Artemis answered as she crossed her arms. "Why?"

"Well from what I can tell about this nest," Kallindra said as held out the egg, showing Artemis. "This is the only egg to survive whatever happened."

"Is that...a dragon hawk egg?"

"Um...yes?" Kallindra replied. "What is a dragon hawk?"

"It is probably the closest you will get to a dragon without it being a dragon," Artemis answered. "They are incredibly rare. That nest was the only one here."

"Oh," Kallindra said as she looked at the egg. "Should I leave it with you?"

"No," Artemis replied with a soft smile. "If you can hatch the egg than the hawk will imprint upon you. And get down here, I am tired of yelling."

Kallindra nodded and peered down at the drop, it seemed much higher to her now than when she was on the ground. Taking a calming breathe, she took a few steps back then ran towards the edge of the nest and jumped.

"Not that way!" Artemis yelled then covered her face with her hand.

Kallindra winced a bit as she landed and stood, brushing her legs with her free hand.

"You would have done that as well," she said with a smile, getting an exasperated sigh from Artemis. "So how do I hatch the egg?"

"Let me see the egg and I can tell you."

Kallindra nodded and handed the egg to Artemis.

"Hmm," she said as she held it up. "Blue shell usually means it is a water hawk, though the black speckling means it is ice."

Artemis glanced at Kallindra, noting her confusion.

"Depending on the element," she continued. "It changes how to incubate the egg. The reason it was here is odd."

"Why?" Kallindra asked.

"In order to incubate ice dragon hawk-" Artemis began as the egg began to crack and shake. "Oh, that explains it. Quickly now."

Artemis quickly thrust the egg back into Kallindra's hands as the cracks spider webbed along the shell. Holding the egg away from her body, Kallindra watched with fascination as the shell broke away to reveal the dragon hawk chick. Icy blue fur like feathers covered its body, its beak serrated like teeth, small sweeping horns sprouted from its head. Cawing softly, its amber draconic eyes locked with Kallindra's.

"Congratulations," Artemis said as she laid her hand on Kallindra's shoulder. "You are a mother now."

"Ha ha, so funny" Kallindra replied. "But why did the egg hatch?"

"Well normally it would need to be encased in ice," Artemis said as she watched the hawk perch itself on Kallindra's shoulder. "It would remain like that until it was time to hatch."

"So it was ready to hatch?" Kallindra asked as she reached up and stroked the hawk's head. "That is why there was no ice?"

"She is going to need a name," Artemis said as she gestured to the hawk.

"Hmm," Kallindra pondered. "How about Sapphire?"

The hawk cawed again and nuzzled Kallindra's cheek.

"Seems she like it," Artemis said as she crossed her arms. "Sapphire will grow quickly, especially here in the grounds. In the mean time, feel the bond you share with her."

Kallindra nodded and closed her eyes, her consciousnesses spreading out and touching Sapphire's mind. She could feel her desire, her hunger, her anxiety, her fear.

"I can feel it," Kallindra said as she opened her eyes. "All of it."

"Good," Artemis replied as she turned away, heading back towards the trees. "Your bond with her is strong."

"What next?" Kallindra asked as she followed, Sapphire still perched on her shoulder.

"First you go back and get rest," Artemis answered as the two walked through the forest. "Once Sapphire has grown more then I will teach you."

"Very well," Kallindra said with a nod.

It was only when she stepped out of the forest in front of the gates of Morningside that Kallindra had realized that they had already left the Eternal Hunting Grounds.

"Sapphire, I need you to stay with Artemis for now," Kallindra said as she stroked Sapphire's feathers.

Sapphire cawed and flew over to Artemis.

"Do not worry," Artemis said as she held up her arm, allowing Sapphire to land on it. "Sapphire will be safe."

Sapphire cawed again as Artemis turned and strode back through the trees.

"Hello Thunan," Kallindra said without looking as the monk approached.

"How are you this day?" He asked her. "I saw you run from town earlier."

"I am...struggling," Kallindra said with a sigh as she turned and face him. "Everything that happened at the monastery, to Kimiko, is all my fault."

"Why do you think that?" Thunan asked.

"How is it not my fault?" Kallindra countered.

"I do not know," he replied with a shrug. "I was not there to see what had happened."

"I let myself get distracted," Kallindra answered. "I let my pride get the better of me and Kimiko paid for it."

"Ah yes, pride," Thunan said with a laugh. "The burden of a foolish man."

"Regardless," Kallindra said as she leaned against a tree. "My argument with Athanasia might have gotten Kimiko killed."

"Kimiko isn't dead," Thunan replied, an icy tone edging into his voice. "She is much stronger than you give her credit for."

"Why do you care so much?" Kallindra asked

"Why shouldn't I?" Thunan countered.

"Because you have only known us for a day," Kallindra answered.

"So it means I should care less about my comrades?" Thunan asked. "Why should the length of time I've spent with you change my opinion?"

"What are you doing out here anyway?" Kallindra asked.

"You're deflecting the question," Thunan replied.

"I know," Kallindra said.

"I've been meditating," he answered. "I wish to understand the true extent of the power Aos Si has gifted me."

"You think there is more than just the lightning?" Kallindra asked.

"Yes," Thunan answered. "Aos Si is a storm god, there is more to storms that just lightning."

"You think you can use wind and water?"

"Why not?" Thunan countered. "While lightning is most attributed to storms, people do forget that wind and water also have a place."

"Then why stop there?" Kallindra asked. "Could you not argue that ice could be part of a storm?"

"That's true," Thunan answered. "Though I have not felt the ability to use any ice magic and I believe that magic would fall into the domain of Thor."

"Right, Northern Storms," Kallindra replied. "Well it is an interesting theory. Keep me in the loop on what you learn?"

"If you wish," Thunan said with a slight bow. "It is past midday, have you eaten yet?"

Before Kallindra could answer, her stomach let out a loud growl. Flushing with embarrassment she stood and followed Thunan back towards Morningside.

***

Over the next few days, Kallindra continued to return to the Eternal Hunting Grounds, each time deepening her bond with Sapphire. As their bond grew stronger, so did Kallindra's abilities.

"You must focus," Artemis said as she crossed her arms. "Let Sapphire be your eyes."

Kallindra sat cross legged in front of Artemis, her vision flickering between her own and Sapphire's. A sudden snap broke her concentration as she fell backwards.

"Gah!" Kallindra cried as she landed heavily on her back.

"What did you do wrong?" Artemis said as she leaned over Kallindra.

"I do not know," Kallindra said as she pushed herself up. "But I am sure you are dying to tell me."

Artemis shook her head and rolled her eyes before walking away.

"I guess not," Kallindra grumbled and leaned back looking up at Sapphire, circling above her.

Kallindra gave a sharp whistle then watched as Sapphire dove at her with incredible speed before slowing and perching on her outstretched arm.

"What do you think girl?" She asked as she stroked Sapphire's feathers. "What am I doing wrong?"

Sapphire cawed softly and ruffled her feathers.

"Yeah, you are probably right," Kallindra sighed. "I just need to keep practising."

Sapphire flexed her wings and took flight, again circling Kallindra as she tried to focus again as she began the evocation of the spell.

I invoke the call of the wilds,
I call upon the strength of beasts,
Allow your spirit to pass through me,
Let your vision become mine,
Eyes of the beast.

This time she was able to hold onto Sapphire's vision for a few moments.

I am getting better at it at least, Kallindra thought as she sighed, *I best find Artemis.*

***

The next day, Kallindra confronted Ryuvin as he approached the blacksmith.

"Ryuvin," Kallindra said as she approached him, her eyes narrow.

"What is it Kallindra?" He asked as he turned and faced her.

"Why are you out?" She asked. "You should be resting. You have yet to fully recover from the monastery."

"I understand what you mean Kallindra," Ryuvin said, still a bit pale from the events at the monastery. "You do not need to worry about it."

"It is just that Serina and I are worried about you," Kallindra replied as she puffed out her cheeks and stamped her foot. "You are pushing yourself too hard."

"As I said," Ryuvin continued. "I am well enough to be able to do some scouting."

Before Kallindra could answer Ryuvin turned and headed towards the gate, leaving her to simmer as she watched him.

"Gods why must he be so thick headed?" Kallindra asked aloud as she rubbed her temples. "And why must I be attracted to him and Serina?"

"You are attracted to me?" A woman asked.

"S-Serina?!" Kallindra gasped and spun around. "It... I

mean..."

Kallindra stammered, her face turning red as she blushed. She stared at Serina, her hand clutched to her chest.

"Okay," Kallindra said as she avoided Serina's eyes. "Yes, I admit it. I think I am in love with you and Ryuvin."

"Oh...That's...I mean..." Serina stammered, her face also turning red.

"I know you both will never feel the same," Kallindra said as she fidgeted. "But I cannot help how I feel."

"For h-how long?" Serina asked.

"Since we left for Jotunheim," Kallindra replied. "When my Mother was flirting with you and Ryuvin. It made me start thinking about finding someone to be with. I know it is pretty naive of me to think I would ever be with you and him but-"

Kallindra was cut off as Serina pulled her close and kissed her lips passionately, Kallindra froze for a moment before deepening the kiss. Eventually pulling away, Serina panted slightly and looked into Kallindra's eyes.

"Truth be told," she said softly. "I have been conflicted lately with my feelings for you and Ryuvin."

"I wish we could be more," Kallindra said as she pulled away. "But I cannot do that to Ryuvin."

"Neither can I," Serina said as she hugged herself.

"We are pathetic," Kallindra laughed bitterly. "Both in love with the same man while in love with each other."

The two women turned away from each other and walked in opposite directions.

Gah! Kallindra thought as she covered her face with her hands, *what the hell is wrong with me? What in the nine hells possessed me to say that?*

***

"Focus," Artemis said as she smacked Kallindra upside the head.

"Gah!" Kallindra exclaimed as she fell forwards. "What the hell was that for?"

"You have been distracted ever since yesterday," Artemis

replied. "If you do not focus than taming a storm howl fox will be impossible."

"I am trying alright," Kallindra said as she sat up. "There is just a lot on my mind."

"You mortals and your notions of love," Artemis sighed and rubbed her temples.

"Do not act like you have never been in love," Kallindra said as she leaned back to look at Artemis.

"No," Artemis said coldly. "I have never been in love. Love is a weakness in the wilds."

"If you have never been in love how can you claim it to be a weakness?" Kallindra retorted. "It can drive us to do impossible things."

"Clearly," Artemis said mockingly as she gestured to Kallindra. "I see it is helping you right now in taming a storm howl fox."

"Did you learn to tame beasts your first attempt?" Kallindra asked, watching as Artemis clenched her jaw. "Yeah, I did not think so."

Artemis sighed and lay next to Kallindra, leaning back on her elbows.

"Then tell me about love," Artemis said flatly.

Kallindra looked over at the goddess and raised an eyebrow.

"Do not look at me like that," Artemis growled. "You said love is not a weakness, so tell me what love is."

"Love is..." Kallindra began as she looked at the sky. "It is that feeling you get in your chest when you are close to someone. It is a warmth that comforts you when you think about them. It is when you feel safe with their arms around you."

"You know," Artemis said as she looked over at Kallindra. "That does not sound so bad."

"That is because it is not bad," Kallindra said with a smile as her mind wandered towards Ryuvin and Serina. "I just wish that I could do more."

"Then why not try?" Artemis asked.

"Because the man I am in love with is engaged to someone else," Kallindra answered.

"And you love her as well," Artemis replied flatly. "I fail to see the problem here."

"Elves are not like Felians," Kallindra said as she stood. "They do not take multiple partners."

"Hmm," Artemis replied as she rolled back and did a cartwheel to stand. "Sounds like you need to figure out what you want. In the mean time, you need to find a storm howl fox to tame."

"I do need to ask," Kallindra said as she moved under the shade of a nearby tree. "What makes a storm howl fox so special?"

"A storm howl fox is gifted with Zeus' lightning," Artemis replied as she moved beside Kallindra. "One of the few beasts to have ever been given his blessings."

Kallindra nodded and gazed out over the fields before her, dotted with clusters of trees, large bushes and rocky outcrops.

"This is not going to be easy," Artemis continued. "Storm howl foxes are masters at stealth. If you want to find one than you are going to need Sapphire's help."

Kallindra looked up to the sky, watching as Sapphire circled above her. Taking a breathe, Kallindra focused her mind on Sapphire, her eyes shifting from her feline eyes to Sapphire's amber draconic eyes.

"You seem to have gotten better at the Eyes of the Beast," Artemis said as she watched Kallindra.

"It is still a bit disorienting," Kallindra replied as her vision became Sapphire's.

"It will pass in time," Artemis said as she leaned against the tree. "For now, use Sapphire to find a storm howl fox, there should be a few north of here."

Nodding, Kallindra directed Sapphire to fly northwards, her eyes scanning the ground from above.

"What does a storm howl fox even look like?" Kallindra asked. "To be honest, I have never even heard of them until you told me they exist."

"They look like a normal fox," Artemis answered. "The only difference is their fur is a dark blue and they have lightning crackling off their body."

"So I am looking for a dark blue fox that is hiding in the shadows of the undergrowth?" Kallindra asked.

"Should not be too hard for you," Artemis said and yawned. "I am going to have a nap while you search."

Is she for real? Kallindra thought to herself as the sounds of Artemis' soft snores reached her ears, *forget her Kalli, focus on the task at hand.*

Through Sapphire's eyes, Kallindra scanned the ground, searching for any hint of movement or sign of the fox. Scanning every bush, every shadow, every rock, she found nothing. Kallindra stopped the spell as pain began radiating from behind her eyes and, with a sigh, rubbed her temples as she sat down. She let out a short whistle and watched as Sapphire flew to her, perching on her outstretched arm. Sighing softly, Kallindra ran her fingers down Sapphire's back, eliciting a caw from her.

"What do I do here Sapphire?" She asked the dragon hawk. "I am at a lose and I do not know how to proceed."

In response, Sapphire cawed again as she flexed her wings.

"Artemis said there should be some to the north," Kallindra replied. "Think we should check again?"

Sapphire cawed a third time then pushed herself off Kallindra's arm and started flying back towards the north.

"Your bond with her is getting stronger," Artemis said with a yawn. "If it keeps up, at this rate you will be able to hear her voice."

"Her voice?" Kallindra asked as she channelled the Eyes of the Beast spell.

"Dragon hawks are unique in that manner," Artemis answered. "Forming a strong bond with one will allow you to hear her voice."

"Is that something you have ever experienced?" Kallindra asked.

"Not personally," Artemis replied with a shrug. "But then again, I never bonded with a dragon hawk before."

"There seems to be a lot of things you have never done before," Kallindra said with a smirk.

"Trust me girl," Artemis said with a wicked grin. "I have had more sex than you think."

Kallindra blushed hard as she listened to Artemis' laughter. It was more joyful than Kallindra had heard before, which made her smile softly. Focusing her attention back to the task at hand, Kallindra had Sapphire scan the landscape, focusing on any type of movement that could indicate where the storm howl fox might be hiding. Minutes turned into hours as Kallindra continued to search, finally snapping, she threw her hands in the air as she fell back onto the grass.

I do not understand, she thought, *Artemis said there were some here, what am I missing?*

She lay still, watching the clouds pass overhead as the afternoon sun slowly travelled across the sky.

Wait that is it, Kallindra thought as she sat bolt upright, *I am looking for the wrong things, instead of movement I should be looking at the shadows.*

Focusing her mind again, Kallindra cast the Eyes of the Beast, her eyes shifting back to Sapphire's as she began scanning the undergrowth, this time the shadows and the lack of movement. After a few minutes, Kallindra found a shadow that was oddly still...too still. She had Sapphire focus her vision on the small shadow and upon closer inspection, saw that it was indeed a storm howl fox.

"I found one, Artemis!" Kallindra exclaimed excitedly. "I found a storm howl fox!"

"Good girl," Artemis replied as she pat her head. "Now because a storm howl fox is extremely skittish I will help you tame it. Come."

"Help me how?" Kallindra asked as she ended the spell's channel and stood to follow Artemis.

"By calling it to you and easing its fear," Artemis answered. "Once tamed, a storm howl fox is a fierce and loyal companion."

Kallindra only nodded as she followed after the goddess. Her presence was different from what Kallindra had become used to. Instead of the tense aura and need to feel on edge, she felt a calm and welcoming feeling.

"You seem...different," Kallindra finally said. "You are not giving off the feeling of hunger, the need to hunt."

"That is because I do not wish to scare my prey," Artemis replied as she glanced over her shoulder. "Not all hunts require the hunger for blood, child."

After a few minutes, they neared the spot where Kallindra had spotted the storm howl fox. It lay curled up beside a rocky outcrop, its eyes following the pair as they approached but made no move to run.

"He will not run," Artemis said. "This is your chance to bond and tame him."

Kallindra nodded and took a deep breath before approaching the fox and kneeling in front of it as it sat up. She reached out with her mind, searching for something to grasp. She could feel the curiosity of the fox, its uncertainty, its need to hunt.

"You feel it, do you not?" Artemis asked as she watched. "Its primal instincts?"

"He is curious about me," Kallindra responded as she held her hand out for the fox to sniff. "I do not think he trusts me."

"Show him he can," Artemis replied as she crossed her arms.

Kallindra sat and crossed her legs as she watched the fox. Its curiosity inching him closer before sitting a few feet away from her and tilting its head, Kallindra in turn tilted her head, mimicking the fox. Each time it changed its posture, Kallindra matched it.

"Hmm..." Artemis said as she watched. "That is an interesting way to gain its trust."

"Well, I figured if I showed that I am like him," Kallindra replied as she rolled onto her back mimicing and watching the fox. "Then he would be more inclined to trust me."

"It seems to be working," Artemis said and nodded towards the fox as he moved closer to Kallindra.

Kallindra sat up and swallowed softly before reaching out to pet the fox. He watched her before sniffing her fingers and eventually pressing his head against the palm of her hand.

"Well done," Artemis said and turned away. "Do not forget to name him."

"Hmm...how about Midnight?" Kallindra asked the fox.

Midnight barked happily in response. Smiling, Kallindra stood and began to follow Artemis as she walked away, Midnight trotting beside her.

***

The sun had begun to set as Kallindra, along with Midnight, made her way back towards Morningside. As she approached the gate she saw Ulrick outside, pacing.

"Why so anxious?" Kallindra asked as she approached.

"It's Lorewind," he answered as he glanced at the fox. "Is that a storm howl fox?"

"Yes," she answered and pat the Midnight's head. "But what about Lorewind?"

"Storm howl foxes are incredibly rare," Ulrick replied. "And Lorewind said she would be back by nightfall, she has yet to return."

"Return from what?" Kallindra asked.

"If I had to guess," Ulrick answered. "Dealing with an angry elemental."

"She should be fine," Kallindra said as walked passed him. "She has Verdag with her."

"The elemental is Nymphia," Ulrick said as he watched Kallindra. "First Daughter of Watroth. She is as powerful as Verdag, if not more."

"What?!" Kallindra snapped and spun around grabbing Ulrick's tunic. "And you let her go on her own?!"

"She did not wish for me to accompany her," Ulrick said as he removed Kallindra's hand.

"Where is she?" Kallindra said as she marched out the gate.

"Where is who?" Lorewind asked as she nearly collided with Kallindra.

"Lorewind!" Kallindra gasped and hugged her tight.

"You're late," Ulrick said as walked up to the women.

Kallindra pulled away with a soft smile then frowned when she looked Lorewind up and down. She was soaked from head to toe, the sleeves of her robes were torn and she bore several cuts along her arms and one on her cheek.

"What in the nine hells happened to you?" Kallindra asked.

"Nymphia wasn't exactly in a talking mood," Lorewind answered with a smile. "But I convinced her in the end."

Holding out her staff, Kallindra saw there was now a blue crystal floating around the head with the green one.

"You could have gotten yourself kill," Kallindra chided then sighed. "Come on, you are soaked, you are going to catch a cold."

Kallindra quickly ushered Lorewind into the tavern and up to her room.

"Get out of those clothes," Kallindra said as she found a couple dry towels.

"I'm fine Kallindra," Lorewind said. "I can do this mys-"

"I said get out of those clothes," Kallindra interrupted as she stepped behind Lorewind. "It is bad enough Kimiko is hurt because of me, I do not need you getting sick on my watch."

"Do you really blame yourself for that?" Lorewind asked as she disrobed.

"Yes," Kallindra answered as she handed Lorewind a towel. "Now sit and use this to dry your body."

Lorewind nodded and sat on a stool in front of Kallindra. The silence was comforting to Kallindra as she gently dried Lorewind's hair.

"You know," Kallindra finally said. "When I found out you went off on your own, I was really worried."

"Kallindra," Lorewind said as she leaned back to look at her. "I am stronger than you give me credit for."

"I know," Kallindra sighed. "But you and the others are like family to me."

"You are family for me as well," Lorewind said with a soft smile. "My body is dry, so I can take care of finishing my hair."

"Alright," Kallindra replied as she handed Lorewind the towel and walked towards the door. "I will get a bowl of stew for you."

"I will meet you down in the tavern," Lorewind said as she continued to dry her hair.

Kallindra smiled and nodded before closing the door.

***

Over the next several days Kallindra had continued to return to the Eternal Hunting grounds, having tamed an iron-hide bear and onyx tiger but mostly to avoid both, Serina and the recently recovered Kimiko.

"You will have to face her eventually," Artemis said to Kallindra as they prowled through a wooded grove.

"Serina? Or Kimiko?" Kallindra asked.

"Both," Artemis answered. "They need to know they can rely on you."

"I know," Kallindra replied as she knelt and studied the trail. "I just do not know what to say. I have never been in this type of situation before."

"Well you need to figure that out," Artemis said as she dropped her voice to a whisper. "In the meantime let us hunt."

Kallindra nodded as they moved quickly through the trees.

***

Evening had fallen as Kallindra approached the tavern in Morningside, as she was about to open the door she heard her name being called.

"Hey Kallindra," Waruk shouted joyously as he and Athanasia approached. "Join us for a drink."

"I will pass," Kallindra said, careful to avoid Athanasia's

gaze, though she knew it would not do much.

"Ah come on," Waruk continued. "I insist."

"She said no Waruk," Athanasia said dismissively. "If she wants to join us she can, she doesn't need you pressuring her."

"Ah fair enough," he said with a smile. "Some other time perhaps."

"Maybe," Kallindra replied and watched as Waruk threw open the door and walked inside then followed.

Kallindra glanced around the tavern, watching as Waruk and Athanasia sat at a table near the hearth with several other orcs. Ryuvin had been sitting in the far corner to the right of the entrance, a plate of untouched food in front of him. Ulrick and Thunan were also sitting at their own table, each with a plate of food, conversing with each other.

"What can I get for you?" Zavabar asked as Kallindra sat at the bar.

"Something that will help me feel better," Kallindra said with a heavy sigh.

"Well usually some warm food helps with that," Zavabar replied. "How about some of the boar stew the cook made?"

"That sounds great," Kallindra replied.

After a few minutes, Zavabar placed a bowl of stew and a mug of cider in front of Kallindra. Nodding her thanks, Kallindra took a spoonful and put it in her mouth.

"Hot," Kallindra gasped as she tried to cool her tongue.

"Of course it is," Zavabar laughed. "It's the only way to eat boar stew. Here, try this bread with it."

Zavabar placed a small plate with a bun next to the bowl before smiling and heading back into the kitchen.

"Does it seem like Ryuvin is acting different?" Serina asked as she approached.

"I do not know," Kallindra replied as she looked at Serina. "Maybe."

Kallindra knew what Serina meant but she was trying to keep her distance when it came to her feelings towards Ryuvin and her.

"You are not a very good liar," Serina giggled.

Kallindra sighed and looked over her shoulder at Ryuvin then blushed as she turned back to Serina.

"You have also been avoiding me," Serina continued. "Is it because of the kiss?"

"Yes," Kallindra said guiltily. "I cannot be in love with you and Ryuvin. You both are already together and I doubt he feels anything for me."

"You may be surprised," Serina answered as she put her hand over Kallindra's. "I've seen him steal a few glances at you."

"Do you think so?" Kallindra asked.

"I have a plan," Serina said as she leaned in and whispered to Kallindra.

"Are you sure that is a good idea?" Kallindra asked, her face red from blushing.

"Positive," Serina replied with a smile and kissed Kallindra's cheek.

***

A few minutes later, Kallindra was in Ryuvin and Serina's room.

I cannot believe I am doing this, she thought as she disrobed.

She went over what Serina had told her in her head. Go up to their room and strip down, that there was a leather collar sitting on the bed for her, a matching one for Serina. She was then to kneel down and wait in the middle of the room, facing the door, for Serina to bring Ryuvin to the room. Doing as she was told, Kallindra picked up the collar and noticed that it was embossed with Serina's nickname for her, Kalli. Blushing harder, Kallindra slipped the collar around her neck and knelt down on floor.

This is so embarrassing, she thought, *I should just leave.*

The sound of footsteps approaching the door made Kallindra's ears perk up, her heart began to race as her tail began to swish from side to side.

"Serina," Ryuvin said from behind the door. "Will you just tell me what you are planning?"

"All in good time," Serina said with a flirtatious giggle. "Now open the door."

She heard Ryuvin sigh, the latch on the handle lifted and the door creaked open. She felt a tingling between her legs as she watched Serina and Ryuvin enter the room, her tail swishing faster.

"What is going on?" Ryuvin asked as he froze in the doorway.

"Isn't she beautiful?" Serina asked as she strode into the room, then stripped and knelt beside Kallindra before putting her own collar on.

Blushing harder, Kallindra stayed still, her hands on her knees. She gasped suddenly when she felt Serina's fingers slip between her legs.

"Mm..." Serina said as she slipped her fingers into her mouth. "She is so wet for you Master, won't you come play with us?"

"Yes, please Master," Kallindra whispered meekly as she fidgeted.

Ryuvin swallowed hard then grinned as he stepped into the room, the door closing behind him.

Chapter 15

Her mind wandered to the events of the previous night. How she ran back to the Monastery to help Ryuvin and the others, only to find him being half carried out by the orc Waruk.

If I hadn't argued with Kallindra, Athanasia thought, *than none of this would've happened.*

Athanasia lay in the bed in her room, her unseeing pale purple eyes staring at the ceiling. As she remembered how Ryuvin brushed off her attempts to help, she could feel tears well in her eyes. She wiped her eyes and sat up, with a sigh she slipped out of the bed and moved over to the wash basin. She splashed some water on her face before using a cloth to wash her body. After which she donned her amour and moved out of the room. As she did, she saw Serina and Mareck speaking. Staying out of sight, Athanasia pressed her back against the wall and listened.

"Why not?" Mareck asked Serina. "Are felians not known for having multiple partners at a single time?"

She did not hear Serina answer as Mareck walked away, descending the stairs.

"Think about it kid," he said as he reached the bottom then exited the tavern.

Athanasia remained where she was as she listened to Serina leave the tavern, eventually descending the stairs, finding and sitting at an empty table.

"Morning Athanasia," Lorewind said as she approached holding a plate of food. "Sleep well?"

"No, not really," Athanasia said as she shook her head.

"Everything okay?" Lorewind asked.

"Not really," she replied with a sigh.

"Did you want to talk about it?" Lorewind asked as she tilted her head.

"No," Athanasia replied flatly.

"Oh," Lorewind said, looking down. "Is it about Kimiko?"

"I said I don't want to talk about it," Athanasia snapped as she slammed her fists on the table.

"I'm sorry," Lorewind said meekly before turning and walking away.

What the hell is wrong with me, Athanasia thought, *I shouldn't have snapped at her like that.*

"Good morning," one of the tavern waitresses said with a friendly smile. "Hungry for some breakfast?"

Glancing up at her, Athanasia nodded.

"How about some eggs with some diced potatoes and fried pork?" The waitress asked.

"Sounds good," Athanasia replied. "Can I get a glass of milk as well?"

"Sure thing," the waitress beamed. "You know, I wanted to thank you."

"What for?" Athanasia asked.

"For protecting the town," she answered before turning and heading towards the kitchen.

"This seat taken?" Waruk asked as he approached the table. "If not, mind if I sit?"

"Go ahead," Athanasia answered as she rested her elbows on the table, head in her hands.

"You going to tell me why you snapped at her like that?" Waruk asked as he leaned back in the chair.

"I really don't know," Athanasia answered. "That was not fair to her."

"Nope, it wasn't," Waruk replied.

"So you're here to what?" Athanasia asked as she glanced at him. "Scold me? Tell me to act my age?"

"Nah," Waruk replied. "Sounds more like something the

boss would do."

"Then why are you here?" Athanasia asked as she sat back. "You don't seem the type to have these types of conversations."

"Ha," Waruk replied with a gruff laugh. "I'm the type that lives in the moment, best way to live really."

"That didn't answer my question," Athanasia said as the waitress approached with two trays of food.

"No I guess it doesn't," Waruk smirked.

"Here you both are," the waitress said with a bubbly smile. "Let me know if there is anything else you need."

"I can think of a few things," Waruk said with a wink.

The waitress blushed fiercely before hurrying away giggling.

"But to answer your question," Waruk said, turning back to Athanasia. "I'm here to eat."

Athanasia covered her face with her hand, only to elicit a laugh from Waruk.

"You're trying to get on my nerves," Athanasia stated as she picked up her fork.

"I'll leave that for you to decide," Waruk replied before taking a mouthful of food.

Athanasia shook her head and began eating as well, a comfortable silence passed between the two. After several minutes, having finished the food on her plate, Athanasia leaned back in the chair and looked over towards the window.

"What you looking at?" Waruk asked as he finished the rest of his food.

"Nothing," Athanasia replied.

"Ah," he said with a huff. "Don't wanna tell me?"

"I did tell you," Athanasia said as she looked back at Waruk, removing her blindfold. "I'm looking at nothing."

"You seem to be able to move around remarkably well," Waruk said as he rested his elbows on the table. "You know, for a blind girl."

"I have learned to compensate with my other senses," Athanasia replied as she replaced her blindfold. "I can see using those."

"So what can you hear right now?" Waruk asked.

"I can hear Roshamrik and Ulrick conversing as they work on healing Kimiko," Athanasia answered. "I can hear Lorewind crying."

"She the one with the horns?" Waruk asked.

Athanasia nodded and stood up, walking towards the door.

"Why she crying?" Waruk asked as he followed.

"Because Kimiko is injured," Athanasia answered as the pair exited the tavern. "And it's my fault."

"How so?" Waruk continued as he placed his hands behind his head. "From what I know, she was injured when you guys were ambushed."

"And because I let my arrogance blind me," Athanasia replied as she clenched her fists. "I should've heard them. Now leave me be."

With that, Athanasia stormed off to the gates and out into the field south of Morningside.

***

A few days later, Athanasia stood at the door to the medical wing.

"The door won't open itself," Waruk said as he approached.

"What do you want now Waruk?" Athanasia asked irritably.

"You gonna go in?" He asked as he leaned against the wall. "Or are you just gonna hover outside the door?"

Before she could answer, the door opened revealing Ulrick.

"I thought I heard you out here, Athanasia," he said and stepped to the side. "You can come in, though if you are here to see Lorewind, I sent her to get some more herbs a few minutes ago."

"I know," Athanasia replied. "That's not why I'm here."

"Ah," Waruk said. "So you are here to see the ninja girl."

"Her name is Kimiko!" Athanasia snapped as she spun

around and grabbed Waruk's throat, slamming him into the wall. "You will do well to remember that."

"You got spirit, girl," Waruk said with a wicked grin and easily pulled Athanasia's hand from his throat, his eyes turning red. "I like that but rage is my domain, careful were you tread."

Athanasia clenched her jaw then shoved passed Waruk and made for the tavern exit. Once outside, she took a few breaths trying to calm herself, her hands trembled, either from fear or adrenaline, she was not sure.

"Just some herbs," Lorewind said, drawing Athanasia's attention. "Ulrick said they will help with Kimiko's wounds."

Not far from where she stood, Lorewind had been conversing with Serina, both unaware of Athanasia's presence.

"Still no change?" Serina asked her.

"No," Lorewind replied sadly.

Athanasia could not listen anymore as she turned and walked away.

Lorewind is hurting because of me, she thought, *I failed them both.*

Frustrated, she punched a nearby barrel, splitting her knuckles open as well as splintering the wood. She continued walking, blood running down her fingers and dripping to the ground. She paid no mind to where she went, only to find herself in front of the Monastery of Belhalus.

"Figured I would find you here," Waruk said from behind her.

"Why are you so persistent?" Athanasia asked as she turned to face him.

"Because you are beating yourself up for no reason," Waruk replied nonchalantly. "From what I see, you and Kallindra are way too hung up on who the fault falls on."

"You know nothing of what happened!" Athanasia shouted, Soran Helios flying into her hand.

"Is that how you want to play?" Waruk smirked and drew his axes. "Fine, let's play."

"Tch, this isn't a game," Athanasia said as she charged at

Waruk. "If Kimiko dies than it's my fault."

"You need to realize," Waruk replied as he parried Athanasia's wild swing. "I get why you feel it is your fault."

"You weren't there," Athanasia said as she spun sweeping her sword low. "You can't possibly understand."

"I didn't have to be," Waruk retorted, jumping over Athanasia's sword. "I know you are blaming yourself, just like princess kitty is blaming herself as well."

"Her name is Kallindra!" Athanasia screamed as she swung her sword hard.

Waruk blocked the blow but was still pushed back, seizing her chance, Athanasia pressed her attack. Her assault relentless as she let her rage consume her.

"You act like you know what happened!" She said as she continued her attack. "You don't know anything about Kimiko! You don't know anything about Kallindra! And you know nothing about me!"

With another hard swing, Athanasia pushed Waruk up against a tree. With a scream, Athanasia attacked again. Waruk rolled to the right as her attack struck the tree, cutting through its trunk. As the tree crashed to the ground, Athanasia began the evocation of a spell.

I invoke thee, Ares, Great Goddess of War,
Grant unto me thy strength,
Send forth your might,
Let my blade cut with thy fury,
Thousand sided strike,
Iaijutsu.

As she finished the spell, Athanasia shifted into a low stance, her sword, the blade now glowing silver as lightning crackled along it, held behind her before swinging it in a horizontal arc in front of her, energy launching off the blade.

Did I just do combat magic? She asked herself, shocked at what just happened.

Athanasia quickly regained her composure as Waruk rolled under the attack.

"Ooh fancy attack," Waruk taunted before charging Athanasia.

They pair continued their battle, neither relenting. The fight continued into the late afternoon, their blades clashing as the sun travelled across the sky. The fight had moved into a clearing away from the monastery, the area torn up from the conflict, as both stared each other down, panting from exhaustion.

"Not gonna give up are you girl?" Waruk asked with a chuckle, blood seeping from the small cut on his cheek.

"Never," Athanasia replied as she spit blood from her mouth. "I will do this all day if I have to."

"Enough!" A man yelled as the two charged each other again, a bolt of lightning crashing down between them.

The blast knocked both Athanasia and Waruk to the ground. As they struggled into a sitting position, Thunan approached them.

"What is wrong with the two of you?" He asked, anger edging into his deep voice.

"Hey she started it," Waruk said as he pointed at Athanasia.

"Oh grow up you muscle headed brute," Athanasia replied.

"I said enough!" Thunan yelled over the arguing pair. "You two are supposed to be comrades, you should be helping each other, not trying to kill each other."

"Believe it or not," Waruk said as he stood up and brushed himself off, no longer panting. "I was helping her."

"What?!" Athanasia fumed as she struggled to her feet. "You call this helping?"

"You obviously care about Kallindra and Kimiko," Waruk answered as he stretched. "Otherwise you wouldn't have been fighting me so hard."

Athanasia stared at Waruk in confusion.

"Look, you and Kallindra have some issues to sort out," he

continued. "And you need to realize that blaming yourselves for being mortal is not going to help you are all."

"He's right," Thunan said as he approached the two. "Kallindra blames herself just as much as you blame yourself. It helps neither you nor her in the long run."

"How would you know what she feels?" Athanasia spat.

"We talked for a moment," Thunan answered. "A couple days ago."

"So I should just accept what happened and move on?" Athanasia asked angrily. "Just forget it happened?"

"No," Thunan replied calmly. "Remember what had happened and learn from it."

"And what am I supposed to learn from this?" Athanasia asked.

"That's for you to find out," Thunan replied as he turned and began walking away.

Athanasia sighed and sat back down.

"Why did you do it?" She asked Waruk.

"Do what?" He replied as he sat cross legged.

"Push like you did," she answered as she lay on her back. "Why go out of your way to help someone you barely know?"

"Should that matter?" Waruk asked as he sat next to her. "Look girl, we all have a part to play here. Plus you seem to need the help."

"I don't need help," Athanasia replied sharply as she looked over at him.

"Of course you do, we all do," Waruk stated as he lay down looking at the clouds. "On this journey we are going to struggle and be knocked down, in order for us to recover we have to focus, move forwards and learn from our mistakes."

Athanasia sighed and sat up, she glanced over at Waruk then stood and held out her hand.

"Let's head back to town," she said. "I'm hungry."

"Sound like a plan," Waruk laughed as he took hold of her hand.

***

Over the next few days, Kimiko had recovered, thanks to Lorewind's new magic, and had been able to start moving around. Athanasia watched from the gates, leaning against one of the posts, as Kimiko and Lorewind conversed with Serina.

"What are they talking about?" Waruk asked as he approached and looked over.

"You assume I can hear them," Athanasia replied as she crossed her arms.

"I know you can," Waruk said with a shrug.

"Serina is just asking how Kimiko is fairing," Athanasia said as she pushed herself off the gate. "Now let's go spar more, you need to add another loss to your count."

"Ha like that is going to happen," Waruk replied with a laugh as he ran out the gate. "Last one there buys the first round tonight."

Smirking, Athanasia raced after Waruk.

"So I believe the count is nine wins for me," Athanasia said as they reached the clearing together. "Seven wins for you."

"Nice try," Waruk replied. "I have eight wins."

"And sixteen draws," Athanasia said as she drew Ryoka Inazuma. "Shall we make it ten wins for me today?"

"I like the idea of nine wins for me instead," Waruk replied as he drew his axes.

"You best work for it than," Athanasia smirked as she charged at Waruk.

***

As the sun began to set, Athanasia and Waruk strolled through the gates to Morningside as the headed towards the tavern.

"New count seems to be fourteen wins for me," Athanasia said. "Eleven for you and twenty five draws."

"I'm curious though," Waruk said, hands behind his head. "Why do you never use both your swords at once?"

"Both Soran Helios and Ryoka Inazuma require two hands to wield," Athanasia answered. "Not exactly weapons that can be wielded with one."

"Sounds like you need to get some muscle's on your arms," Waruk laughed then noticed Kallindra. "Hey Kallindra, join us for a drink."

"I will pass," Kallindra said, as she carefully avoided Athanasia's gaze.

Looks like she doesn't want to talk to me, Athanasia thought

"Ah come on," Waruk continued. "I insist."

"She said no Waruk," Athanasia said. "If she wants to join us she can, she doesn't need you pressuring her."

"Ah fair enough," he said with a smile. "Some other time perhaps."

"Maybe," Kallindra replied as Athanasia and Waruk entered the tavern.

"So, we never decided who is buying the first round," Waruk said boisterously, drawing the attention of several orcs. "Let's figure out now, you and me."

Sitting at the table, Waruk propped his elbow up and held out his hand.

"Get ready to spend some gold," Athanasia replied with a smirk and did the same.

"Ready?" One of the orcs asked as she held their hands.

With their hands suddenly released, both Athanasia and Waruk flexed hard, trying to pin the other's hand to the table. All around them the orcs cheered for one or the other, neither giving any ground.

"Ha not bad girl," Waruk taunted. "But you aren't winning this one."

"Keep talking old man," Athanasia replied. "We both know it's only a matter of time until you lose."

The pair fought for several more minutes, through gritted teeth, sweat rolling down their necks, until, finally Waruk could not longer hold and Athanasia slammed his hand to the table. A loud cheer echoing through the tavern.

"Ha, that's right I win," Athanasia said, arms above her head in victory. "Looks like you have to pay up old man."

"Okay girl," Waruk said over the cheering. "Round two,

this time we drink."

"Oh you are on," Athanasia replied confidently.

***

Sunlight streamed through the window to her room as Athanasia groaned and rolled over.

"Ugh my head," she said aloud as rubbed her forehead with the heel of her hand. "What the hell happened last night?"

A shuffling in bed beside her drew her attention.

"Mm..." the tavern waitress moaned softly as she stirred, her eyes opening. "Good morning."

"Um..." Athanasia replied, realizing she was naked. "Did we?"

"You don't remember?" The girl asked.

Athanasia thought for a moment.

"I remember drinking with Waruk," Athanasia began as she rubbed her temples. "It's a bit hazy though. I barely remember coming up to the room."

"Mhmmm," the waitress said as she slipped out of the bed. "Do you remember what you said?"

"I think so," Athanasia replied, the throb in her head slowly fading. "Something about Kallindra riding Ryuvin hard."

"Well not only that," the girl giggled. "That you were a virgin."

Athanasia looked up at the girl, her face turning red.

"Don't worry," she giggled. "We didn't do anything. You said you wanted your first time to be with the one you loved. So we just cuddled and fell asleep."

"I'm sorry," Athanasia said as she looked at the floor.

"Don't be," the girl said with a smile. "I think it was very sweet and hope you find that special someone soon."

The two women dressed quickly and stepped into the hallway.

"I did have fun last night though," the waitress said gleefully before kissing Athanasia on the cheek and skipping away.

Athanasia sighed and made her way to the tavern and ordered food. It was then that she noticed Kimiko and Kallindra sitting at a table conversing with each other.

Well, she thought, *here goes nothing.*

Plate of food in hand, Athanasia took a breathe and made her way over to the table.

"I am sorry," Kallindra said. "If not for my pride-"

"And had it not been for my arrogance," Athanasia said as she approached. "May I?"

Kimiko nodded and watched as Athanasia sat down between her and Kallindra.

CHAPTER 16

Lorewind sat in a chair beside Kimiko's bed in the medical wing of the tavern. It had been five days since the Knights cleared out the monastery where Kimiko was gravely wounded. Her condition had barely changed, her breathing was shallow, her dark skin pale, sweat constantly beading on her brow, the bandages around her midsection stained with blood.

"Sitting by her side day in and day out will do nothing," Ulrick said as he approached with fresh bandages.

"What else should I do?" Lorewind asked as she rubbed her sleep deprived eyes.

"If I had an answer I would tell you," Ulrick replied. "In the mean time, you can check the general store for herbs. There may be some I know will help Kimiko."

Lorewind nodded and rubbed her eyes before standing and walking towards the door.

"Just make sure she-"

"Don't worry Lorewind," Ulrick said, cutting her off. "She's in good hands."

Lorewind made her way towards the general store, she barely paid heed to anything around her as her thoughts constantly drifted back to Kimiko.

"Ah hello love," Nusha said as Lorewind entered the shop. "How are you?"

Lorewind looked over at Nusha, she was Zavabar's twin sister, the only difference was that Nusha was slightly shorter, wearing a sleeveless green tunic and brown leggings.

"As well as I can be," Lorewind answered. "Given the circumstances."

"Don't you worry," Nusha replied. "I'm sure your friend will recover soon. Now was there something you needed?"

"I was hoping that you would have any medicinal herbs," Lorewind said as she approached the counter.

"Hmm," Nusha pondered. "I think Rodrick brought some in yesterday. Let me check."

Lorewind nodded and watched as Nusha disappeared behind the curtain that lead to the back of the shop. She then began wandering up and down the few isles, each ladened with a variety of items, most of them trinkets.

"Alright," Nusha said as she returned with a few bundles of herbs. "Rodrick found a few different herbs that should help."

"Thank you Nusha," Lorewind replied as she paid for the herbs.

"No worries," Nusha said with a warm smile. "It will be nice to see all you Knights back on your feet."

Lorewind gave a small bow before turning and heading towards the door, her thoughts again drifting back to Kimiko as she exited the store as Serina walked by.

"Oh, hello Serina," Lorewind said. "How are you feeling?"

"I'm well," Serina answered. "What's that?"

"Just some herbs," Lorewind answered. "Ulrick said they will help with Kimiko's wounds."

"Still no change?" Serina asked.

"No," Lorewind said sadly, tears welling in her eyes. "There is only so much Roshamrik and Ulrick can do. I feel so useless right now."

"Didn't Roshamrik start teaching you healing magic?" Serina asked.

"He said he would," Lorewind answered. "It is different for me than it is Ulrick."

"How so?" Serina asked.

"Ulrick already has some knowledge of healing because of Artio," Lorewind answered. "Verdag can't help me at all with it."

"That is why you need to draw on a different element,"

Roshamrik said as he hobbled up to them.

"Which element would that even be?" Serina asked the elderly orc.

"Water," he replied as he leaned on his cane. "If you wish to tap into your potential you must learn to harness the element of water."

"I just wish I knew how," Lorewind said, her head down.

"Patience child," Roshamrik replied, resting his hand on her shoulder. "All things take time. You will learn how."

"You can do it Lorewind," Serina said with a smile. "I know you can."

"Thank you," Lorewind said with a nod. "Both of you."

Lorewind and Roshamrik made their way back towards the tavern, leaving Serina to her own devises. As the entered Lorewind glanced back over her shoulder towards Serina and watched as she walked towards Kallindra and Ryuvin before looking back to Roshamrik.

"When can we start my training?" She asked him as they approached the medical wing.

"Tomorrow," Roshamrik said. "Meet at the gates of the town at dawn."

***

Lorewind stood at the gate, fidgeting and pacing, the sky slowly changing as the sun crept over the horizon.

"You are up early," Thunan said as he approached her. "Is there something wrong?"

"No," Lorewind replied. "Roshamrik said he would teach me to use the elements. What of you?"

"I am usually awake at this time," Thunan replied. "Having lived in the monastery for as long as I have it is just second nature."

"So what are you doing?" Lorewind asked.

"I am going into the woods to meditate," Thunan answered. "I wish to commune with Aos Si."

"To what purpose?"

"There is much of this power I do not understand,"

Thunan answered as he hefted the quarter staff. "If I am to be her champion I must control the storms within myself."

"You have doubts?" Lorewind asked, shifting her weight.

"Don't we all?" Thunan countered before bowing and walking towards the woods.

***

Not long later Lorewind and Ulrick followed Roshamrik through the woods.

"There are many ways to wield healing magic," Roshamrik said as he eased himself onto a fallen log. "There are those that heal through the spirits to reinvigorate the body."

"That is what Artio has been teaching me," Ulrick said.

"That is traditionally how druids and shamans heal," Roshamrik nodded. "There are others that call upon the light to mend wounds, this is the more widely spread practise."

"That is how you heal?" Lorewind asked.

"You are correct," Roshamrik continued. "Healing by any means simply increases the body's regenerative speed."

"Is that why you only heal in short amounts?" Lorewind asked.

"It is child," Roshamrik answered. "The body can only handle so much before it shuts down."

"So how do you know what is too much?" Ulrick asked.

"When healing, you can feel the flow of energy," Roshamrik answered. "You can feel how much the body can handle."

"What are the other methods to heal?" Lorewind asked.

"There are two others," Roshamrik said. "Both considered lost arts and are extremely rare to see any that heal with these practises."

"I have heard rumours," Ulrick said. "Of a tribe hidden in eastern Jotunheim that used water magic to heal."

"That is one of the lost practises," Roshamrik replied. "The other is through necromancy."

"How?" Ulrick asked.

"While necromancy has been known as death magic," Roshamrik answered. "The truth of it is the manipulation of life energies, it is that manipulation that heals wounds."

Is that true Artio? Ulrick asked.

Yes, Artio replied, *there has not been a necromancer in nearly a thousand years that could use their powers to heal.*

"How am I supposed to use water magic?" Lorewind asked.

"How did you learn to summon Verdag?" Ulrick asked.

"I-I don't know," Lorewind answered. "He told me, that the day I had summoned him we were in grave danger, and I had spoken in the ancient Terran language. A language I have no knowledge of."

"Interesting," Roshamrik pondered. "It would seem that the elements themselves called to you to summon Verdag forth."

"Is that something that can be replicated?" Ulrick asked. "Summoning an elemental when in dire need?"

"Perhaps with some," Roshamrik answered. "Elementals that are guardians like Verdag, or warriors such as Bluthel, First Son of Temra."

Even though he is my cousin, Verdag whispered, *I find him a bit....too eccentric.*

"Elementals that lean towards the pursuit of knowledge tend to be more reserved," Roshamrik continued. "Nymphia, First Daughter of Watroth, is one such elemental."

It is interesting to hear Nymphia described as such, Verdag whispered, *it is true that she is more reserved and seeks knowledge but she can be quiet volatile.*

Do you have any suggestions as to summoning her? Lorewind asked.

No, Verdag answered, *because you will not be able to summon her.*

Wow thanks for the vote of confidence, Lorewind snapped.

You misunderstand me My Lady, Verdag replied, *you will not be able to summon her because she is already here.*

Meaning?

She is here, Verdag answered, *upon the realm of Therago and she is close.*

"Roshamrik," Lorewind said. "Are there nearby lakes or wide, deep rivers nearby?"

"There is a lake," Roshamrik answered. "No one goes near it though."

"Why?" Ulrick asked.

"A few years back," Roshamrik began. "One of the town hunters had been tracking a herd of deer, when he followed the trail to the lake he had seen several large boats on the water. They seemed to be hunting something in the lake, which was odd."

"Odd in what way?" Ulrick asked.

"Well they had heavy equipment meant, weapons meant for hunting and killing dragons" Roshamrik continued. "It was not long before the ships were attacked by something from beneath the waves."

"You think it may have been a dragon?" Ulrick asked.

"It is difficult to say," Roshamrik answered. "There has been no trace of dragons in this area for several generations."

"Which way is the lake?" Lorewind asked.

"It is about two kilometres north," Roshamrik answered. "Why?"

"Because that is not a dragon," Lorewind said as she set off towards the lake. "It is Nymphia."

"I shall accompany you," Ulrick said as he stepped in behind her.

"No," Lorewind replied. "This is something I need to do alone. Besides, you have your own training to do."

Ulrick nodded reluctantly.

"I shall return to Morningside by nightfall," Lorewind said.

Ulrick watched as Lorewind strode through the trees.

"Will she be okay on her own?" He asked.

"She has strength within her heart," Roshamrik answered. "I have every bit of faith in her."

Roshamrik stood and looked up to the sky.

"You each have a part to play," he said as he hobbled up to

Ulrick, placing a hand on his shoulder. "None of you can stand alone. Now let us continue your training. One of the abilities of a druid is their beast form."

"The ability to assume the form of the many beasts of the wilderness," Ulrick replied. "Artio has been guiding me but there is only so much she can teach with the power difference between us."

I am sorry, Ulrick, Artio said to him, *it does not help I have not had a student in centuries.*

I don't blame you Artio, he answered her, *it probably doesn't help I've never done magic before.*

"Let us begin," Roshamrik said. "We shall start with something simple, the wolf. Merge. Sit."

Ulrick nodded, merged with Artio and sat cross legged, eyes closed.

"Extend your awareness into the land around you," Roshamrik continued. "Feel the spirits of the beasts. Feel their energy, their strength."

Ulrick could feel the surge of energy flowing into him.

That is it, Artio said, pride filling her voice, *feel the spirit of the wolf, let it become one with you.*

Ulrick opened his eyes, no longer the green and gold, they were simply golden wolf eyes.

***

The trek to the lake took Lorewind almost twenty minutes. She stood and gazed over the crystal clear water, the sun reflecting off the water as fish leapt into the air.

It is so peaceful here, Lorewind thought as she stepped close to the shore, the waves lapping against her feet.

She is here, Verdag said.

Just then, something breached the water's surface. It moved with such speed that Lorewind only saw its tail before a wave came rushing at her. She took several steps back as the water rushed up around her calves.

Was that her? Lorewind asked.

I believe so, Verdag replied, *and judging by that reaction, she is not happy.*

Any idea on how to get her attention? Lorewind said as she moved along the shore.

I can think of one way, Verdag answered.

What's the plan?

There is a spell, the Maw of the Mountain, Verdag said, *it can be dangerous.*

Aside from jumping into the lake with a pissed off elemental, Lorewind said as she moved down the shore, *there really is no other option.*

Very well, Verdag said, *I shall teach you the spell.*

Lorewind nodded and found a large flat rock. Sitting cross legged, laying her staff behind her, Lorewind closed her eyes and began meditating.

I'm ready, she said.

Then let us begin, Verdag replied, *just like when I taught you the earthen trap, you must open your mind.*

Lorewind took a deep breathe, trying to relax as best she could.

You are tense My Lady, Verdag said.

I'm sorry, Lorewind replied, *I can feel her power from here, her rage is...overwhelming.*

Something happened to her, Verdag said, *I do not think this is a good idea.*

Too late, Lorewind said as she opened her eyes, *she knows I'm here.*

She watched as a shape cut through the water towards her only for it to suddenly stop, a wave of water rushed towards her, crashing against the rock she sat on. She looked down into the water, the draconic eyes of the elemental staring into her own. She watched as it retreated back into the deeper water, its tail swinging up sending water crashing over her.

"Well at least she didn't try to kill me," Lorewind coughed.

It is a start, Verdag answered, *she is more bestial than I remember.*

Hopefully your spell will get her back, Lorewind replied.

Closing her eyes again she refocused, doing her best to not let Nymphia's rage overwhelm her. She let the knowledge, that Verdag offered, pour over her. She clenched her head as pain flared in her skull before she opened her eyes and stood. She pressed her fists together and began the evocation of the spell.

Unyielding earth I beseech thee,
Allow me to channel your power,
Let me shape stone to my will,
Become a fissure and swallow all in thy path,
Maw of the Mountain.

As she finished the evocation, Lorewind thrust her hands forwards then brought them together, the clap echoing over the water as the ground beneath her feet rumbled.

I hope this works, she thought to herself.

***

Ulrick paced back and forth at the gate to Morningside, the last vestiges of sun turning the sky a mix of red and orange as it set over the trees giving way to the stars.

"Why so anxious?" Kallindra asked as she approached, a blue and white fox next to her.

"It's Lorewind," he answered as he glanced at the fox. "Is that a storm howl fox?"

"Yes," she answered and pat the fox's head. "But what about Lorewind?"

"storm howl foxes are incredibly rare," Ulrick replied. "And Lorewind said she would be back by nightfall, she has yet to return."

"Return from what?" Kallindra asked.

"If I had to guess," Ulrick answered. "Dealing with an angry elemental."

"She should be fine," Kallindra said as walked passed him. "She has Verdag with her."

"The elemental is Nymphia," Ulrick said as he watched Kallindra. "First Daughter of Watroth. She is as powerful as Verdag, if not more."

"What?!" Kallindra snapped and spun around grabbing Ulrick's tunic. "And you let her go on her own?!"

"She did not wish for me to accompany her," Ulrick said as he removed Kallindra's hand.

"Where is she?" Kallindra said as she marched out the gate.

"Where is who?" Lorewind asked as she nearly collided with Kallindra.

"Lorewind!" Kallindra gasped and hugged her tight.

"You're late," Ulrick said as walked up to the women.

Kallindra pulled away with a soft smile then frowned when she looked Lorewind up and down. She was soaked from head to toe, the sleeves of her robes were torn and she bore several cuts along her arms and one on her cheek.

"What in the nine hells happened to you?" Kallindra asked.

"Nymphia wasn't exactly in a talking mood," Lorewind answered with a smile. "But I convinced her in the end."

Holding out her staff, Kallindra saw there was now a blue crystal floating around the head with the green one.

"You could have gotten yourself kill," Kallindra chided then sighed. "Come on, you are soaked, you are going to catch a cold."

***

The next morning, Lorewind sat next to Kimiko's bed, her condition unchanged. She leaned in closer and cupped Kimiko's cheek as her eyes welled with tears.

"Just hang on a bit long," she whispered. "I have the power to help now."

Do not fear Lady Lorewind, Nymphia whispered, her voice calming and motherly, *the Dragon's Melody will be of great assistance to Kimiko's recovery.*

What must I do? Lorewind asked.

Relax, Nymphia replied, *you are too tense and you need to calm yourself.*

It is difficult, Lorewind said as she closed her eyes, *I care greatly for Kimiko.*

I know child, Nymphia said soothingly, *it is for her sake you must calm the turmoil in your heart and your mind.*

Lorewind took a few calming breaths before she sat in the chair next to Kimiko's bed, her eyes closed.

I am ready, she said to Nymphia.

Her head began to throb slightly as Nymphia's knowledge of the spell poured into her mind.

It feels different, Lorewind said, *opposed to when Verdag taught me the Maw of the Mountain.*

Unlike Verdag, Nymphia replied, *I am used to sharing knowledge with mortals and I know how to ease that pain when it is shared.*

Lorewind then placed her hands over the bandage covering Kimiko's side, took a deep breath then began the evocation.

> *Life giving waters come forth,*
> *Flow to my will,*
> *Through the chorus of Dragons,*
> *Give me the strength to heal,*
> *Dragon's Melody.*

Her hands began to glow a soft blue, she felt the energy flow between herself and Kimiko, A gentle melody in the air, which she somehow knew made Kimiko feel more at ease.

That is all you can do for now, Nymphia whispered, *she may be a strong woman but she can only handle so much, just like yourself.*

Reluctantly Lorewind pulled away, the chorus of draconic song still lingering in the air.

I wish I could do more, Lorewind replied.

As do all who have a heart such as yours, Nymphia said, *there is only so much anyone can do regardless of their strength.*

Lady Lorewind, Verdag whispered, *you should get some rest.*

You're both right, Lorewind replied with a sigh and leaned back into the chair.

"You did well child," Roshamrik said as he hobbled over. "Not many can take to using a lost art so easily."

"Nymphia was a great help," Lorewind replied wearily. "Though I'm not used to this type of drain."

"That spell is fairly advanced," Roshamrik said as he placed a hand on her shoulder. "The drain on your strength will be high until you become stronger."

"I feel so powerless sometimes," Lorewind said, clearly downcast. "Compared to the others I'm just a tag along. I can barely handle one spell without becoming exhausted or passing out."

"It is fair to feel that way," Roshamrik began. "When you compare yourself to others, especially others as talented as those in your Order."

Lorewind looked up at Roshamrik.

"But do realize that you all have strengths and weaknesses," Roshamrik continued. "Like you, they have struggles of their own, weaknesses that gnaw at their spirit. They find strength in each other, without you they can never be whole, just like you can never be whole without them."

"You make it sound like they are my family," Lorewind replied.

"Would that be so terrible?" Roshamrik asked.

Before Lorewind could answer, the door to the medical wing flung open and Ulrick entered.

"How is Kimiko?" He asked as he approached.

"She is doing much better," Roshamrik answered as he pat Lorewind on the shoulder. "Thanks to Lorewind and her magic."

"Come on," Ulrick said to Lorewind as he held his hand out to her. "Let's get you some breakfast."

With a nod, Lorewind took Ulrick's hand and followed him back towards the tavern.

"How is she?" Ryuvin asked as the two exited the medical wing, his complexion still pale.

"Much better," Ulrick answered. "Thanks to Lorewind's

new magic."

"She still needs more time," Lorewind said with her head down. "I couldn't heal her fully. I'm sorry."

"Lorewind," Ryuvin said as he approached and placed a hand on her shoulder. "Do not be sorry, you are helping more than you think."

"We were just about to get some food," Ulrick said. "Care to join us?"

"Not this time," Ryuvin answered. "I have many things to take care of still."

"Well, don't push yourself to hard," Ulrick replied

"Yes," Lorewind said. "Please make sure to rest as well. You were barely able to walk on your own when you came back from the monastery."

"I will be fine," Ryuvin said coldly before walking away.

"He isn't fine," Lorewind said to Ulrick.

"You're right," he replied with a sigh. "Ryuvin has been taking this all on his shoulders."

"I'm worried about him," Lorewind said and sighed.

A loud grumble from Lorewind's stomach caused her to blush.

"Right food," Ulrick laughed as he continued towards the tavern.

"Hey don't laugh at me," Lorewind huffed as she chased after him.

CHAPTER 17

"Do you know why you were chosen?" The man asked as he sat on the ground with his legs crossed.

"It is the way of the clan," the young girl replied as she sat behind him. "Every family must provide one child to continue the Ways of Shadow."

"Good," he replied and looked at the young girl. "You will become a great shinobi, Kimiko."

"I will make you proud, To-san," young Kimiko said as she bowed her head to her Father.

"I know you will," he said to her and stood. "You will be the best of the next generation."

***

Kimiko remained unconscious in the medical wing of Morningside, although vaguely aware of her surroundings. Reliving the memories that she held close, memories she had never shared with anyone.

***

She continued her exercises, like she did daily from a young age, always keeping in mind what her Father told her the day she was chosen all those years ago.

"You must be silent," the instructor said as she paced back and forth. "To make a single whisper of sound is to betray the code."

Suddenly she hurled a rock into the trees where they trained, it was followed by a cry of pain as another of the drow students fell from his hiding place.

"Now change locations," the instructor commanded as she

continued hurling rocks in seemingly random locations, each striking a student.

The training went on for hours and eventually ending with Kimiko as the only one not found.

"Excellent," the instructor said as Kimiko approached. "You would all do well to learn from Kimiko-chan."

"How do you do it?" A young drow asked her as they walked back towards the barracks.

"Do what?" She replied.

"All of it," he answered. "You are so much better than anyone here in training, perhaps even the clan. You must have some secret."

"I have no secret," Kimiko answered.

"There must be something," he said stepping in front of her. "Come on, some magic spell maybe."

"Ranin," Kimiko sighed with a shake of her head. "There is no magic spell, or special item. It is all just the skills we have learned."

She remembered the lessons well. Training hard, since the age of four, to become the greatest of her clan.

The years continued to pass and Kimiko only became stronger, smarter and feared amongst the other students. Few dared to approach her as the training became more intense and dangerous. Many students either died or were sent back in shame, like Ranin was.

"Tonight will be the final lesson you all have to learn," the instructor had said as she stood before them. "You will each fulfill an assassination contract that we have been requested of, you have three days."

The contract was simple, Kimiko being one of the first to return. After the three days had past, Kimiko and the other eleven students stood before their instructor.

"And with that you have completed your training," the instructor said as each student was gifted an onyx dagger. "This dagger is a symbol of our clan. Now repeat the clan creed."

The students in unison began to speak.

We are the faceless among the faces.
We are the blades within the night.
We are the silent shadow.
We are shinobi.

The training was seared into the very fibre of her being. The first life she took to become who she was. That was the way of her clan.

***

As the years continued to pass, Kimiko's clan continued to operate within the shadows of the world, her clan became one whispered in fear. Once it was learned you were a target of one of their contracts, there was nothing you could do but wait for death.

"Do you ever wonder if we should be doing this?" One of the shinobi asked Kimiko.

"This is what we are," Kimiko replied flatly. "We have a mission, we will complete it."

"And does this target deserve death?" Another asked. "His death might only advance someone's own self interest."

"And that matters to us why?" Kimiko asked coldly as she looked at the other two. "We have a job to do."

The others nodded as they all pulled on their masks and descended from the roof and into the crowd, vanishing within the midst of the people.

***

It was a simple contract, in hindsight she should have realized the obvious trap. Her target was out in the open and she made easy work of the contract, or so she though. Kimiko had become overconfident and it cost her everything. She was betrayed by someone that knew the ways of her clan but she never learned their identity. With her mission a failure and her team dead, Kimiko vanished.

***

It had been nearly thirty years since her failure, doing whatever she needed to survive. For a time she had joined a mercenary company. She started to make a name for herself when the clan came *for her, she was forced to kill them then vanished again. She had learned her lesson and worked odd jobs here and there, never staying in the same place for more than a fortnight.*

She could not remember the last time she ate as she crouched in the shadows watching carriage, escorted by four elven knights, approach. She was so focused on the carriage that she failed to notice the creature come up behind her. When she finally did, she spun and barely managed to block its attack as it sent her flying from the brush, across the path of the carriage and crashing into a tree before falling to the road. Searing pain shot through her right shoulder, her left leg and her stomach. Looking down she saw branches impaled through her body.

"To arms!" Yelled one of the knights as he drew his sword.

Six ogres charged from the trees towards the carriage. Spitting blood from her mouth, Kimiko forced herself to her feet.

I will not die without a fight, *she thought to herself.*

Blood running down her face and into left her eye, Kimiko let out a battle cry and charged at one of the ogres, daggers drawn.

***

Kimiko awoke, heavily bandaged, in what appeared to be some sort of hospital. She lay still, gauging her surroundings. The window to her left, the setting sun poured light into room she was in, to her right was another bed, the man sitting in the bed looked over at her, a bandage wrapped around his chest and over his right arm.

"We are on the second floor of the hospital," the man said calmly. "You could survive the jump in theory, although in your condition I have a feeling the fall would kill you."

"I cannot stay here," Kimiko groaned as she sat up, fresh blood seeping into the bandages covering her body. "I need to leave."

"Far be it for me to try and stop you," the man said and gestured to his missing right arm with a smirk. "As you can see I am a bit short handed at the moment."

Kimiko huffed out a chuckle as she forced herself, unsteadily, to her feet, pain flaring through her body.

"You really should rest," the man continued. "You are not going to make it far."

Kimiko ignored his warning and took a step, the moment she put weight onto her left leg she collapsed, crashing into the nearby table and knocking the glass jug over, shattering on the ground upon impact.

"Miss," a woman said as she came running over, obviously a nurse. "You need to stay in bed and rest."

"I had just told her that," the man said with a chuckle. "She did not want to listen."

"You shush," the woman said as she gave him a venomous glare. "You cause enough trouble with how often you are here, Vamir."

"You wound me," Vamir said as he dramatically placed his hand on his chest. "I only come here to see the such an exquisite beauty."

The woman's face turned red, Kimiko was not sure if it was because she was angry or flustered. She then turned back to Kimiko and reached for her arm which Kimiko batted away.

"Please miss let me help you," she said as she knelt beside her. "You are severely injured."

"Do not touch me," Kimiko spat as she slapped the nurse's hand away and forced herself into a seated position panting heavily. "What happened to the knights?"

"Dead," Vamir said as he walked over, standing at the end of her bed. "You and I are the only two that survived the ogre attack."

"It is my fault," Kimiko said as she rest her head on the edge of the bed, her breathing steadying. "I was careless and let them get the jump on me."

"Would anything have changed if they did not find you?" Vamir asked.

"Your men would still be alive," Kimiko answered.

"Is that so?"

"Yes," Kimiko replied. "The ogres would have attacked, I would have waited just long enough to save you and the nobles in the carriage. They would have given me a reward and I would have left."

"You say that as if you know what happened," Vamir retorted. "You collapsed after you had killed two, so you did not realize there were actually twenty of them."

"I could have handled twenty ogres had I not been-" Kimiko said but was cut off as a loud grumble came from her stomach.

"Ah," Vamir chuckled. "Hunger, the bane of good soldier."

"I am not a soldier," Kimiko replied.

"Then what are you," Vamir asked, his eyes narrow. "You are obviously well trained and you do not hesitate to kill."

"Whatever she is does not matter," came another woman's voice.

"Your Majesty," Vamir and the nurse said together as they bowed and stepped away from Kimiko's bed.

She must be the Queen, Kimiko thought as she watched the heavily pregnant woman approach.

"What is your name?" The woman asked coldly.

Kimiko looked into her silver eyes, she could feel the weight of her magic pressing against her. It was suffocating. She had never felt anything like this before.

"M-my name is Kimiko," she answered nervously, a bead of sweat running down her neck.

Is this fear? Kimiko asked herself.

The Queen stared her down for moment before turning to the nurse.

"Make sure she is given food," she said then looked back at Kimiko. "You will remain here until you have fully recovered."

Kimiko nodded and watched as the Queen turned and walked away with the nurse. Once she left, Kimiko let out a breathe she had not realized she had been holding.

"Still thinking about leaving?" Vamir asked as he sat back in the bed.

"Is she always that...terrifying?" Kimiko asked.

"Believe it or not, no," Vamir answered. "She is actually one of the sweetest women you will ever meet, I think the mood swings from the pregnancy coupled with the attack has her on edge."

"Okay you two," the nurse said as she returned with a tray of food. "As per the Queen's orders."

She placed the tray on the bedside table and helped Kimiko

back into the bed, propping the pillows up so Kimiko could remain seated.

"Venison and pheasant stew with potatoes, carrots and broccoli," the nurse said with a smile. "There is also freshly baked bread with apple and raspberry cider to wash it down. I hope you enjoy."

"Do I not get anything?" Vamir asked.

"You can go to the mess hall on the first floor if you are hungry," the nurse answered as she set the tray gently on Kimiko's bed.

"Thank you," Kimiko said softly to the nurse.

The nurse smiled again and left.

***

A few days later, Kimiko lay in the bed looking out the window. She was still weak and could barely walk. The sound of the door opening caused her to turn and look. She watched as Ninthalor approached her with a friendly smile.

"How are you this morning, Kimiko?" He asked, his hands enveloped in the sleeves of his robes.

"Exhausted," Kimiko said as she groaned and sat up, blood seeping into the bandages again. "I hate this, being stuck in this bed."

"Your body needs time to recover, Kimiko," Ninthalor told her as he stepped bedside her bed.

"Is that not what your magic is supposed to do?" Kimiko asked as she groaned again. "To completely heal my wounds?"

"My magic merely speeds up the process," Ninthalor answered as slowly removed the bandages on her arm. "Your body has limits. Too much and it will shut down."

Kimiko sighed, and looked out the window, a whisper of movement catching her attention. She looked back over towards the door and saw a young elf boy slip behind one of the beds.

"We have company," she said and nodded towards the boy.

"That would be Prince Ryuvin," Ninthalor said as he continued to removed the bandage. "His curiosity clearly is getting the better of him."

"There is no point hiding," Kimiko called the young Prince. "I know you are there."

She watched as the boy meekly approached, his head bowed

slightly. He looked up at her, his silver eyes filled with a mix of fear and curiosity.

"Ryuvin," came a woman's voice causing him to jump. "What are you doing in here?"

"I-I am sorry Mother," the Prince said and looked down. "I wanted to see the scary elf lady."

Ninthalor coughed back a laugh as he placed his hands on the wound still in Kimiko's shoulder.

"There are questions I have for her," he continued.

"I do not know how you manage to keep sneaking out of your studies," the Queen said as she hobbled over to him. "But you can ask when she has recovered. Serina, take him back to your classes."

It was then that Kimiko noticed a young elf girl behind the Queen.

"Yes, Your Majesty," Serina nodded. "Come on Ryuvin, if we finish early we can play in the garden with Jassin."

Ryuvin smiled as he chased after Serina. Kimiko looked to the Queen and saw the warm smile as she watched them. Turning back to Kimiko, the Queen's icy expression returned, though it seemed forced.

"Interesting," Kimiko said aloud.

"What is?" The Queen asked.

"How you pretend to be a cold person," Kimiko answered.

"Oh?" The Queen said.

"I saw how you watched your children," Kimiko continued. "The expression now is forced."

"Wait," Ninthalor said in shock as he looked at the Queen. "Is that true?"

The Queen sighed and nodded.

"I have never really been one for being cold," the Queen said. "I care about my people as a Mother cares for her children. It is a practised expression I use when necessary, but Serina is not my child."

"I understand," Ninthalor said and turned back to Kimiko.

"My name is Amilia Ashgrove," the Queen said to Kimiko. "Queen of Avantharia."

"Why did you bring me here?" Kimiko asked.

"Because you needed help," Amilia answered.

"If not for Her Majesty's magic," Ninthalor said as he began wrapping a clean bandage around Kimiko's shoulder. "You would be dead right now."

"Then I owe you my life," Kimiko said.

"You owe me nothing," Amilia replied.

Kimiko then pulled the knife from the tray next to the bed and slice open her finger.

"By my blood," she began as she drew a symbol on her chest. "I swear this oath, I am yours to command until my final breathe and beyond."

The symbol glowed before it turned into a red mist that travelled towards Amilia's hand.

"Blood magic," Ninthalor gasped.

"Are you sure about this?" Amilia said.

Kimiko struggled out of the bed. When Ninthalor moved to stop her, Amilia waved him back. Dropping to her knees, Kimiko bowed forwards at Amilia's feet.

"Yes, Amilia-sama," Kimiko answered.

"My first order," Amilia said as she looked down at Kimiko. "Tell me what you are."

"I am the faceless amongst the faces, the blade in the night, the silent shadow," Kimiko answered as she looked up at Amilia. "I am shinobi."

"So you are an assassin?" Amilia asked.

"No, Amilia-sama," Kimiko answered. "I am more than that."

"Explain." Amilia commanded.

"I was part of a clan," Kimiko said. "We followed the way of shadow. We accepted contracts for many things; assassinations, protection, espionage, sabotage, to name a few. Each member of the clan was skilled in all of these, many believed I was the best amongst them. My clan holds many secrets. Secrets that can start wars, create heroes and destroy kingdoms. I know enough to bring ruin to my clan. They will come for me."

"Is that why you wished to leave?" Amilia asked.

Kimiko nodded.

"How do I find your clan?" Amilia asked.

"You do not find the clan," Kimiko answered. "The clan finds you."

Amilia pondered for a moment before looking back at Kimiko.

"Rest now," Amilia said and turned away. "The sooner you are well the sooner you will be on your feet."

***

"Hello Kimiko," a familiar voice said.

Sitting on the bed, Kimiko looked towards the window. She could barely see the man against the night sky.

"Hello, To-san," Kimiko said as she looked into her Father's eyes.

"It has been a long time," he said to her. "Thirty-five years."

"I failed my mission," Kimiko answered. "To return would mean death."

"So you chose exile instead?" Her Father asked.

Kimiko only nodded.

"To what purpose?" He asked.

"Because in exile, I shall live with my failure until the end of my days," Kimiko answered. "Are you here to kill me?"

"No," he answered. "I am here for the Queen."

"If you touch her," Kimiko said, anger flaring in her eye. "I will kill you."

"Dear child," he laughed. "If I was here to harm her I would not be speaking with you. I am here because she was searching for the clan."

"To what ends?" Kimiko asked.

"For you," he answered. "She told me of the blood oath you swore to her. I am here for another oath. So long as you live you will speak nothing of the clan or its secrets. You will not teach our ways to anyone."

"I understand," Kimiko said.

"Swear it," her Father said.

"I swear," Kimiko said. "That I will speak to no one of the clan secrets nor train any in the way of shadow."

Her Father nodded and turned back towards the window.

"It is unlikely we will ever meet again," he said wistfully. "Know that I will always love you."

"Goodbye Father," Kimiko whispered as he vanished.

***

Light filtered into the room causing Kimiko to stir. Slowly she opened her eyes, sat up and looked around.

This is all too familiar, she thought.

She looked down at Lorewind, half in a chair half on the bed, sleeping. Kimiko smiled and bushed Lorewind's hair from her face causing her to stir.

"Kimiko?" Lorewind asked sleepily as she rubbed her eyes.

"It is me," Kimiko answered and smiled.

Lorewind teared up as she hugged Kimiko tight.

"I was so worried," Lorewind said as tears began to roll down her cheeks. "I'm so happy you're awake."

"What happened?" Kimiko asked.

"We brought you back to Morningside," Lorewind began. "Roshamrik and Ulrick were able to heal you."

"How long was I unconscious?" Kimiko asked.

"About seven days," Ulrick said as he entered the medical wing. "And Lorewind helped with the healing."

"We were worried you weren't going to wake up," Lorewind said.

"Well you were worried," Ulrick said. "She was-"

"Ah good you're awake," Barubar said as he walked in, interrupting Ulrick. "I shall fetch Ryuvin."

***

Over the next few days, Kimiko began exercising to regain her strength. Lorewind rarely left her side.

"You do not need to need to accompany me," Kimiko panted, sweat coating her brow, as she glanced at Lorewind. "I do not wish to take you away from whatever you have been studying."

"I don't mind," Lorewind replied, affection filling her eyes. "I enjoy being with you. I mean doing this, walking."

Kimiko smiled to herself as Lorewind became flustered.

She is in love with you, Vigil whispered.

And I her, Kimiko replied as they walked around the blacksmith.

"How are you feeling Kimiko?" Serina asked.

Looking away from Lorewind, Kimiko saw Serina approach.

"Serina-sama," Kimiko said and bowed. "I am recovering, I was able to do several laps around the town."

"You need to rest," Serina said told her before turning to Lorewind. "Make sure she gets those bandages changed."

"I will," Lorewind replied with a nod before turning to Kimiko. "Okay, you've wandered enough for now, time for new bandages and rest."

Kimiko nodded and slowly made her way back to the tavern with Lorewind.

"What have you been studying?" Kimiko asked as they entered the tavern.

"Roshamrik has been teaching Ulrick and I healing magic," Lorewind answered. "I felt helpless and couldn't sit by doing nothing."

"I understand," Kimiko said and cupped Lorewind's cheek. "I thank you for everything you did to help."

Tears welled in Lorewind's eyes again as she kissed Kimiko's palm.

"It's more than that," Lorewind said. "I-I love you."

"I know, Lorewind-san," Kimiko said with a soft smile. "I love you as well."

Lorewind smiled and kissed Kimiko softly before pulling back.

"I was able to summon a new elemental," Lorewind said, smiling proudly as she changed the subject. "Nymphia, Daughter of Watroth."

"A water elemental?" Kimiko asked.

Lorewind nodded happily.

"I am proud of you," Kimiko said with a warm smile.

Lorewind beamed and took Kimiko's hand, pulling her towards the medical wing.

"Come," she said. "Let's get those bandages changed."

Kimiko nodded with a smile and let Lorewind pull her along.

***

As the sun broke over the horizon, Kimiko awoke and sat up, the pain in her side was nothing more than a dull ache now. She looked over at Lorewind and smiled as she brushed a strand of hair from her face. Slowly, she shifted out of the bed and donned the simple cotton tunic, leggings and boots she had been wearing over the passed few days. Quietly she slipped from the room and headed towards the tavern, a soft click of another door closing made her turn around to see Kallindra slipping out of a room.

"Good Morning Kallindra-san," Kimiko said. "Why are you coming from Ryuvin-sama and Serina-sama's room?"

Kallindra blushed and looked away.

"Ah, I see," Kimiko continued as she noticed Kallindra's dishevelled hair. "Fun night?"

"How are you Kimiko?" Kallindra asked, clearly wanting to change the subject.

"Recovering," Kallindra answered and began to walk down the stairs. "Come, let us get something to eat, I wish to talk with you."

Once sitting at a round table with a plate of food Kallindra spoke.

"I am sorry," she began. "If not for my pride-"

"And had it not been for my arrogance," Athanasia said as she walked up beside them, a plate of food in hand. "May I?"

Kimiko nodded and watched as Athanasia sat down between her and Kallindra.

"My point is," Kallindra continued. "Is that it is our fault you were injured. Our fault you nearly died."

"It is our failure," Athanasia said as she pushed the eggs on her plate around with her fork.

"Long ago," Kimiko began. "I failed as well, I lost everything. My home, my clan, my family. I eventually came to realize that failure is a part of life. We should not be afraid to fail, because in failure we learn to succeed."

"Kimiko is right," Roshamrik said as he hobbled to the table. "It is okay to struggle and fail, from time to time, that does not make you a failure. It is okay to be afraid when you fall, but never forget to keep picking yourself back up."

The three women looked at each other then back to Roshamrik.

"The world will be full of people that want you to struggle, to make you afraid to keep standing," he continued as he leaned heavily on his cane. "Just do not forget the world also has people that will be there to guide you when you are lost, to help you stand when you fall."

"We are in this together," Kimiko said to the others. "We are a family, and families are bound to argue."

Kallindra and Athanasia both nodded and smiled.

"Remember young ones," Roshamrik said as he hobbled away. "You do not need to carry the weight of the world on your shoulders alone."

The three watched as Roshamrik entered the medical wing.

"So Kallindra," Athanasia said as she turned back to her with a smirk. "I'm surprised you aren't having difficulties walking after that pounding Ryuvin gave you last night."

Kallindra choked and sputtered on the water she had been drinking.

"W-w-what are you talking about?" Kallindra stuttered, blushing fiercely.

"I was wondering why you came out of his room this morning," Kallindra said as she rested her chin in her hand. "You never did answer my question earlier."

"Oh I think she had a very fun night," Athanasia said with a giggle. "I'm surprised you didn't hear her."

"You guys are being so mean," Kallindra said. "It was my first time."

"Oh," Athanasia said, a slight blush forming on her cheeks. "You were a virgin?"

Kallindra nodded.

"Are you a virgin as well Athanasia-chan?" Kimiko asked.

Athanasia's blush grew more vivid as she gave an embarrassed nod.

"Well then," Kimiko said with a smile. "It seems that your onee-san has a few things to teach you."

"Onee-san?" Kallindra and Athanasia said in confusion.

"From where I am from it means big sister," Kallindra said. The two nodded.

"I always wanted a big sister," Athanasia said. "Having brothers was never very fun."

"At least you have siblings," Kallindra said. "I am an only child."

"Well then," Kimiko said as she steepled her hands on the table. "I shall give you some advice."

CHAPTER 18

It had been a little over two weeks since the events of the Monastery, Kimiko having nearly fully recovered since then. During this time, Ryuvin had received news that the Avantharian outposts had been fortified, as well as the contingent of soldiers sent to the Central Plains had been reinforced with a contingent from Amenthur as well as a unit from Sandara, led by Patridale. Reports had been flooding in, small towns had been eradicated and several small skirmishes with the mordian, most of which indicated few survivors, if any. The most troubling report being the destruction of Silverriver, the kingdom of the north eastern plains. From all reports, they had met the mordians on the open plains in full force; their legendary cavalry standing no chance.

"I don't like this," Thunan said as he crossed his arms. "Silverriver has one of the greatest armies in the realm. For it to fall so easily…"

Ryuvin glanced around the room they occupied, given to them to use courtesy of Zavabar.

"This is indication that now, more than ever, we must stand united," Ryuvin said as he leaned on the circular table in the centre of the room. "Regardless of feuds between nations, we must look passed that if we are to save Therago."

"If only it were that simple," Kallindra replied as she leaned back in one of the several chairs, next to Serina. "News is going to spread across the realm, Silverriver held many nations in check."

"And with it gone," Kimiko continued from where she leaned against the wall, still slightly pale. "There will be those that will use this as a chance to strike at their enemies as well as those looking only to protect themselves."

"Ha!" Waruk spat as he slammed a mug of ale onto the table. "They're either full of arrogance or they're fools. The decimation of Silverriver and its cavalry should be testament to that."

"A cavalry that would have been useful in the coming days," Ulrick stated flatly as he sat in another chair, reading reports.

"What are the chances that other nations will rally to aid us?" Lorewind asked hesitantly from where she was sitting beside Kimiko.

"Latest reports," Kimiko said, holding a rolled up scroll. "Indicate that several of the tribes from Jotunheim have mobilized and are sending scouting parties throughout the north. Even the dwarven kingdom of Ysegarde is gathering their forces."

The Knights continued discussing the reports, rumours gathered from travellers and plans for their next move in finding a dragon shaman, when suddenly one of Mareck's men burst through the doors.

"Forgive the interruption," he said as he knelt down. "But we just head that Dacorvia has begun to march against Mystaria."

"Seems like it has already started," Kallindra sighed and crossed her arms. "I am not surprised Dacorvia is the first to make a move."

"How many?" Ryuvin asked.

"Early reports say seven thousand," the bandit replied. "They will reach Mystaria is four days."

"Ryuvin," Serina chimed in as she stood. "If we ride hard we can get there first."

"Serina," Ryuvin replied as his silver eyes locked with her emerald. "This is not a simple war, the forces against us are much worse than anything we have ever faced."

Ryuvin, something is here, Kayle whispered, *something...fa-*

miliar.

Zana suddenly rushed into the room.

"Quick...at the gate..." she panted frantically. "Warrior...arms in chains...looking for the Knights."

The Knights rushed after Zana as she lead them back to the gates. Sure enough, a warrior awaited them. She wore grey leather leggings, unadorned black greaves and a simple studded leather baldric covered her pale body. Auburn hair spilled from beneath a red hood, chains coiled around her arms and chest, a sword, wrapped in red cloth, on her back.

Dovaria, Kayle hissed.

I do not like this, Altareon whispered.

"Why are you here, Dovaria?" Ryuvin called to the fallen angel.

She did not move, yet Ryuvin could feel her gaze on him, he could feel her fury, her overwhelming power. She did not answer, the tension in the air building. After several moments of silence, she spoke, her voice rumbling through their bones.

"I have come to deliver justice," she said.

"You are not Justice," Ryuvin replied, a drop of sweat running down his temple.

"I do not speak to you," she answered as she stepped forwards.

"We cannot beat a god," Athanasia whispered, her hand grasping the hilt of Soran Helios. "At least not one as powerful as she."

"No, you cannot," Dovaria said as she pulled the sword from her back. "Now step aside."

She continued forwards, passed the Knights and stopped in front of Serina. Towering over her, Dovaria presented the sword to her.

"Excalibur has long been away from the planarverse," she said. "I failed in the duty Ao had tasked to me on the day of my birth. But you, one who has always believed in justice, true justice, shall carry this blade."

Serina blinked and hesitantly reached for the hilt but

stopped and pulled her hand back.

"What will happen if I take the sword?" She asked.

"You will gain the part of me that I had lost millennia ago," Dovaria answered.

Serina nodded and, with a deep breathe, reached out again, her hand closing around the white leather hilt. Light enveloped Serina, vanishing as quickly as it appeared. She now wore armour that was identical to Ryuvin's, the only difference was that both wings embossed on he back were angelic. A pale reddish gold orb floated between her and Dovaria.

Hello Serina, a gentle voice whispered, *I am Dovaria the Archangel of Justice.*

You are that which she lost? Serina asked.

Yes, the angel replied, *when I was exiled, my sense of justice was lost and sealed with Excalibur.*

"She will guide you where I was lost," the goddess said, her voice wistful.

"I shall wield Excalibur as you once did," Serina said as she strapped the white leather sheath to her back. "And bring justice to Therago."

Dovaria nodded and turned, walking back towards the gates to Morningside.

Her wings, Kayle gasped, *they are gone.*

On Dovaria's back, two large parallel gashes ran down her shoulder blades where her wings would have been, the wounds looked fresh.

"Dovaria," Ryuvin called. "What happened to your wings?"

"I cut them off after my exile," she replied without looking back. "A fallen angel should not have the grace of her wings."

With that, she conjured a portal and disappeared. The rest of the Knights then looked to Serina, their newest member.

"What?" She asked when she realized they were staring.

"Looks good on you," Kallindra said, a hint of flirtation in her voice then leaned in and whispered. "Does this mean I outrank you in the bedroom as well?"

Serina blushed hard before glancing at Ryuvin.

"Gather what provisions we need," he ordered. "We ride for Mystaria within the hour."

The seven other Knights nodded and dispersed. Lorewind and Kimiko went to the general store, Athanasia and Waruk to the stables, Thunan and Ulrick headed to the medical wing in the tavern, and Kallindra headed out the gate, a black and grey tiger running up beside her. Alone with Ryuvin, Serina turned to him.

"It looks like I'm part of this now," she said to him.

"Serina," Ryuvin began. "This is not some sort of game. Two weeks ago Kimiko nearly died because of me, what if-"

"Stop right there," Serina interrupted. "You think I'm not aware of the risks? And that Kimiko's injury is your fault? Look what has happened since. Everyone has become stronger. Kallindra has learned to tame beasts, Lorewind now has Nymphia. Ulrick can shift into different animals and is more adept with his healing. Athanasia can use combat magic. Waruk has better control over his rage state. And Thunan can use wind and water magic as well as lightning."

Ryuvin sighed and brushed his hand through his hair. He knew all of what she said was true.

"I know these past two weeks have been the hardest for you," Serina continued. "You can't keep blaming yourself for what happened at the monastery. All you are doing is thinking about is the what if's. What if I was stronger? What if I was faster? What if I was a better leader? Ryuvin, all of us would follow you to the edges of the planarverse and beyond."

"She is right Sir," Thunan said, causing Ryuvin to turn and see the rest of the Knights.

"You held us together through all of this," Ulrick said.

"Yeah, let's be honest boss," Waruk said. "We were a pretty big mess these last several days."

"Had it not been for your determination," Kallindra interjected. "Who knows what would have happened. We all looked to you for strength."

"The Magus had once told me," Lorewind began. "That in our darkest moments, when we stare into the abyss, we will see it stare back at us. In those moments, when the light has all but faded, what will you do? Will you shrink away? Or will you stand defiant against its gaze?"

"We are the Knights of Medusal," Athanasia said.

"And you are our leader, Ryuvin-sama," Kimiko continued.

"And together," Ryuvin said, drawing his sword and raising it to the sky. "We shall stand defiant!"

The Knights raised their fists into the air, and the townsfolk, who gathered during Serina's speech, cheered loudly. Less than an hour later, Ryuvin, with renewed confidence, led the Knights out of Morningside and towards Mystaria.

"I best be off," Mareck said to Roshamrik as they watched the Knights.

"I do not suppose you can be convinced to stay?" the elderly orc asked.

"After a speech like that?" Mareck laughed. "No, my people need me, now more than ever. The Thrones of the Jarnherrar have sat empty for long enough."

Roshamrik nodded and watched as Mareck walked down the road.

"May Aremto speed your journey," the orc muttered. "Jarnherrar Jormungandr."

Chapter 19

The night was calm, the moon hidden behind the clouds. His black armour blending him into the shadows. He watched, crouched silently in the fields outside Mystaria, as eight black garbed warriors rode dire wolves hard towards the city. He watched as they spoke quickly with the gate guards then entered the city. He watched as the gates closed behind them. He waited several moments before slipping away from his position, unaware of the shadow watching him.

***

Kimiko watched, from her shadow, as the Dacorvian scout retreated from his position.

What do you think Vigil? She asked as she left the shadow and sat on the dead scout next to her.

On one hand if you kill him we don't find the army, Vigil replied, *on the other, Dacorvia has no information about us.*

True, she replied with a sigh.

I have an idea though, Vigil said with a hint of glee.

Kimiko smirked as she listened to Vigil's plan, then moved back to all the corpses of the scouts before following the last one.

***

"Commander White," the scout said as he knelt down.

He was in a large tent, furs covered the ground and in the centre was a round table, with a map, surrounded by several men, their black and red armour gleaming in the light of the lanterns.

"Where are the others?" An older officer asked.

Strong jawed, with a clean cut beard and short salt and

pepper hair, cold brown eyes. His armour was battle worn, unlike the other officers, bare muscular arms covered in scars and a wolf fur draped over his back.

"I don't know Sir," the scout answered, keeping his head bowed.

"I sent fifteen of you," White said, anger edging into his voice. "How do you not know?"

White watched the scout for a minute then sighed.

"I will deal with that later," he said as he pinched the bridge of his nose. "Report."

"Mystarian watch hasn't changed," the scout said. "But eight warriors in black rode hard for the city and were granted entrance."

"Could they be part of the forces that destroyed Silverriver?" One of the officers asked.

"Unlikely," another answered. "They are probably part of the elven forces in the Central Plains."

"They rode dire wolves, Sir," the scout said.

"There have been several reports of a group of warriors fitting that description," a younger officer replied.

"They did enter the-" the scout began but was cut off as a spike of shadow speared through his body, blood splattering the top of the tent.

White leaned over the table, eyes wide.

"Sorry about that," came a woman's voice, cold and sinister.

The officers whirled around to see a black garbed woman sitting lazily in the command chair, one leg hanging over the arm, twirling a large dagger on her finger.

"Could not leave the count at fourteen," she smirked, her needle like teeth making her featureless face all the more unsettling.

"You are responsible?" An officer asked as he drew his sword.

"Oh?" The woman asked. "Was that not obvious? Well you can have them back I guess."

With a flick of her finger, a shadow quickly enveloped the table. When it dispersed, the bodies of the scouts, face frozen in horror, lay piled on the table.

"You will pay for this assassin!" The officer shouted and rushed the woman.

It was brief, but White saw the woman's taunt and how effective it was.

"Stop!" White commanded, but it was too late.

She moved, faster than anything he had seen before. The officer let out a gurgle as his hand flew up to his throat then crumpled to the ground, a spray of blood spattering the chair. When White looked up, the woman was gone. The guards, from outside the tent, had rushed in to witness the event unfold.

"Search the camp!" White ordered.

The woman's mocking laugh filled the tent. Fear filled the guards' eyes.

"Now!" White shouted.

Terrified, the guards quickly scrambled out of the tent.

"We march at dawn," White said as he addressed the officers.

Saluting, the officers left the tent. Meanwhile, Kimiko smiled from her shadow then quickly left the camp.

Do you think it worked? She asked Vigil as she moved through the trees.

Soldiers talk, Vigil replied gleefully, *rumours will spread, I can already taste their fear.*

Kimiko smirked and made her way back to Mystaria, about an hour later she was outside the walls. Her shadow climbing effortlessly up to the ramparts. Once on the wall, she stepped out of her shadow, just as a soldier was walking by. She stared at him, and smiled. Not too far away, Kallindra and Ryuvin stood watching the fields, her ears suddenly flicked around.

"Kimiko is back," she said.

"How do-" Ryuvin began but was interrupted by a scream.

The two ran to the source only to find Kimiko crouched on the battlements and the solider shakily holding his spear pointed at her.

"Stand down soldier," Ryuvin commanded as more troops arrived. "Kimiko, report."

"I dispatched fourteen scouts in the field and followed the last to their camp about an hour west of here," she began as she released her merge with Vigil. "After a successful infiltration, I dealt with the fifteenth as well as an officer. They march at dawn."

"Good work, Kimiko," Ryuvin replied and turned.

"Ryuvin-sama," Kimiko said. "Balthazar White is leading them."

"Of course he is," Ryuvin replied bitterly. "Go and get some rest."

"I have heard of General Balthazar White," Kallindra said as she glanced at the gathered troops. "Are what the stories say about him true?"

"Cold, calculating and utterly ruthless? Yes," Ryuvin began. "His only redeeming quality is that he cares for the men under his command, he is not known to be reckless. Although it seems like he was promoted since the last time I met him."

"You fought against him?" Kallindra asked.

"No," Ryuvin answered. "Dacorvia had requested aid during the Red Fang Uprising just over twenty-five years ago. My Father sent me with a sizable force to cement an alliance. We won the battle but White had ordered his men butcher every prisoner captured. Father withdrew our forces when he learned of this."

"Sir," one of the nearby guards said. "What should we do? Mystaria has no formal military, just the City Watch."

Ryuvin looked at the men and women gathered, both on the ramparts and the ground below.

Remember Ryuvin, Kayle whispered to him, *true leadership.*

"Dacorvia has sent their best general and ten thousand troops," another guard said. "Why even fight? It's hopeless."

Hopeless. The word echoed in Ryuvin's head. He looked down to the people gathered, the Knights amongst them.

"You ask why we fight?" Ryuvin began. "Is it for glory? Or perhaps for honour? Maybe instead of asking why you fight, you should ask something else. Ask what is worth fighting for?"

His words echoed across the silent crowd as he looked up to the sky for a moment, a patch of star visible through the clouds.

"We stand here, on the eve of battle," he continued. "Against overwhelming odds. None would fault you for feeling fear, but look around you, at the faces of those next to you, your friends and family. Look at what you stand to lose if you do not fight. Believe me when I say that a battle is only hopeless if you believe it so. Know that so long as one person holds than the light is never truly gone. So long as a single person believes, that hope will never fade. So take heart! Know that you do not stand alone. We shall stand together to face the forces that are at our doors and we will be victorious! So now, I ask you, when I stand before them, who will stand with me?!"

"I will," Kimiko said without hesitation.

"As will I," Kallindra continued.

"And so will we," Serina called out from the crowd.

Slowly the gathered crowd began to follow suite, calling out their support.

"I am Ryuvin Ashgrove," he continued as he took the gold orb containing Kayle. "And let it be known that today, the Knights of Medusal have returned. And today, we show the world that we will stand against the darkness!"

Ryuvin merged with Kayle and rose up above the city, light radiating off him. He flew above the cheering crowd and across the city causing people to look up. Word spread through the city quickly, the Knights of Medusal have returned. They would protect the people. A beacon of light to guide them through the darkness. A beacon of hope.

Chapter 20

He watched from across the field. He could see the Mystarian guards scurrying back and forth on the wall, frantically trying to get their forces in order. He did not care, his forces will easily overpower them once they reached the wall. What bothered him, were the nine black garbed warriors marching across the field towards his forces.

"Commander White," an officer said. "Your orders?"

"Hold here and prepare for combat," White said, not taking his eyes from the warriors. "Let us what they want."

White and his officers spurred their horses. As they approached, he noticed a drow and thought she seemed familiar but pushed the thought aside.

"I am Commander Balthazar White of Dacorvia," he said calmly. "Who leads you?"

A young elf stepped forward, silver eyes meeting his brown.

"Well if it is not Prince Ryuvin Ashgrove," he said in an almost mocking tone. "You are a long way from Avantharia. Does your Father know you are here?"

"I am here of my own accord," Ryuvin replied calmly. "For my purpose is beyond those of my own kingdom."

"You elves," White replied. "Always thinking you are high and mighty. Why are you here?"

"I have an offer for you," Ryuvin answered. "Stand down, send a contingent of forces to the Central Plains and aid the forces there."

"Aid them against what?" White asked.

"The mordian," Ryuvin answered flatly.

White and the officers laughed.

"The mordian are a myth boy," White jeered. "So what will happen if I refuse?"

"Then we will stop you," Ryuvin replied as he drew his sword and raised it to the sky. "Know that you will stand against the Knights of Medusal and you will lose."

Behind him, on the city walls, a standard was raised above the gates, black banner with a gold roaring lion. White then noticed that more forces had appeared on the wall, the academy mages. An elderly looking man stood outside the gates.

"Hmm, so you convinced Headmaster Frandle to help," White said, his tone light. "Not that it will matter. I will not stand my army down and any that resist shall die."

"Then make peace with your gods," Ryuvin replied coldly. "For you shall see them soon."

Ryuvin and the Knights turned and started back towards the city but the drow stopped.

"I meant to ask," she said as she looked over her shoulder with an unsettling smirk. "How troublesome was your camp after I left last night?"

White watched as she walked away, his jaw clenched.

"Sir," one of the officers said, grabbing his attention. "The Knights of Medusal are said to be the greatest warriors of old, is it wise to stand against them?"

White did not answer, he sat, with narrowed eyes, and watched as the Knights walked back towards the city. After several moments he looked to his officers.

"The Knights of Medusal are just stories," White replied. "All they are meant to do is coddle the weak. We are Dacorvia, we take what we want because we are strong."

The officers gave a quick cheer before riding back to the Dacorvian army.

***

Back at the city gates, Ryuvin and the Knights looked back across the field as the Dacorvian army because to mobilize.

"Headmaster Frandle," Ryuvin said as he turned his attention to him and bowed. "I thank you for the aid."

The Headmaster was an elderly man wearing simple blue robes with long white hair and grey eyes, he was a bit taller than Ryuvin and held himself with a dignified posture.

"This city is my home," he said, voice calm and deep. "I will not stand idly by as barbarians march on its gates."

"Are your people ready?" Ryuvin asked.

"As ready as they can be, I have assigned them the best I could," he answered. "Most are but students, I am just worried they will be overwhelmed."

"I understand," Ryuvin replied and bowed again. "The Knights and I will hold the majority of the forces, I only ask that you do what you can from the wall."

Frandle nodded then bowed and returned to the city, the massive iron gates closing behind.

"Our best option, as I said," Ryuvin began as the others gathered around. "Will be to hold the front line outside the city gates. The Mystarian Guard and mages can give us some support from the walls as White will not be testing our strength with small skirmishes. He will send his entire army at us."

"What kind of units are we looking at?" Kallindra asked as she unslung her bow. "Any cavalry?"

"No," Ryuvin answered. "White assumed that the battle would take place on the walls, not the field before the city. He will have brought mages of his own as a precaution. There will be a good portion of archers as well, which he would use to keep the defenders pinned while the foot soldiers pressed to the walls. He will have ladders and other potential sieges weapons but the main concern will be The Breaker, once he forces had a footing on the walls, he would have used it to breach the gates."

"What's a breaker?" Waruk asked.

"The Breaker, not a breaker," Athanasia replied.

"Ah okay...what is it?" Waruk asked again.

"A Dacorvian siege machine," Kimiko answered. "Long range, fire a concentrated blast of magical energy capable of destroying almost anything it hits."

"Athanasia," Ryuvin continued as he turned to her. "Can you stop it should it fire?"

"Nothing will breach The Warbringer's shield," she replied with a nod. "Of that I promise you."

Ryuvin nodded and turned back to the others.

"Show no mercy, do not break," he said. "If some get passed you it will be up to Athanasia and the city defenders to take care of them. We will not falter."

The Knights nodded and Athanasia took up her position about twenty feet from the city gates, the others charging out to the field roughly sixty feet from the wall and spread out in a line. The Knights readied themselves for the coming battle. Ryuvin had merged with Kayle. To his right, Serina had merged with Dovaria, her gold armour gleaming in the sunlight as she flex her crimson wings. On his left, Kimiko pulled her headband off to reveal her magic eye as she merged with Vigil. When a horn sounded in the distance, Ryuvin watched as the Dacorvian archers readied their bows and began an evocation.

Light of Yggdrasil shine forth,
Become a shield,
Protect those that stand beneath thy glow,
Let it be a sanctuary from that which would do harm.
Sanctuary of Light.

Ryuvin raised his hand up as he finished the evocation of the spell, a pale golden light enveloped them and spread out over the area, creating a dome, the mages also casting protective barriers to shield those on the wall. Arrows rained down upon the dome of light, disintegrating upon impact.

"Nice trick Boss," Waruk called out as another horn bellowed. "Looks like the real fun is about to begin."

"Remember," Ryuvin called out as he watched the Dacorvian infantry charge. "We hold this line! For Therago!"

The Knights let out a battle cry as the army surged towards them. Lorewind now summoned Verdag, his roar shaking the ground. Kallindra already losing arrows into the charging foot soldiers, had called her beasts; Midnight, her storm howl fox, Griz, a large iron hide bear, her and Ebony, an onyx tiger, from their slumber in the Eternal Hunting Grounds. The infantry clashed against the Knights, expecting to easily overwhelm them, what they did not expect was that the line they held did not budge. The Mystarian guard watched in awe as the held, cutting through the enemy soldiers with ease. They watched as Waruk, Ryuvin and Serina danced, their blades a blur, as they dispatched soldier after soldier. They watched as Verdag easily batted aside the soldiers that got close to him and Lorewind weaving earth magic. As Thunan moved like a whirlwind, lighting crackling off his staff and as Ulrick shifted effortlessly between his beast forms. Though it was Kimiko that terrified the enemy most. Dacorvian soldiers pulled screaming into their own shadows or watched as their comrades would die in a spray of blood as shadows spikes impaled their bodies, those that were not stood little chance as they stood paralyzed with fear as she descended upon them; her feature less face and smile being the last thing they see. Those that were able to get passed the line came face to face with Athanasia, as she stood fast before the gate, her swords a blur as she switched effortlessly between the two.

"How you holding up girly?" Waruk called over to Lorewind as he cleaved into the skull of a soldier with his axe, blood spraying up his arm.

Lorewind glanced over at him quickly but did not answer. She slammed her staff into the ground as she began the evocation of a spell.

> *Daughter of Watroth, I call to you.*
> *Come forth, she who rides the waves,*
> *Grant me your aide.*
> *Nymphia, I summon you.*

A massive geyser erupted in front of her sending soldiers flying. Taking shape, the geyser formed itself into a serpent then solidified. Nymphia shook the excess water from her greenish blue scales. Landing in front of Lorewind, she coiled her serpent like body protectively around her. She had a long narrow white snout with two horns that broke through the dark blue main running down her neck that then turned into a webbed spine, running all the way to her fish like tail.

"Thank you for answering my call, Nymphia," Lorewind said with a bow.

"Of course Lady Lorewind," Nymphia replied as she idly batted aside a group of soldiers with her front leg as they charged at her.

"You deal with these troops," Verdag said as he crushed the solider in his grasp. "I shall protect our Lady."

Nymphia nodded and turned her attention to the charging Dacorvian forces. Her roar shook the ground as she surged forwards, her powerful legs propelling her as she crashed upon them like a wave.

***

Elsewhere, a small force of ten Dacorvian troops had infiltrated the city and were making their way towards the citadel.

"Time is of the essence," the leader said. "If we can find the Dragon Heart for Commander White than the city will fall."

"They say a monster guards the heart," one of the men said.

"Just a silly rumour," the leader replied.

***

Back on the battlefield, a soldier ran up to White.

"Commander White," he said as he knelt down. "The Breaker is ready."

White surveyed the battlefield, a third of his forces were already dead, barely any were getting through the Knight's front line and even the ones that did fell to the one protecting the gates and the archers on the wall.

"Fire The Breaker, we can still win this," he ordered then spurred his horse into a charge. "All forces forward! For Dacorvia!"

***

A low rumble caused Ryuvin to look up. He saw White charging forwards, his troops, with renewed courage, followed. Ryuvin watched as a massive ball of crackling magical energy flew at the gates.

"Athanasia!" He called.

Athanasia turned her attention towards the ball of magic and began the evocation for her spell.

I invoke Athena, Goddess of War and Wisdom.
Send forth your shield,
Let it be the wall that stands against all thrown against it.
Shield of the Warbringer.

A massive shield of golden fire formed on her left arm, throwing it up as the blast hit. The ball pushed her back, her feet sliding against the ground as she slammed her claymore into the earth and gritted her teeth. She felt her feet grind to a halt and, with a battle cry, pushed back against the magical energy.

***

The Dacorvian forces were in full charge as the ball of magical energy faded.

"Commander White!" An officer yelled and pointed to the gate. "Look!"

White looked towards the gate and his face paled. It was unscathed, the warrior in front stood to her full height, a golden shield on her left arm.

"So what's your plan now White?" Came a voice from above him.

Hovering above him, was an angel, with red wings, a bastard sword wreathed in pale gold flames in her hand. White looked around, his men had lost the will to fight. Their charge halted. Ahead stood the Knights of Medusal, around them lay the bodies of more than half his army.

***

In the citadel, the infiltration team cornered a group of mages, too young to be on the wall to help, their only protection were two older girls. Both were beautiful and in their late teens to early twenties and wearing the white and blue robes of the academy. One had short blonde hair with brown eyes, her clenched fists crackled with lightning. The other had long bluish black hair tied into a single braid, she stood back and tried to block the children.

"Who are you?" The blonde girl demanded.

"Lily, be careful," the other girl whispered.

"Shut up Argenta," Lily said as she looked over her shoulder at Argenta, anger and disgust in her eyes.

"Stand aside girl," the leader said with a step forward.

Lily blasted the ground in front of him with lightning, forcing him to stop.

"I said who are you?" She asked again.

"Lily," Argenta gasped. "Don't."

"For the last time," Lily snapped. "Shut up."

"You should've listened to your friend," the leader laughed. "You're too weak to stop us."

He stepped forward again, Lily unleashed another blast of lightning. Though it bounced harmlessly off his armour. He laughed again and rushed her, his sword plunging into her stomach. Lily gasped and staggered back before falling to her knees, blood quickly soaking her robes.

"Lily!" Argenta cried.

"Give me the Dragon Heart," the leader said as he stepped passed Lily. "If you do, I will let you live."

"D-don't do it Argenta," Lily said as she coughed up blood. "He...he is lying."

"So you protect the Dragon Heart?" He asked with a mocking laugh and turned to his men. "Look boys, here is your monster. Nothing but a scared little girl."

"Are you sure she is a monster?" One soldier asked. "She

doesn't look like one."

"Maybe she is one of those shapeshifters," another replied. "I hear they are revolting in their true forms."

"Well whatever she is," the leader said. "She clearly isn't much of a threat."

The men all started laughing as they watched Argenta try to shield the children with her body. Argenta looked passed the leader to Lily, laying in a pool of blood clutching her wound trying to stem the bleeding. The laughs echoed in her mind, memories flashing of the other students laughing and calling her a monster. Turning, she knelt in front of the children.

"Close your eyes," she whispered to them. "It will be over soon, I promise."

The children nodded, shutting their eyes tight and covering their ears. Argenta let out a ragged breathe and stood.

"You say I'm a monster," she said, magical energy surging around her as she turned, blue eyes now gold. "Then perhaps I shall show you the monster."

***

"So what's your plan now White?" Serina asked, Excalibur, wreathed in pale gold flames, in hand as she hovered above him. "Your charge has falt-"

She was cut off by an earth shattering roar, the likes of which had never been heard of. The sound shook the very earth itself, the Dacorvian forces stumbled and fell.

"It cannot be," Nymphia said, fear in her voice, as she looked towards the city. "Kossathia."

"That is impossible," Verdag replied as he crouched protectively over Lorewind. "The Primordials made a pact to never come to Therago."

All watched as a massive blast of fire enveloped part of the citadel.

"Ryuvin!" Serina called to him.

Both she and Ryuvin launched themselves towards the citadel.

"Hurry Serina!" Ryuvin yelled back to her.

They arrived to the citadel to find the area collapsed, rubble sliding from the spire to the street below.

"What in the nine hells happened here?" Serina asked in horror.

This was dragon magic, Kayle whispered to Ryuvin, *but not just any dragon magic.*

What do you mean? Ryuvin asked.

This was Primordial, Altareon answered.

"Whoever did this is powerful," Ryuvin said to Serina as he flew closer. "Be on your guard, I sense a strong magical barrier."

"I sense it as well," Serina replied as she flew down beside Ryuvin. "Could it be the girl we are looking for? Argenta?"

The rubble started shifting again, causing Serina and Ryuvin to move away for safety. As the rubble fell away, a small dome of magic was revealed, inside was a girl, arms outstretched and shaking as she maintained the spell. Behind her, a group of small children and a young women, her robes soaked in blood.

"Are you Argenta?" Ryuvin asked.

The girl looked up to him.

***

The dark closed in around them, the light of the barrier dim, she was not even sure what she had done. All Argenta could remember was an earth shattering roar and a blast of fire before the citadel collapsed on top of her. She could not even remember casting the barrier. Behind her, Lily lay on the ground, the bleeding had not stopped as the blood pooled beneath her. Argenta knew she was dying and could do nothing to save her, she could barely hold the barrier up. Tears stung her eyes as she clenched them shut, her arms trembling. The rubble shifted and fell away from the barrier.

"Argenta?" Came a voice from above her.

She opened her eyes and looked up to the voice. Wreathed in light were two angels, one with white wings like fresh fallen snow, the other with wings as crimson as the morning sun. The light reflecting off their golden armour.

"Who are you?" She asked.

"We are here to help," the crimson winged angel replied.

"Please," Argenta pleaded. "Save Lily."

Exhaustion took hold, her strength taxed, Argenta collapsed as the two angels flew to her.

CHAPTER 21

That evening, Argenta paced back and forth in her room. It was not a very large room, big enough to fit a bed, desk, wardrobe and full length mirror. She stopped and looked into the mirror again for the countless time. After the events of the Dacorvian assault and her use of whatever magic that was in the citadel, Argenta had changed. Stripping off her robes, she stared at her naked reflection, tears filling her now blue and gold draconic eyes. Her pale skin now had dragon like scales over her pear shaped hips, as well as along the cleavage of her average sized breasts, back, neck and shoulders. Her teeth were more fang like and her hands felt stronger, her nails more like talons.

She sobbed and fell to her knees, tears spilling over her cheeks and hands. Monster. That word echoed in her mind. It is what the Dacorvian soldiers called her. It is what the other students call her, all over the fact her magic is different. Her body shook, sobs wracking through her, she braced herself with her right arm to keep from falling.

I truly am a monster, she thought.

There was a knock at her door.

"Argenta?" A soft voice of a woman called to her. "Are you okay?"

"Go away!" Argenta screamed.

She listened, through sobs, as the woman walked away, she thought she could hear the faint sounds of conversation. A few moments later, the door burst open and Argenta scrambled to cover herself.

"Haven't you heard of knocking?!" Argenta yelled, tears staining her cheeks.

"Lorewind already tried that," the woman said as she strode into the room. "You screamed at her."

"Get out!" Argenta cried as she tried to cover her body.

"Why?" The woman asked.

"I'm naked!" Argenta answered. "Can't you tell?!"

Gods who is this woman? Argenta thought, *is she an imbecile?*

"Well no actually I can't," the woman replied and pointed to her blindfold as she sat on the bed.

Argenta looked at the woman, she wore a cuirass that left her midsection exposed, the left pauldron was larger than the right, on her right arm was a tattoo of reddish gold fire, her left arm had a chain mail sleeve and her leggings were loose fitting, all of which was black with gold trim. Argenta's eyes lingered on her toned abs before she looked up to her face. Her purplish black hair was tied in a warrior braid, a black blindfold covered her eyes.

"See something you like?" The woman asked cheerfully.

Argenta blushed and looked away.

"I know you," she said, still avoiding looking at her. "You're Athanasia, Kensei of Sandara. You were the one that stopped Dacorvia from breaching the walls."

Athanasia threw her head back and let out a joyous laugh. The sound was sweet to Argenta.

"It took more than just me," Athanasia said as she leaned back. "My friends did most of the work, I just stood in front of the gates."

Argenta heard the story. She heard how nine warriors stood before the city. How they fought against an army of over ten thousand strong.

"Though I'm sure the story will change," Athanasia continued. "With each retelling something will change. Today it will say ten thousand troops. Tomorrow maybe a million. We might even be depicted riding dragons."

"That doesn't bother you?" Argenta asked.

"Should it?" Athanasia responded.

"Because that isn't the truth, it changes how people look at you," Argenta spat angrily. "People will look at you and see something you're not."

"And how should people see me?" Athanasia asked calmly. "Should they look at me and see a blind girl pretending to be a warrior? Should they look at me and feel pity?"

"T-that isn't what I meant," Argenta replied, caught off guard by Athanasia's remark.

"Regardless," Athanasia continued. "How people perceive me does nothing to change who I am."

"That's easy for you to say!" Argenta barked as fresh tears spilled down her cheeks. "Look at you!"

"Again," Athanasia replied with a smile and looked at Argenta. "I can't, I'm blind remember?"

"You're not funny," Argenta replied bitterly. "But you're gorgeous and I'm a monster. Inside and out."

"I may be blind," Athanasia sighed and leaned forwards. "But that isn't what I see."

Argenta turned and looked at her.

"I see a girl with a tortured soul," Athanasia continued. "A girl that has been hurt because she is different. A girl that has fought against who and what she is, and I don't blame you. Just know that you can continue fighting against this world but where will that leave you? Alone, filled with anger and fear, lashing out at anyone around you."

Argenta looked down at the wood floor of her room.

"Or you can embrace what you are," Athanasia continued as she stood and knelt beside her. "See that there is nothing to be afraid of. You can stand beside friends that will be there for you. People that will fight beside you, people that will share your pain, people that will help you stand when you fall."

"How can you be so sure?" Argenta asked, more tears rolling down her cheeks.

"Because it happened to me," Athanasia answered, a hint of melancholy in her voice. "More recently than I would care to admit."

Athanasia sighed again and leaned over, brushing Argenta's tears away with her thumb.

"Do you want to know what I truly see?" Athanasia continued. "I see a beautiful girl looking for where she belongs."

Argenta looked at Athanasia, suddenly aware of how close they were. She could feel Athanasia's breathe tickle her lips. Argenta felt her cheeks flush and leaned in, her lips pressing tentatively against Athanasia's. For a moment, Argenta thought she would pull away, then felt Athanasia pull her close, deepening the kiss. She gasped slightly as Athanasia playfully bit her lower lip. Suddenly, Argenta pulled away.

"I'm sorry," she said as she looked away. "I shouldn't have done that."

"If it was an issue I wouldn't have kissed you back," Athanasia responded with a smile then kissed her cheek.

"But can someone like you be with someone like me?" Argenta asked meekly.

"Why not?" Athanasia countered.

"Because you are a hero," Argenta answered. "And I'm a monster."

"No you aren't," Athanasia replied. "And I'm sure the kids you saved would agree that you are a hero."

"Can I even be a hero?" Argenta asked and looked back at Athanasia.

"You can be whatever you choose to be," Athanasia answered. "And if that means in love, then be in love."

Argenta smiled and kissed Athanasia again.

"Thank you," she said.

"Don't thank me just yet, get dressed," Athanasia said with a chuckle. "There is a world that needs saving and we need you."

***

"Her power is incredible," Kallindra said as she addressed the others. "A true monster."

She crossed her arms and looked at the other Knights then leaned back in the chair she was sitting in, crossing her legs. They gathered around a large, round oak table, the room looked as it was used for astrology.

"Monster is a relative term," Thunan replied as he leaned forwards, placing his hands on the table. "I'm sure the Dacorvian infantry would call us monsters."

"We did kill a lot of em," Waruk said with a smirk, his arms crossed as he put his feet up on the table. "Was I the only one counting my kills?"

"Four hundred eighty one," Ulrick answered from where he was sitting next to Thunan.

"Ha!" Waruk laughed joyfully. "Not bad animal boy. I had six hundred and nine."

"Are we really doing this?" Serina asked and looked around then sighed. "Fine, one hundred ninety two."

"I didn't know I was supposed to count," Lorewind said sheepishly and fiddled with her hands.

"Two hundred thirty-three," Ryuvin said.

"Not bad Boss," Waruk said as he stood and flexed. "But you're going to have to do better than that."

"One thousand four hundred and twelve," Kimiko said from where she leaned against the wall.

"You know that doesn't surprise me," Athanasia said as she strode into the room, Argenta behind her. "Argenta, I would like to formally introduce you to my friends."

Argenta swallowed nervously.

"Let's start with our fearless leader," Athanasia said as she gestured to Ryuvin. "Ryuvin Ashgrove, Crowned Prince of Avantharia."

Ryuvin turned to Argenta and gave a slight bow.

"A pleasure to finally meet you," he said with a smile. "Though I would hardly say I am fearless."

"Next is his fiancee," Athanasia continued as Serina stepped up beside Ryuvin. "Lady Serina of House Althara."

"It's good to see you are well," she said with a warm smile.

"The brooding drow leaning against the wall is Kimiko," Athanasia continued.

"I am not brooding," Kimiko said to Athanasia.

"Yeah sure, whatever you say," Athanasia replied with a dismissive wave. "The one beside her is lover, Lorewind."

"Why would you say that?!" Lorewind squeaked and covered her face, blushing hard.

"Are you a daemon?" Argenta asked.

"I am not," Lorewind replied as she removed her hands, still blushing. "But with my appearance, I can understand why you ask."

"The muscle headed orc is Waruk," Athanasia said as she continued to introduce the others. "He's all smash first, ask questions later."

"Hey!" Waruk began then paused as if thinking. "Okay that is true most of the time."

"Only most of the time?" Kimiko asked as the others laughed.

"The shirtless one is Ulrick," Athanasia said, causing him to blush a bit. "He is from one of the tribes in Jotunheim. The Isvandrere I believe."

Ulrick replied with a nod.

"I've heard few stories of your tribe," Argenta said, her eyes lighting up with curiosity. "I would love to hear more."

"I would be happy to share," Ulrick replied.

"The felian beside him is Kallindra," Athanasia said as she gestured to Kallindra. "Princess of Falcion."

"I heard that Falcion was destroyed, but any new we received was vague," Argenta said and looked down. "I can't even begin to know the pain you must have felt."

"It could have been worse," Kallindra said as she looked down at the table. "I am thankful for having allies such as Ryuvin and Avantharia."

"And finally, we have Thunan," Athanasia said and gestured to the monk to her right. "Monk of the Belhalus Monastery."

Thunan only bowed to Argenta with a polite smile.

"When I was first found, there were two angels," Argenta said as she looked around at the Knights. "Was it just my imagination?"

"No," Serina answered. "That was Ryuvin and I."

"Each one of us has the power of an immortal or god," Ryuvin continued. "For those of us with immortals, we merge our souls with theirs to unlock the full potential of our power. Serina and I have angels."

"You also have that daemon guy Boss," Waruk said and smirked. "You should use him more, he makes you more badass."

"Yes," Ryuvin said as he rolled his eyes and looked back to Argenta. "I, as well as Lorewind and Athanasia, have more than one. I have Kayle, Commander of the Angelic Legions, and Altareon, the Daemon King."

"We all have our strengths," Lorewind said softly. "But we all have our weaknesses as well."

"So how exactly do I fit in?" Argenta asked as she looked at each of the Knights. "No god or immortal has ever spoken to me, and Athanasia said you needed me. What am I supposed to do?"

"Pardon the interruption," Headmaster Frandle said from the door. "There are some people here that would like to meet the one that protected their daughter."

Stepping back, he gestured for the people to enter. A well dressed young man, with short black hair and a clean cut beard, entered with his wife and young daughter.

"Is that her?" He asked as he knelt down beside her and gestured to Argenta.

The girl smiled and nodded. Standing, he turned and bowed low to Argenta.

"Thank you for saving my Lydia," he said, still bowed. "She is the world to my wife and I."

Argenta looked at the girl and realized she was one of the children she protected in the citadel.

"If there is anything we can do," the wife began and curtsied. "Please let us know. My husband, Cameron, owns the McToth Trade Company."

Argenta was at a lose, unsure of what to say. Suddenly, Lydia ran up and hugged her tight.

"Thank you again for saving me, Miss Argenta," Lydia said and looked up, her brown eyes sparkling. "I know mommy and daddy say things about you, but I am glad you are not a bad person."

Argenta looked at Lydia's parents and noticed they could not look her in the eye and shifted uncomfortably.

They see the monster, she thought to herself, *why wouldn't they?*

It all came flooding back to her. The insults, the threats, the fear, the hate, the anger. Everything fought inside her head. Then she remembered Athanasia's words as they cut through the chaos in her mind.

You can continue fighting against this world but where will that leave you? Alone, filled with anger and fear, lashing out at anyone around you.

She looked around at the Knights as Athanasia's words continued to echo in her mind.

You can stand beside friends that will be there for you. People that will fight beside you, people that will share your pain, people that will help you stand when you fall.

She looked down to Lydia and placed her hand on her head. Tears filled Argenta's eyes. Lydia smiled up to her, it was pure and innocent, before returning to her parents.

"Can we go see Miss Lily now?" Lydia asked as the family left the room.

"Like I said," Athanasia said as she stepped up beside Argenta. "You can be a hero if you want to be."

"I...I think I would like that," Argenta replied and looked at the others. "I want to come with you."

"There is one other that wishes to speak to you, Argenta," the Headmaster said from the hallway.

Argenta turned back to see a woman enter the room. Sparkling hazel eyes, long flowing chestnut hair, a white sleeveless gown and shawl, flecked with gold, covered her flawless body. She was the pinnacle of beauty.

"Hello Argenta," she said, her voice sweeter than honey. "I

have finally found you."

"I'm sorry," Argenta said. "But who exactly are you?"

"Oh forgive me, I should have realized," the woman replied, sorrow edging into her voice as she did an elegant curtsy. "I am Aphrodite."

Waruk suddenly perked up and opened his mouth.

"Aphrodite?" Serina asked before Waruk could say anything. "As in Goddess of Love and Beauty?"

"Yes," Aphrodite answered with a sigh. "But it would seem that history has forgotten that I am Ao's wife."

She looked back over at Argenta, a motherly affection filling her eyes.

"It was one hundred years after the ascension of the first gods; Thor, Odin, Ra, Tyr, Hades, Kali, Athena and Ares," Aphrodite continued. "Therago worked to rebuild itself. New kingdoms arose from the ashes. That is when I met them, Ao and Oa, or at least their mortal avatars. They had come to help rebuild Therago."

"Valtherol mentioned this," Kallindra said. "That the dragons had rebuilt the world before."

"I know of at least one time," Aphrodite continued. "Eventually the heart took over. Ao and I married and had two children, the first of the True Dragonblooded. We Ao had returned to Yggdrasil, I followed. We would send a part of us to Therago, to be born upon the mortal plane to continue the bloodline."

Aphrodite's expression suddenly changed, her eyes filled with pain and regret.

"But eventually, like all things, it ended," Aphrodite continued, sorrow filling her voice. "A talented young man, Deveran, wanted power. Easily manipulated by a being of pure evil, he was taught a spell to steal the power from another and began to hunt down the Dragonblooded. Eventually he hunted down all those born with the dragon blood, even hunting the dragons themselves, almost to the point of extinction, those that survived retreated to the lost places of the world. And thus the world was left without the Dragonblooded"

"What does that have to do with me?" Argenta asked.

"When Deveran came for you," Aphrodite answered. "She sacrificed herself so that you would live."

"Why would Deveran come for me?" Argenta asked, eyes narrowed.

"Because you have the blood of dragons in your veins," Ryuvin said. "You are a descendant of Ao."

"No, she is much more," Aphrodite replied, her eyes welling with tears. "Argenta, you are my child, born into the world from my avatar. The daughter I lost all those centuries ago."

"Lost?" Kallindra asked.

"When Deveran came for her," Aphrodite said as she looked over towards Kallindra. "My avatar did something to send her to this era in time, I do not know how for he killed my avatar and took her soul. It is the only part of me I that had never returned."

As she said this, Aphrodite shifted the shawl around her shoulders to reveal her missing left arm.

"I don't understand," Serina said. "If it was your avatar, why didn't you use your powers?"

"Because I was never in direct control of my avatar," Aphrodite answered. "When our avatars died, their memories of the life they had would return to us. Ao knew something was wrong when felt my avatar die, my arm withering away, and my memories never returning. Ao assumed control of his avatar and, with Oa's help, hunted Deveran and killed him but the souls of those he killed were never found."

"I am sorry you had to feel that pain," Kimiko said and gave a respectful bow.

"Thank you," Aphrodite replied before turning back to Argenta. "I knew in my heart that I had a child, that she was alive. When you used your power I was finally able to find you. My baby girl, my Argenta."

Tears welled in both Aphrodite and Argenta's eyes as she ran forwards and hugged her mother tight. She finally had her answer, she was not a monster, she was Ao's daughter.

"This power you wield," Aphrodite finally said as she pulled away from Argenta slightly. "If you are not careful, it will consume you."

"How do I control it?" Argenta asked hesitantly.

"You must learn your limitations," Aphrodite answered. "Do not be afraid to ask for help if you struggle."

"You're not alone anymore, Argenta," Athanasia said as she took Argenta's hand in her own. "The ten of us are in this together."

Argenta smiled softly at Athanasia then looked back at Aphrodite

"What about my father?" She asked.

"Planar travel is different for him," Aphrodite answered. "For the Primordial Dragons, they need an avatar to enter the mortal plane, and that takes times, he does love you though."

Argenta's eyes welled up with tears again as she nodded.

"We have something for you as well," Lorewind said as she picked up the tome given to them by Valtherol.

"The Book of Dragons?" Aphrodite asked when she saw the thick red and gold tome. "Where did you find that?"

"King Valtherol gave it to us," Ryuvin answered. "He is how we learned of Argenta, in a sense."

After a quick recount of their journey thus far, Aphrodite nodded and sighed.

"This is only the beginning," she said. "You are going to be tested and pushed to the breaking point. I pray that you all will have the strength to carry on."

"If we have faith in ourselves," Ulrick said as he stood. "And a trust in each other then we can succeed."

"So long as we stand together," Serina said as she looked to the others. "We will not fail."

***

She opened her eyes, sunlight flooded her vision as her eyes adjusted. She sat up and winced in pain. Looking down at the bloodied bandages wrapped around her stomach. She replayed the previous day in her head. How the soldier thrust his blade through her body. She remembered Argenta's magic, beautiful and terrifying. She remembered how Argenta pulled her to safety as the citadel started collapsing. A knock on the door snapped her out of her memories.

"Who is it?" She called out.

"It's Argenta," came the reply. "Can I come in?"

"Yes," Lily answered after hesitating.

Lily watched as Argenta entered the room. She was different, she walked with a new found confidence. She was wearing a form fitting cuirass with her midsection exposed, pauldrons, bracers, greaves and a tasset with chain mail protecting her arms. Underneath the cuirass, she wore a black thigh length tunic, a gold chain like belt around her waist, black knee high boots, black finger-less gloves and black leggings, a long gold train of sheer silk flowed behind her.

"How are you feeling?" Argenta asked her.

"Why do you care?" Lily retorted bitterly. "We are not friends. Or are you just here to laugh at me."

"Why would I do that?" Argenta asked calmly.

The question shocked Lily. She looked at Argenta, genuine confusion in her eyes.

"True, we aren't friends," Argenta continued. "But why should that matter? You're hurt and I wanted to know if you are okay."

"I am not okay," Lily replied angrily as tears filled her eyes. "I almost died and I will never be able to walk again. I was powerless against that man. He laughed as he stabbed me, he was going to let me die and I needed a monster to save me."

The tension was heavy in the air as Lily wiped the tears out of her eyes. She looked up at Argenta, she seemed calm but Lily doubted that. They stared at each other for awhile.

"Say something damn it!" Lily snapped, finally breaking the silence.

"I wanted to give you some time to calm down," Argenta replied as she sat on the end of the bed. "I can't say I know what you are feeling but I want you to know I'm glad things turned out like this."

Argenta paused and looked at Lily.

"I don't mean that you are hurt," she continued, slightly flustered. "I mean that if it wasn't for how you and your friends treated me, I wouldn't have been so afraid to use my magic and I wouldn't have been able to find my mother."

"But I treated you like garbage," Lily said unable to look at Argenta. "All because your magic was different from ours. We tormented you, my friends-"

Lily stopped mid sentence with a realization.

If they were my friends, she thought, *why did they not visit me last night?*

"They never were friends, were they?" Argenta asked.

The question made Lily laugh. She always had people following her around, she was the popular student, the best at magic. But now what was she?

"No they were not," Lily finally answered. "Maybe they hoped that being around me would benefit them in some way. But now? I guess they want nothing to do with a crippled girl. Looks like karma caught up to me and I've hit rock bottom."

"Well the only way left to go is up," Argenta said thoughtfully. "Rock bottom can be a good foundation, so why not use where you are now to grow and become better? You have a chance to change who you are, not everyone gets that."

"Where is all this confidence coming from?" Lily asked. "Yesterday you were this terrified girl, easily pushed aside. Now your...your...well this."

Argenta laughed as Lily gestured to all of her.

"And why are you dressed like that?" She asked.

"Because I am leaving," Argenta answered.

"Argenta," a woman said from the doorway. "It's time we meet the others.

Lily caught a glimpse of the muscular woman then saw how Argenta's eyes sparkled.

"You love her?" Lily asked.

"Yes...maybe...I don't know," Argenta replied sheepishly.

"At least I think I do."

"Who is she?" Lily asked.

"Athanasia," she answered.

"Wait, what?!" Lily gasped. "She was the one that kept the gates from falling."

"I know," Argenta replied.

"And you are one of them now?" Lily asked, still shocked. "A Knight of Medusal?"

"I am," Argenta answered with a warm smile then stood. "I can't stay any longer, but I'm glad you're okay."

Lily watched as Argenta left her room. The silence lingered as she stared out the window for several minutes.

"Only way left to go is up," Lily said aloud to herself. "A chance to change who I am, huh?"

"Good morning Lily," Headmaster Frandle said as he stood in the doorway. "You look lost in thought."

"Good morning Headmaster," Lily replied and fidgeted slightly. "Would it be too much trouble to ask for a favour?"

***

"All set to go?" Ulrick asked Athanasia and Argenta as they approached the gate, hand in hand.

"Argenta!" Someone called out causing her to turn and see Lily in a wooden wheelchair, Headmaster Frandle pushing her.

"Go ahead," Ryuvin said. "We can wait."

Argenta nodded before walking over to Lily and the Headmaster.

"I thought about what you said," Lily said as Argenta approached. "About having a chance to change who I am. I know there is nothing I can say right now that will change our past but I truly am sorry."

"Maybe when all this is over and I come back," Argenta said, her smile warm and comforting. "We could be friends?"

"I-I would like that," Lily replied, smiling back. "But can...can we start as of today?"

Argenta nodded and hugged Lily. They embraced for a short moment before parting.

"Now get going," Lily said, a tear rolling down her cheek as she smiled. "There is a whole world out there and, when you come home, I want to hear all about it."

Argenta nodded with a smile, tears in her eyes, as she turned back to the city gates and the Knights. Lily watched as they rode through the gates. A small group of students drew her attention, girls she once called friends.

"Finally, the monster is gone," one said.

"Yeah, good riddance," said another.

"Hey!" Lily yelled at them. "She is a better person that you ever will be, from where I am, you are the monsters, so back off."

"Or else what?" The first girl sneered. "You know what she is."

"Yes I do," Lily said and looked back to the gate, watching the Knights fade into the distance. "She is a hero and my friend."

Epilogue

"I'm telling you," the man said to his companions. "Only nine of them stood against Dacorvia's might. Over a hundred thousand troops."

"I heard they entered the battlefield riding dragons," another said.

"Don't make me laugh," one man said. "Dragons haven't been seen for hundreds of years."

Across the tavern, at the bar, a woman in a black cloak watched the men conversing.

"What can I get ya?" The tavernkeep asked as he walked up, cleaning a mug.

"Ale and information," the woman replied as she turned to him.

"What kind of information?" He asked as he picked up a clean mug and turned.

"Any rumours, or talk, of strange monsters," she answered.

"What are ya? Some sort of monster hunter?" He asked.

"In a sense," the woman replied.

He looked back over his shoulder, the hood hiding most of her face, his eyes locked onto her purple, then shrugged and turned back.

"Only thing I've heard recently was about some small fishing village," he said as he filled the mug. "About six days east of here. Word is no survivors, the people torn apart, it was like a pack of-"

When he turned back, the woman was gone, a few gold

coins left on the counter where she was sitting.

***

In the weeks following Dacorvia's attack on Mystaria, word had begun to spread of the return of the Knights of Medusal. Slowly, reports of the mordian increased, most were still small skirmishes across different areas of the Plains. Thought it was not until the fall of Dacorvia did the other nations start taking notice. Almost a month after Balthazar White returned, with what was left of his forces, Dacorvia was attacked. With their forces crippled and moral at a low from their defeat, the kingdom fell within days. Any and all reports were vague and inconsistent, the only detail that remained the same was of a strange sickness spreading from the fallen kingdom, the same sickness that was spreading from Silverriver, the crops withered, rivers dried and all wildlife fled.

***

Ryuvin sat with his back against a tree, looking up at the stars. He looked to his left and smiled. The rest of the Knights sat around the campfire, laughing and talking amongst themselves. He looked back to the stars.

"Copper for your thoughts?" Serina asked looking over at him, the others doing the same.

"Just thinking about how much has changed in the past six months," he said, a slight smile on his face. "Back when all this started, and where we are now. Honestly there is no where else I would rather be."

"It's nice," Argenta said, sitting in Athanasia's lap and snuggling close to her. "To finally have a family."

"Family huh?" Waruk said with a joyful huff. "Am I the lovable uncle?"

"I was thinking more along the lines of the crazy cousin," Kallindra replied, sitting next to Serina and holding her hand.

Laughter echoed from around the campfire.

"We should get some rest," Thunan remarked as he saw Lorewind yawn. "I will take first watch."

"Sounds like a plan," Waruk said as he stood and stretched.

"A bit of shut up will do this crazy cousin some good."

Ryuvin shook his head and smirked as they all followed suit, each going to their tents. He watched as Kimiko half carried Lorewind, as Athanasia kissed Argenta along her neck before the tent flap fell closed.

"Coming Ryuvin?" Kallindra asked, drawing his attention to her and Serina.

They were standing by the tent the three of them now shared. Ryuvin only nodded and stood, letting Serina and Kallindra take his hands as he followed them into the tent.

The End.

Manufactured by Amazon.ca
Bolton, ON